colin Bateman

the Seagulls have Landed

D1324623

Also by Colin Bateman for Hodder Children's Books:

Reservoir Pups
Bring Me the Head of Oliver Plunkett

GALWAY COUNTY LIBRARIES

colin Bateman

the Seagulls have Landed

Hodder
Children's
Books

a division of Hodder Headline Limited

For Matthew

Copyright © 2005 Colin Bateman

First published in Great Britain in 2005
by Hodder Children's Books

The right of Colin Bateman to be identified
as the Author of this Work has been asserted
by him in accordance with the Copyright,
Designs and Patents Act 1988.

10 9 8 7 6 5 4 3 2 1

All rights reserved. Apart from any use permitted under UK
copyright law, this publication may only be reproduced,
stored or transmitted, in any form, or by any means with prior
permission in writing of the publishers or in the case of
reprographic production in accordance with the terms
of licences issued by the Copyright Licensing Agency and
may not be otherwise circulated in any form of binding or
cover other than that in which it is published and without a
similar condition being imposed on the subsequent purchaser.

All characters in this publication are fictitious and
any resemblance to real persons, living or dead,
is purely coincidental.

A Catalogue record for this book is available
from the British Library

ISBN 0 340 87782 0

Typeset in Palatino by Avon DataSet Ltd,
Bidford-on-Avon, Warwickshire

Printed and bound in Great Britain by
Bookmarque Ltd, Croydon, Surrey

The paper and board used in this paperback by
Hodder Children's Books are natural recyclable products
made from wood grown in sustainable forests.
The manufacturing processes conform to the environmental
regulations of the country of origin.

Hodder Children's Books
a division of Hodder Headline Ltd
338 Euston Road
London NW1 3BH

GALWAY COUNTY LIBRARIES

J184.464
€9.00

GALWAY COUNTY LIBRARIES

One

Babies!

You would think that Eddie Malone, hero, warrior, gang leader intent on world domination but still not quite in charge of his own apartment, would have had enough of babies. And you would be quite right. After all, he had once rescued twelve of them from a murderous gang. That was more than enough to do with babies to last him a lifetime. Several lifetimes, in fact. He couldn't stand them, which made it all the more annoying for him that his mother was on the verge of giving birth to one. She wasn't actually due for another five weeks, but if the preceding eight months were anything to go by, well, then Eddie's life, already made a misery by the constant demands of his nagging mother, was about to get an awful lot worse.

It was all get this, get that, get this, get that. Oh Eddie, I'm too tired, get this, get that. Oh Eddie, would you be a love and get this, get that. Oh Eddie, just this once, get this, get that. Oh Eddie, run into my bedroom, get this, get that. Oh Eddie, I forgot this, I forgot that, would you be a darling and get me this or get me that. Really, you should never contemplate taping your mother's mouth shut, but Eddie came quite close to it on several occasions.

Take, for example, the night when his mother was lying on the couch watching *Coronation Street* and Eddie was trying to finish a complicated English homework for his class at Brown's Academy the next day. She couldn't get comfortable, which wasn't surprising really.

'Oh Eddie,' she moaned. 'I'm the size of a house.'

'Yes you are.'

When he next looked up from his homework, he saw that she was crying. 'What's wrong?' he asked innocently.

'You said I was the size of a house,' his mother wailed.

'No, *you* said you were the size of a house. I merely agreed.'

'Well you didn't have to agree!' she exploded. 'You could have said I was quite neat. Or that I looked beautiful or that I was . . . *blooming*.'

Eddie rolled his eyes and said, 'You are blooming. You are blooming well the size of a house.'

And that set her off roaring again.

There was no pleasing some people.

Take food, for example. Eddie wasn't exactly a chef, but with his mother almost too large to squeeze through the door into the kitchen – and even when she did manage it she claimed that the cooking smells made her feel sick – it fell to him to prepare their breakfast and evening meal. But not for Mrs Malone anything straightforward – oh no, that would be too easy. Eddie could rustle up a boiled egg or two. He could make oven chips. Toast was a particular speciality. Bacon even. But oh no. His mother would take a long look at their well-stocked fridge or freezer and decide that she wanted precisely what wasn't there.

'I want . . . fresh pineapple,' she would say, it being ten o'clock on a Sunday night in Belfast, when fresh pineapple probably wasn't even available at that late hour in Hawaii, or wherever it was pineapples came from. And then she would add as if it was perfectly normal, 'and I want French mustard with it.'

'You are barking mad,' Eddie would say.

'I'm not mad, Eddie, that's not nice. I'm just hungry.'

'Then have a chip, have a Jaffa Cake.'

'But I want fresh pineapple and French mustard!'

And so nothing would do her but she had to have pineapple and mustard, so Eddie would be forced to go out and try to track them down, which usually meant venturing into dangerous parts of the city where his reputation as a fearless warrior wasn't quite as ... well, even *he* had to admit, he didn't quite have a reputation yet, despite vanquishing the Babysnatchers and playing a major part in the rescue of the head of Oliver Plunkett.

The city was ruled by the gangs – the Reservoir Pups being the largest and most powerful and most dangerous and most likely to string Eddie up. There were also the Strand Road Agitators, the Ramsey Street Wheelers, the Church Hill Regulars and literally dozens of others. Eddie's own gang was so informal that it lacked even a name, and, indeed, much in the way of members. There was Mo, of course, his albino friend who packed a mean punch, for a girl. There was Gary Gilmore who had been known to put together some interesting inventions, which invariably blew up, usually by accident. There were Sean and Pat, who both lived over a hundred miles away, which was no use to anyone. And ... that was about it. The Gang of Two, Sometimes Three. So when it came to tracking down obscure and bizarre foods for his insane mother, it usually fell to just Eddie to brave the cold, dark streets of his adopted city by himself. He had been chased, he had been attacked, he had been forced to jump rivers, dive out in front of speeding cars and hide himself in stinking dumpsters just to avoid being caught by his enemies. All in the name of – well, pineapple and French mustard.

But he hadn't failed her yet. She was his mother, and he loved her. However, sometimes he loved her less than at other times.

For example, when he arrived home after three hours of very dangerous adventures with the pineapple and the mustard, she had hardly looked up from the TV. She just said, 'I've changed my mind. I had some toast when you were out.'

At times like that, he really didn't love her at all.

Bernard Scuttles, father of the upcoming child, and the man who made Eddie's life a misery even more than his mother, tried to explain her behaviour.

'Eddie,' he said, 'when women are pregnant they sometimes behave irrationally. They develop strange tastes in food. It's to do with their hormones and the chemicals in their body. They also get very sensitive about their body weight. You shouldn't make fun of her for being . . . heavy.'

'Well, can I make fun of you then, because you've no excuse for being a fat pig?'

'Eddie.'

'Unless you're pregnant. Are you pregnant? Or did you swallow a rhino?'

'Eddie . . .'

'Or a whole herd of them?'

'One more word . . .'

'What? Like fat slob? Oops, that's two . . .'

'I'm warning you . . .'

'And did the rhino have a piano for breakfast?'

'Right that's it . . .'

And Scuttles struggled out of his chair and came after him, but he wasn't about to catch Eddie, gang leader and action hero. Eddie was off and running.

Eddie's father had also run off. Off to England with the local doctor from the small village where Eddie had spent a very happy childhood. He hadn't heard from him since, which just destroyed Eddie every time he thought about it. He'd thought his dad had loved him and that they'd been great friends as well. But now it seemed that he had never loved him, otherwise why hadn't he been in touch? Eddie thought for a while that there must be something more to it: that his dad had been kidnapped by aliens, or gone off on a secret mission to Brazil, or somewhere. However, Eddie somehow doubted that aliens would have chosen to kidnap his dad, who had worked as an engineer in the Belfast shipyard. Much more likely that they'd go for the American president or whoever had won *Pop Idol*. And when was the last time a shipyard worker had been sent on a secret mission? Eddie had to accept that his dad was gone for good. It was nearly a year now. Certainly his mum had accepted it. She was basically living with Scuttles now.

One day, when he'd had another row with Scuttles, his mum had taken him to one side while Scuttles went outside for a smoke.

'Eddie,' she'd said, 'we have a new life now.'

'I know that.'

'And I like my new life.'

'I know that too.'

'And it's been very difficult for you and you've gotten into quite a lot of trouble.'

'I've rescued—'

'Eddie – you've been in trouble.'

Eddie sighed. 'Yes, I know.'

'But I love you more than ever.'

'I love you too.'

'But you have to accept that your father isn't coming back, and that we have Bernard now.'

'*You* have Bernard now.'

'No, son. Like it or not, *we* have him. I love him, and you will grow to love him.'

'I think not.'

'Well, then, you're just making it difficult for yourself. He's really a lovely man. I just don't understand why you have to give him such a hard time.'

'I give *him* a hard time? I think not. I think the other way round.'

His mum put her hands on her hips, and sighed. 'Two men in the house,' she said, 'I always knew it wouldn't be easy.' She reached out and ruffled his hair. 'I want you to try to get on with him, Eddie. For me.' She patted her stomach. 'This little one is coming into the world soon, and I want him to come into a happy family. And that means that we love and respect each other. Will you try for me?'

Eddie looked at her pink cheeks and her moist eyes, and couldn't help but say, 'I'll do my best.'

She kissed the top of his head and smiled down at him. 'That's my boy. Now, I want you to go out there and be nice to him. It's difficult for him as well, you know.'

Eddie took a deep breath, then nodded, and turned for the door.

'Eddie,' his mum said, and he stopped and looked back at her. 'I am very proud of you, you know.'

'I know, Mum.'

Eddie opened the door.

Scuttles was leaning on the wall outside their front door. The apartment was on the eighteenth floor of the nurses' quarters, which sat beside the dark edifice of the Royal Victoria Hospital where his mum worked and where Scuttles was head of security.

Eddie leant on the wall beside him and looked out over the blinking lights of the city. It looked quite beautiful, and not at all like the dangerous place Eddie knew it to be. One day, of course, he would rule it all. Although that day seemed a million years away.

'So, she gave you the talk, then,' said Scuttles. He kept his eyes on the city.

Eddie glanced at him. 'The . . . ?'

'All about how we have to get on, for the sake of the baby, that I'm not as bad as you think.'

'Yeah, she gave me the talk.'

Scuttles nodded. 'I had the same. So,' he said, 'what do you think?'

'What do I think about what?'

'About us having some sort of truce.'

Eddie shrugged. 'What do you think?'

'I don't know. What do you think?'

'I'm not sure. What do you think?'

Scuttles shrugged.

They stood for another minute. Eddie could see the steam coming off his breath, and off Scuttles' as well. They watched below as an ambulance, its siren screeching, its lights flashing, roared into the hospital complex.

'I suppose,' Eddie said, 'we could ... well, we could ...'

'Try,' said Scuttles.

Eddie nodded. Scuttles turned then and put his hand out to him.

'We should shake on it, then.'

Eddie, somewhat reluctantly, reached out his own hand. Scuttles clasped it.

'So ... ah, what exactly are we shaking on?' Eddie asked.

'We agree we'll try and get along, and we'll stop annoying your mother by fighting all the time.'

'OK,' said Eddie.

'Just one thing, though,' Scuttles said, and suddenly his grip became a lot firmer, 'I want you to know . . .' and his face came closer and his eyes were suddenly sharp and powerful and menacing, 'I want you to know that as far as I'm concerned . . .' and now he was really squeezing hard, crunching the bones in Eddie's hand together, 'that you're still a little gutter rat and troublemaker and you make your mother's life miserable and as soon as we've had our baby and your mother goes back to work, I'm going to make sure you suffer, I'm going to make sure your life is every bit as—'

But he stopped then, because Eddie was suddenly squeezing back and with a strength he really didn't know he had.

'And I want you to know,' Eddie spat back, 'that you're the biggest fattest stench barrel I've ever met and that as soon as this baby is born I'm going to do everything in my power to make sure my mother dumps you and you go back into the cesspit you crawled out of . . .'

Behind them the door to the apartment opened suddenly and Eddie's mum looked out.

There was sweat rolling down Eddie's brow – and down Scuttles' as well. Both of them grimaced with the pain of pulverising each other's hands.

But his mother couldn't see that. All she saw was her two boys shaking hands.

'I'm so happy you've sorted it out,' she beamed.

Eddie and Scuttles glared at each other, and then released their hands.

Eddie stuck his hand immediately into his pocket, and massaged it against his leg. Scuttles put his behind his back, flexing it again and again, trying to get some life back into it.

'Come on in, boys – I've made spaghetti and ice-cream sandwiches.'

Eddie rolled his eyes as she turned back into the apartment.

'Lovely,' said Scuttles and went after her, though not before giving Eddie another of his scathing looks.

Eddie remained outside for another minute, looking out over the city. They had shaken hands on a peace agreement, but it was really just another declaration of war. Scuttles was the enemy, and he would be defeated, however long it took. Eddie was a gang leader. He was a hero. He would overcome Scuttles in the same way that he had overcome the Babysnatchers and returned the head of Oliver Plunkett.

He was Eddie Malone, man of action.

'Eddie! Get your jim-jams on, it's time for bed!' his mum shouted from inside.

Eddie sighed. *He* knew he was a superhero – it was just the other people in his life who needed convincing.

Two

Eddie had never heard of the Seagulls before the day he went shopping with his mother. He didn't read newspapers, he rarely watched the television news, so he didn't know who or what they were. Apart from the fact, of course, that they were birds. But *these* Seagulls, the Seagulls that were going to cause him so much trouble, certainly weren't birds.

It was a Saturday morning – school over for another week, a perfectly nice and sunny morning he would much have preferred to spend in bed with the curtains drawn, sleeping or playing on his Gameboy Advance SP. But no, here he was in the middle of Belfast guiding his circus-tent-sized mother on what she said was her last shopping trip before the baby would be born. 'I just need to buy a couple of things for her,' she said.

Eddie said, 'Her? Do you know it's a girl?'

'No, of course I don't, Eddie – I mean, not officially. Nobody's told me. But a mother knows. Believe me, a mother knows.'

'Yeah, right,' said Eddie.

'I do. You, when you were in here,' and she ran her hand over her stomach again, 'you were always kicking and causing trouble – a sign of things to come. This little darling, you'd hardly know she was there.'

Eddie looked at the size of her belly. She was no longer as big as a house. She was as big as several houses, and their garages. She was an entire housing estate on legs. She moved only slightly faster than a tortoise with arthritis. Eddie suspected that she was expecting triplets. Or indeed, twenty-seven children, plus their cots. He thought his mother and her bump were probably visible from space. But he decided not to comment. He was learning, slowly.

'Well,' he said, with a shrug of mild disbelief, 'if you're certain.'

Eddie hated shopping only marginally less than he hated Scuttles. Shopping with his mother in such an enlarged state was like normal shopping but much, much slower.

So they spent the morning lumbering from one store to another in the centre of Belfast while his mum looked for baby clothes for a girl and Eddie got more and more frustrated. Luckily, his mum became so engrossed in what she was doing that Eddie was occasionally able to wander off without her really noticing. He poked his head into other shops more in line with his own interests – there was a Game for PlayStation stuff, there was an HMV for music and CDs, a newsagents for sweets. It was while he was coming out of this newsagents, clutching a bag of crisps, that he had his first encounter with the Seagulls.

The thing about the centre of Belfast was that nobody really controlled it. No gang was in charge. It was understood that gang members were free to come and go without fear of wandering into enemy territory, as long as they didn't roam about in large groups. One or two gang members together was considered OK – but more than that, say half a dozen, that wasn't allowed. So when Eddie came out of the newsagents and saw a gang of more than a dozen coming towards him, he froze. He'd been in the city for long enough now to recognise the different gangs – a particular style of dress, the way they wore their hair, the type of shoes or boots they wore – but this lot were different. They were moving at speed, and all along the pavement people were getting out of their way. As they drew closer Eddie realised what the major difference was. They weren't Irish. Irish boys were invariably very pale skinned, and usually quite freckled. But this lot were – well, he couldn't really tell. Their skin was dark, swarthy, but not black. Their hair was dark. They wore black jeans and black T-shirts and black boots and their hair was cropped short against their heads. They didn't even look like a typical Belfast gang – more like an army. And the closer they got the more it appeared that they were moving in a military formation – two rows at the front and back, one line on either side, and in the middle of this rectangle three boys and a girl. The boys were helping to carry the girl – she didn't appear to have any power in her legs and her head was slumped forward. Now that they were almost upon him he could hear that she was groaning; one of the boys patted her head and made sympathetic noises. Then he shouted forward, towards a tall, muscular boy who appeared to be their leader.

'Alexander!' But then he followed it with a word in a language Eddie did not recognise. This 'Alexander' shouted something back, then urged them forward.

Eddie was still standing stock-still in the middle of the footpath, blocking their way. But that wasn't going to stop them. Before Eddie could move, Alexander shoved him hard, and he staggered backwards. His fall was only broken by the window of the newsagents, which rattled behind him. The gang marched on past without a second glance. They'd just swept him out of the way like he was a fly.

A moment later the newsagent appeared in his doorway, and Eddie was just about to start making an excuse about banging into the window when he realised that the newsagent wasn't looking at him at all, but after the retreating gang. The newsagent just shook his head and spat after them: 'Bloody Seagulls!'

Then he turned back into his shop. Eddie looked after the gang, watching as they rounded a corner and disappeared from sight. Who on earth were they? And what had the newsagent meant by calling them Seagulls?

Intrigued, Eddie moved towards the corner, and cautiously peered around it. He saw that a crowd had gathered about thirty metres up, on the far side of the street, and then he saw an ambulance pull into the kerb. He couldn't see any of the gang members – but perhaps the girl they'd been carrying, who'd looked deathly pale, had finally succumbed to whatever illness she'd been suffering from. Two paramedics jumped from the back of the vehicle, and the crowd parted to allow them to approach what Eddie could now see was a large figure lying on the footpath – but it was only when a blanket was pulled away that he realised he knew exactly who it was.

'Mum!' he cried, and charged across the road.

'I should never have left her! I should never have left her!'

He was in the front seat of the ambulance, speeding towards the Royal Victoria Hospital. They wouldn't let him into the back with his mum. How sick did that mean she was? He was terrified. He was supposed to be looking after her, but he'd wandered off and now she was lying in the back of the ambulance, dying for all he knew. She'd been white and panting and crying and calling out Scuttles' name.

'It's OK,' the driver said, 'it's all right . . .' but the speed at which he was driving suggested that it was neither OK nor all right.

'What's wrong with her?' Eddie demanded.

'She's having a baby—'

'It's more than that!'

The driver blew air out of his cheeks, but didn't answer.

'Can't you go any faster?' Eddie demanded.

It was just something to say. He doubted if the ambulance actually could go any faster.

Eddie rubbed at his brow. His head was pounding. He felt like throwing up. How could he have left her like that?

It only took five minutes to get to the hospital; but it felt like an eternity. They screeched into the parking bay outside the casualty department. Eddie dived out of the passenger seat in time to see his mum carefully lifted down from the back of the ambulance. Nurses emerged through the swing doors and escorted her into the main body of the hospital. They recognised his mum, of course, and looked all the more worried for it.

Eddie hurried along beside her as they raced down a corridor. At one point she opened her eyes and held her hand out to him. Eddie grasped it and said, 'I'm sorry, Mum, I'm sorry . . .'

She shook her head, she squeezed his hand. She whispered something. He couldn't quite make it out and bent closer as he ran beside her. 'Get . . . Bernard . . .'

And then one of the nurses stopped him in his

tracks outside another set of doors. 'You can't go any further, son,' she said, then pushed through the doors after his mother. Eddie stood there, almost too shocked to move.

His mother was in there, and there was clearly something seriously wrong with her. And they weren't allowing him in.

Scuttles.

He had to find him.   ~~J184.464~~

Not because he wanted Scuttles to know, or to have anything to do with the birth of the baby or even the possible death of his mother. But because it was her wish.

Eddie hurried back down the corridor towards the elevators. He jumped in and hit the button for the eighth floor, where Scuttles had recently overseen the installation of a new suite of ultramodern offices for his security team. Eddie was all in favour of tight security in a hospital; but it annoyed him that a big thick gorilla like Scuttles was in charge of it.

He arrived at the eighth and charged into Scuttles' office – just in time to see the big fat gorilla standing with his arm around a woman in the grey uniform of the security staff. She was laughing and smiling up at him and he was grinning down at

GALWAY COUNTY LIBRARIES

her. But he froze as he saw Eddie, and quickly removed his arm from her shoulders. She glanced around as well and the smile quickly faded from her face – she blushed, and hurried out of the office.

'What the hell do you want?' Scuttles snapped, moving back behind his desk.

He had caught Scuttles with his arm around another woman.

But this wasn't the time.

'Mum . . .' Eddie said, and that was all he could manage.

It was enough. Scuttles' face went pale. 'Good God!' he said. 'Is she . . . ?'

Eddie still couldn't find the right words.

Scuttles jumped out from behind his desk and grabbed Eddie by the shoulders. 'Where is she, boy? Where is she?'

'Casualty,' Eddie whispered.

Scuttles' mouth dropped open a little, and he looked just as horrified as Eddie felt. He let go of his shoulders and raced out of the door, leaving Eddie standing there, feeling very frightened and very alone.

Three

Two hours later, and he was sitting in the waiting room outside the delivery suite. But it was more than just the simple birth of a baby. Eddie could tell that by the worried looks the nurses kept giving him. They were very nice. They kept offering him Cokes and biscuits, but he couldn't eat or drink. Something dreadful had happened to his mum.

Eventually Scuttles emerged, looking very worried. The top button of his shirt was undone and his hair was damp with sweat. He sat down beside Eddie and said, 'She has very high blood pressure. It's not looking good.'

'For Mum or the baby?' Eddie asked.

'Both,' said Scuttles.

Scuttles lifted one of the Cokes the nurses had left for Eddie, opened it, took a long drink, then set it down again.

'Can I see her?' Eddie asked.

'Best not,' said Scuttles.

And he didn't fight it. He didn't want to see his mum . . . dying. He wanted to see her smiling and laughing and teasing, the way he knew her.

'I'd better go back in,' Scuttles said. He stood up. He looked back down at Eddie. 'She's a fighter, Eddie – just like you.' He winked, then turned and re-entered the delivery suite.

Eddie slumped back down in his seat.

A little while later, he wasn't sure how long, a soft voice said, 'Eddie?'

He glanced up. A small girl, with white, white hair, almost as white as her skin.

'Mo . . .' Eddie said vaguely.

She was wearing a white T-shirt and jeans and she was nervously passing a baseball cap from one hand to the other. Second in command of his gang. The strategist. The planner. Mo knew more about schemes and plotting than anyone. She had fooled an entire city into thinking that her former gang, the Andytown Albinos, were a huge and fearsome outfit – when in fact it comprised precisely one member. Herself. And now she was in a gang that was twice as big. Her and Eddie. She was, as Scuttles would no doubt say, his partner in crime.

'I called for you,' she said. 'One of the neighbours told me . . . How is she?'

Eddie shrugged. He felt like crying. But he

wouldn't, of course. He was a gang leader and hero.

'How long have you been sitting here?'

Eddie shrugged again.

'Have you eaten?' Eddie shook his head. 'Come on then, we'll get something upstairs, there's a staff canteen.'

Eddie shook his head. 'We're not staff.'

Mo grinned. 'I stole some vouchers. We can eat free there for the next six weeks.'

Eddie managed a smile in return. 'I'm not hungry.'

Mo crossed to the doors of the delivery suite; she put her hand against the plastic windows in them to shield against the glare and tried to peer through, but after a few moments she just shook her head and turned away again. 'Scuttles in there?' she asked. Eddie nodded.

'What's he doing?' she said sarcastically. 'Securing the perimeter?'

'He thinks they're dying.'

Mo turned and gave Eddie a hard look. 'Well, what the hell would he know? He's a security guard.'

Eddie had to admit she had a point.

She came towards him, putting her hand out.

'Well come on then – we haven't done a tour of the hospital in ages; if he's in there he won't be able to give us a hard time. Come on, Eddie. You're not doing any good just sitting there. Whatever will be will be, you know?'

Eddie sighed again. He supposed she had another point. His legs were stiff from sitting in the same position and his head was pounding. Maybe a walk would do him some good. Eddie stood. Mo still had her hand out, but he didn't take it. He didn't feel right about holding her hand. They were a gang, not boyfriend and . . . well, you know. Eddie smiled awkwardly and walked ahead of her. She skipped after him and looped her arm through his. That wasn't quite as bad. Perhaps people would think they were brother and sister. Perhaps they would think he was merely helping a very odd-looking patient get some exercise or go to the toilet. Because Mo looked very strange indeed. Like a walking ghost. He didn't notice it any more – but everyone else did.

They wandered from floor to floor. For future reference they checked to see if Scuttles had changed the location of the security cameras; they found out which doors had alarms on them; which exits required security codes. Mo had some counterfeit 50ps which she used to liberate some sweets from a vending machine. Several times they were actually chased by security guards but easily gave them the slip. For whole minutes at a time Eddie was able to forget that his mother was so dangerously ill.

They were moving through the wards on the fourth floor when Eddie stopped suddenly by one of the beds. The sick girl he'd seen in town before his mother's collapse – one of the . . . what had the newsagent called them? Seagulls. She was lying unconscious, hooked up to all sorts of medical equipment, her dark skin gleaming with sweat.

'Who's that?' Mo asked. 'Do you know her?'

Eddie shook his head. 'I saw her in town. She was part of a gang I've not seen before. You know some outfit called the Seagulls?'

'You haven't heard of the Seagulls?'

'Would I be asking if I had?'

'You really haven't heard of them?'

'No, Mo.'

'You haven't heard of the Seagulls?'

'Mo! How many different ways can I say it? I haven't heard of them!'

'You should get out more, Eddie.'

She moved closer to the bed and lifted a chart from the bottom of it. 'Rotavia Mislovich.'

'Is that a name or a disease?' Eddie asked.

Mo rolled her eyes, and quickly scanned the rest of the chart. Then she shook her head and tutted. 'Thought as much,' she said.

Eddie couldn't help but laugh. 'What are you now, Dr Mo?'

'You don't have to be a doctor to know what this is.' She looked down at the girl. 'You bloody fool,' she said. She replaced the chart and nodded for Eddie to follow her out of the ward. Eddie hesitated for a moment, looking down at the poor girl. Her lips were moving slightly, she was whispering something in her fever, something he couldn't make out. Perhaps it was in her native language, because she certainly wasn't from Belfast.

When Eddie caught up with Mo at the end of the corridor, she'd already used her counterfeit coins to liberate two bottles of Coke from another vending machine. They sat in a waiting area and drank for a couple of minutes before Mo began to tell him about the Seagulls.

'You remember the earthquake in Ruritania?'

'What earthquake? In where?' Eddie asked.

'The huge earthquake – whole cities were knocked down – in Ruritania.'

'Rura-where?'

'Eddie, for goodness' sake. For a smart guy you're as thick as two short planks.'

Eddie wasn't sure if that was what you called a back-handed compliment or a direct insult, but he let it lie. 'OK, so I'm useless at Geography. Where is it exactly?'

'Turn left at Albania,' said Mo.

'I've heard of Albania,' said Eddie.

'And you know where it is?'

Eddie nodded. Then quickly said,' 'No idea.'

'OK, well – it's next to Ruritania.'

'Ah, said Eddie. 'Clear as mud.'

'Well it doesn't really matter. Ruritania is a really poor country, and one of the reasons it's really poor is that it keeps having earthquakes. Every time they finish rebuilding their cities another one comes along and knocks them down again.'

Eddie shrugged. 'So what?' he said.

Mo shook her head. 'Eddie, sometimes you really . . .' She sighed. 'Last year they had a really, really bad earthquake, whole cities were flattened, thousands died. You must have read about it.'

'I don't think we got a paper that day.'

'Well, first there was the earthquake, and then there was a disease which spread because of all the people living rough, and thousands more died. And then there was a civil war because everyone was fed up with getting sick and having nothing to eat and dying. So eventually all the countries in Europe got together to help, and they each agreed to take a certain number of refugees. About two thousand of them came here to Belfast.'

Eddie nodded again. 'So what?'

'Well – they like it here.'

'It's not that nice,' said Eddie.

'It is compared to Ruritania. They have homes that don't fall down, they have food and the government gives them money.'

'I haven't seen them around town.'

'That's because you wander around in a daze, Eddie.'

That was probably a fair point. Eddie spent so much time thinking about master plans and world domination that he sometimes wasn't aware of what was going on right in front of his nose.

'OK – so two thousand came to Belfast. And that includes kids, and those kids have formed a gang.'

'A big gang,' corrected Mo.

'And they all wear black. Very dramatic. And they call themselves the Seagulls.'

'Well, yes and no.'

'What do you mean, yes and no?'

'Well, the Seagulls, it's like a nickname, for all of them; everyone who came over from Ruritania.'

Eddie nodded. 'Like they call the Irish Paddies, or Americans Yanks.'

'Well, not quite. People started calling them Seagulls because – well, because they think they're like, well, seagulls, that there's thousands of them, and you can't get rid of them, and they're dirty, and they're scavengers and they steal and generally cause trouble.'

'And are they like that?'

Mo shrugged. 'I don't really know. The thing is, when they formed the gang, they decided to call themselves the Seagulls just out of badness. To show they didn't care what people thought.'

Eddie was thinking about the map he'd made at home that showed which gangs controlled which parts of the city. As far as he was aware there weren't any areas which weren't already under gang control. He pointed this out to Mo.

'You're right, there aren't any. When the refugees arrived it wasn't like there were hundreds of spare houses to just give them, so while the government tried to sort it out they decided to put them in an old army camp just outside the city. It was supposed to be just for a few months, but they're still there and there's no sign of them moving. Thing is, nobody wants a Seagull living beside them. Nobody likes them. So they're going to stay in that camp for ever. That's their territory, and no one I know has ever been inside it. Far too dangerous. Best left alone.'

'Well, fair enough,' said Eddie, 'as long as they stay in there, leave us alone, it doesn't worry me. But what were so many of them doing down here today? We're not meant to travel in packs downtown.'

'Well, I suppose they feel safer that way – and they don't pay attention to the rules anyway. Besides, they were probably down trying to sell some crush.'

'Crush?'

'Crush.'

'What on earth's *crush*?'

Mo shook her head incredulously. 'Eddie, I'm starting to get seriously concerned about you, and what planet you live on. Crush is crush. I know you're from some tiny village in the country, but you've been here long enough to know about crush. Everyone knows about crush. Crush is half the reason everyone hates the Seagulls; crush is the reason that girl is lying half dead in the bed down there. Crush, Eddie, *crush*.'

'I haven't the faintest notion what you're—'

'Eddie!'

But it wasn't Mo who interrupted; it was a nurse, barging at speed through the swing doors behind them. He vaguely recognised her as a friend of his mum's.

'Eddie – thank goodness,' she said, fighting for her breath. 'I've been looking for you everywhere!'

Eddie jumped to his feet. 'Mum! Is she . . . ?'

'You're wanted . . . down there . . . right now!'

'But is she . . . ?'

Her face was flushed, and she could still hardly catch her breath. 'Just give me a moment, I'll be fine in a . . .'

But Eddie couldn't wait. He was off and running, with Mo racing down the corridor behind him.

They hit the elevators.

Mo pressed the button for the second floor where the birthing suite was situated. Eddie drummed his fingers against the back of the lift; his face was pale, his breathing laboured. He looked at Mo. He was on the verge of tears.

'What if she's dead?' he asked.

'She won't be.'

'But what if she is? What am I going to do?'

'She'll be OK.'

Eddie shook his head. 'Everything's gone wrong this last year; why should this be any different? I left her alone. I shouldn't have left her alone. It's all my fault.'

'It's not, Eddie, you know it's not.'

The elevator doors opened and they pounded down the corridor to the waiting room – and found Scuttles sitting on a chair with his head in his hands. Eddie froze. Scuttles' shoulders were shaking. Eddie could see bloodstains on the cuffs of his shirt.

Mo saw them as well. This time she did take Eddie's hand and he didn't mind in the least. He couldn't move. He couldn't speak.

His mother.

His *mum*.

And then Scuttles looked up and there were tears in his eyes and on his cheeks and for a moment he didn't seem to recognise Eddie. When he opened his mouth, words wouldn't come.

Eddie forced himself forward. Mo let go of his hand. He went down on his knees before Scuttles and said, 'Mum?'

Scuttles finally focussed on him. He dragged the sleeve of his jacket across his face, and rubbed his fingers into his eyes. 'I'm sorry,' he said. 'I never cry.'

Eddie sighed. 'It's OK,' he said.

Scuttles began to cry again. Between the tears he managed to say, 'I'm just so happy.'

'Happy?'

Scuttles nodded.

'Happy? My mum . . . ?'

'She's going to be OK.'

A wave of warm relief swept through Eddie. She was OK! She was alive! She was . . .

'And . . . and . . . and . . . the baby, the little girl, is she OK as well?'

This time Scuttles shook his head. 'No Eddie . . .'

And the warmth in his soul began to freeze . . .

But Scuttles was laughing now. 'Eddie – it's not a little girl . . . it's a little boy . . .' And then Scuttles slipped off the chair and was on his knees beside Eddie. He clutched Eddie's shoulders and gave him a gentle shake. 'Eddie – you have a little brother, and I have a son. A little Bernard Junior.'

And then the crying started anew.

Eddie rocked back on his heels.

His mum was fine!

He had a little brother!

A Bernard Scuttles Junior!

And suddenly Eddie didn't know whether to laugh or cry.

Four

Eddie mightn't have known whether to laugh or cry, but the baby certainly did. He chose crying. He cried throughout his three-day stay in the hospital. He cried on the way home. And when he got home he cried all day and all night and drove all of them completely insane. Eddie supposed he was crying so much because he'd realised that he had Bernard Scuttles for a father, and also because Bernard Scuttles was trying to persuade Eddie's mother to christen him Bernard Junior. Fortunately, Eddie's mum was having none of it.

'We'll call him Victor,' she said. And half an hour later: 'We'll call him Stephen.' And the next day: 'I think Frederick's a good old-fashioned name.' And the following week: 'What about Richard?' And five minutes later: 'What do you think of Dominic?' Eddie began to think that if this indecision went on much longer it would begin to emulate his own gang's situation – the Gang With No Name and the Baby With No Name.

Eddie was decidedly undecided about the baby.

Insofar as it was small and pink and peed and pooed and yes, cried – it was like any other baby. But it was also his little brother. *He* was his little brother. Not *it*. But in the days and weeks since *he* had returned home Eddie had had blessed little to do with *him*. His mother was there all the time, seemingly unaffected by what had by all accounts been her brush with death, and when his mother wasn't there Scuttles was, doing a very good impression of a doting father. He fed the baby, he changed the baby, he took it for long walks so that Eddie's mum could rest. In fact one hundred per cent of their time was spent with the baby in one way or another, which left precisely zero per cent for Eddie – either with the baby, or with his mother.

And he didn't mind one bit.

In fact he preferred it.

Some children would feel frozen out, or jealous, and would generally react badly to a new arrival in the family, but Eddie thought it was great. He was left alone to do his own thing; and with Scuttles focussed on the baby, he had no time to argue with Eddie, which was just fine as well.

So Eddie and Mo and occasionally Gary ran wild and free over the city. Or at least over the few streets where it was possible for them to run wild and free without the Reservoir Pups attacking them. The Pups, under the wheelchair-bound, vicious and vengeful Captain Black, blamed Eddie's gang for many things, but most recently for the burning down of their headquarters. The fact that they now had a brand spanking new HQ was neither here nor there. As far as Captain Black was concerned Eddie was right at the top of his Most Wanted list. And Eddie had to admit, Captain Black probably had a point. There was no getting away from the fact that his comrade Gary *had* actually burned the headquarters down and then rubbed salt in the wound by giving an interview about witnessing the event live on national TV. It didn't take an idiot to put two and two together.

It didn't stop them, though. It just meant that they had to be careful. The shorter, colder days of winter were coming in, and they were able to operate much more freely in the darkness. Scuttles was spending so much time with the baby that it even became safe for them to return regularly to the hospital. Eddie had settled well into life at Brown's Academy and even made a number of friends. Because most of them came from quite rich families they were reluctant to travel to the poorer areas where Eddie lived after school – their bright purple uniforms made them stand out a mile, which meant that they were perfect targets for the Reservoir Pups. But Eddie had been to their houses several times and was always made perfectly welcome. At least as far as Brown's was concerned he now had what money couldn't buy – street credibility, or coolness. When he had started there he had boasted about his role in capturing the Babysnatchers and been despised for it. So when the events surrounding the theft of the head of Oliver Plunkett had been played out, Eddie had kept his mouth shut. Nevertheless his classmates had found out, and they seemed to appreciate his new-found modesty.

So this was a *good period* for Eddie. He had a new brother whom he liked but didn't have much to do with, he had Mo to pal around with outside of school and at weekends, he had friends in school he could visit when he liked, and Captain Black and the Reservoir Pups didn't seem able to cause him any trouble at all. Life was pretty wonderful.

And, of course, it was much too good to last.

One Saturday morning Eddie woke to find his mum searching through his wardrobe.

'Mum?' he said groggily. She ignored him. He glanced at the alarm clock on his bedside table. 'It's only eleven o'clock.'

'*Only*,' his mum said sarcastically. 'When I was your age I had a job at eleven o'clock on a Saturday.'

Eddie yawned. 'When you were my age ... it was a very long time ago.' He closed his eyes.

His mum stood back from the wardrobe with her hands on her hips and tutted. 'Right. There's nothing else for it. We're going shopping.'

'What?' Eddie moaned, already half asleep again.

'Patrick Anthony is being christened next week, and you have bugger all to wear. You have seven and a half minutes to get up, washed, and have your breakfast.'

She moved to the bedroom door.

Eddie said, 'What?'

'Seven minutes and counting,' said his mum.

After a lot of shouting back and forth, they left twenty-three minutes later, his mum complaining all the way that she knew apples that got better washes. Eddie had two Jaffa Cakes for breakfast. It was *Saturday*, for God's sake; the day of rest (although technically, of course, Sunday was supposed to be the day of rest). Eddie grumped all the way to the car, thankful that at least Scuttles was being left behind to look after the baby.

While they were driving into the city centre Eddie said, 'Patrick Anthony?'

His mum beamed. 'Patrick Anthony Malone.'

'That's what you're calling it?'

'*Him*, Eddie. Him. He's your little brother. Not an *it*.'

'Paddy Malone?'

'Patrick Anthony Malone. It has a certain class to it, don't you think?'

'It might have, but he'll be called Paddy, which hasn't, frankly.'

'Patrick, Eddie, not Paddy.'

'Well how come I'm Edward, but I get Eddie?'

'Well,' his mother said, 'we made a mistake with you.'

'Gee, thanks,' said Eddie.

'I don't mean it like that. It was your father's fault. I insisted on Edward, he kept calling you Eddie. And it stuck. Unlike your father, who ran away with Spaghetti Legs.'

Eddie slumped down in his seat.

'We're going to buy you a suit,' said his mum.

'I'm not wearing a suit,' said Eddie.

Ten minutes later they were in the suit shop. Eddie had long ago come to the conclusion that despite his finest efforts, life with his mother was one long series of losing battles, whether it was over his choice of clothes, school, or who she shared her bed with. One day, when he ruled the world, things would be different. In the meantime he had to suffer the indignity of trying on a series of horrendous suits while his mum poked and prodded at him and came out with comments like 'His bum's too small' while the shop assistant, who was only about three years older than him, grinned stupidly at her.

Eventually they bought a suit which his mum described as 'a bargain' and Eddie as 'the least bad'. When they emerged from the shop they saw an ambulance sitting across the road, with two paramedics kneeling beside someone lying flat out on the pavement. While Eddie was happy to ignore it, his mother, being a nurse, took a professional interest and led him across to see if she could be of any assistance. As they drew closer Eddie saw that the figure on the ground was wearing the black uniform of the Seagulls, but only had a brief moment to see a teenage boy's face before the paramedics raised a blanket and covered it up.

Which meant: the Seagull was dead.

Eddie stopped where he was at the edge of the pavement. During his fight against the Babysnatchers he had been forced to lie on an old woman's dead body to escape his pursuers, and he never wanted to get that close to a dead body again. His mum let go of his hand, and knelt down beside the paramedics, who appeared to recognise her.

'Dear God,' she said. 'It's not another one?'

The paramedics nodded sadly, then lifted the body on to a stretcher and loaded it into the back of the ambulance. As they drove slowly away, Eddie said, 'What did you mean, Mum – "It's not another one?"'

His mum shook her head. 'We see them all the time at the hospital. Them kids and their bloody crush.'

Crush.

Eddie hadn't even thought about it in weeks, not since they'd seen the girl in the hospital – what was her name, Rotavia ... *something*? Mo knew what crush was, but with all the fuss about his mum nearly dying and then bringing Paddy (!) home, he hadn't asked her again. Now it had claimed another victim – whatever *it* was.

He asked his mum on the way back to the car.

She said, 'Never you mind.'

'Mum, for goodness' sake, just tell me. I'm a big boy now.'

'You're a big boy when I say you're a big boy.'

They walked in silence for another minute. Then Eddie said, 'Fair enough. I'll just ask one of those kids in the black clothes. You know, the Seagulls. They'll tell me what—'

His mum stopped suddenly. She grabbed him by the shoulders and said, 'Stop that right now. You're not to go near those bloody Seagulls, they're trouble, do you hear me?'

'I hear you,' Eddie said.

'Good.'

She turned and walked on. Eddie caught up and said, 'Why are they trouble?'

'They just are.'

'More trouble than me?'

'You're a different kind of trouble, Eddie. They're just . . . trouble with a capital T.'

'In what way?'

'In lots of ways. Just stay away from them.'

'Do you mean they don't have manners? That they burp and don't say excuse me?'

'No, Eddie.'

'That they fart and blame it on someone else?'

'No, Eddie, and don't say fart.'

'Well, what sort of trouble then?'

'Just trouble.'

'OK. Fair enough. But next time I see one of them I'm going to ask them about crush. Seeing as how you won't tell me.'

His mother let out a long, resigned sigh. 'All right, Eddie, have it your way.' They stopped for a moment to let the traffic pass before they could cross a road. 'Crush is a drug. It's a horrible, addictive drug which destroys peoples' lives and causes an agonisingly painful death.'

Eddie nodded. He had already more or less guessed as much. 'But if it's horrible and destroys lives and causes agonising death, why do people take it?'

Mum shook her head, then led him across the road. 'Well, why do people do anything bad, son? Because they're stupid.'

'But it must have something going for it.'

She rolled her eyes. 'Yes, of course it does. It makes you feel great for about five minutes, but then you feel miserable afterwards, so you need another crush, and then another, and then another and before you know it you're stealing and robbing to pay for your crush but you can never get enough of it and eventually you take so much of it that your heart just explodes and you die.'

'Oh,' said Eddie.

'I see them in the hospital all the time, son, all those bloody Seagulls. If it's not the kids, it's their parents – they're all addicted to it, and they're dying off like flies in the winter.'

They walked along quietly for a while. Then Eddie said, 'They probably don't like being called Seagulls.'

His mum nodded, then gave him a gentle smile. 'You're right, son. And I shouldn't.' She reached up and ruffled his hair. 'You are trouble, but you know the difference between right and wrong. I want you to promise me you'll never get involved with those kids, or their crush.'

Eddie nodded.

'I want you to promise me.'

He didn't see what the big deal was. 'I've no intention of—'

'Then just promise.'

'All right. I promise.'

'Good, that's a good boy. Because a Malone always keeps his word.'

Eddie laughed to himself. *A Malone always keeps his word.* Like they were the royal family or something. His mum tried to direct him down a street to the left, but Eddie resisted.

'Mum – the car's down here.'

'I know. There's just a couple of shops I want to pop into down here . . .'

'But you promised we were going home.'

'I won't be a minute.'

And she led him on, nevertheless; completely oblivious to the fact that she too was a Malone.

Five

Eddie was standing in the school playground on Monday morning when Gary Gilmore came hurrying up, his face flushed with excitement. He grabbed Eddie's arm and said, 'Where is it?'

'Where's what?' Eddie asked, shaking his arm free.

'The place we have to go to.'

'I've no idea what you're talking about.'

'Eddie – come on, I know it's a secret, but you can tell me; we're all in this together.'

'We're all in what together?'

'The gang.'

'Yes,' Eddie sighed, 'we are certainly in a gang together.'

'So where is it then?'

'Where's what?'

'The place!'

'What place?'

'Where we're having the thing.'

'What thing?'

Gary Gilmore winked at him. 'The *thing*.'

'Gary – will you just bloody tell me what you're talking about.'

Gary looked a little crestfallen. 'Sor-*ry*,' he said, 'there's no need to snap. I just thought we had to keep it hush-hush.'

'Keep *what* hush-hush?'

'The thing . . . in the place . . .'

Eddie rolled his eyes. 'Good God help me!' he exclaimed. 'Will you just tell me, Gary?'

Gary bit on his lip, glanced around to make sure they weren't being watched or listened to, then drew closer and his voice fell to a whisper. 'The meeting. The special meeting.' He nodded at Eddie, who just looked blankly at him. 'The Alliance, Eddie. All the gangs are going, everyone's talking about it, but nobody knows where it is, it's only you leaders who know, but you can tell me, I'm your friend, I won't tell anyone, swear to God.'

Eddie's mind was racing. The Alliance was an agreement between most of the gangs not to infringe on each other's territory without permission; to respect each other's members – i.e. no stealing from or fighting with fellow members; and it was also a device through which certain gangs got together to plan and execute military operations. Eddie wasn't exactly sure who the

Council Members of the Alliance were – although he guessed Captain Black was one of them. However, he supposed that Captain Black didn't always get his own way with the Alliance – otherwise he would have been able to stop Eddie's little gang from crossing the city at all. If the Alliance issued an instruction it became law, and anyone who ignored it was in big trouble. Eddie had only ever met the Alliance leader once. Billy Cobb was a friendly enough member of the Ramsey Street Wheelers who had signed Eddie's own gang up to the terms and conditions of membership of the Alliance. But that was the last Eddie had heard of the Alliance, and that was more than six months ago. Now, evidently, there was a meeting being held, but what it was about, or when it was to be held, or where, Eddie had no idea. But of course, he wasn't about to admit this to Gary Gilmore. Instead he gave a little shrug. 'I can't really say,' he said.

'Oh Eddie – come on.'

'I'll tell you when the time is right.'

'Eddie, come on. This is driving me nuts.'

'You shouldn't even know about it, Gary. What did you hear?'

'I heard it's about the Seagulls. There's so

many of them now. People are worried they're going to break out of their camp, try to take over other territories. Is that what it's about Eddie, is it?'

'I can't say,' said Eddie. But he winked at Gary. 'As soon as I'm allowed to say, you'll be the first to know, Gary.'

'Yeah, right,' said Gary. He turned and began to tramp unhappily away.

Eddie sighed. The playground was its usual frenzy of early morning activity, but he stood exactly where he was. The Alliance was calling a special meeting of the gangs, but he hadn't been invited. What did that mean? Was it really about the Seagulls? Or was it about the fact that in order to have his gang join the Alliance, Eddie had lied outrageously to Billy Cobb?

When Eddie emerged from Botanic Station on his way home, he automatically glanced around to see if his old friend Barney, who had once been a body washer in the hospital, but more recently had worked as a lollipop man, was in his usual position – but no, not today, nor indeed for the past two weeks. Instead he saw Mo, sitting on the station wall, looking anxious.

'What's up with you?' Eddie asked as he breezed up to her.

'You heard about the Alliance meeting?'

Eddie nodded.

'It's tomorrow night,' she said.

Eddie nodded.

'Do you know where?' she asked.

Eddie shook his head.

'Or do you know, and you're just not prepared to tell me?'

'I don't know. Honestly.'

She gave him a long hard look; he gave her one back. 'You're sure?'

'Mo, if I knew, I'd tell you.'

She nodded, finally, and seemed to accept that he was telling the truth. 'Well,' she said, 'if you don't know, the obvious next question is, why don't you know?'

'What do you mean?'

'Well – we are part of the Alliance, aren't we?' Eddie nodded. 'Then why haven't we been invited to the meeting?'

'Well,' said Eddie, almost without thinking, 'who says we haven't?'

'But you said you didn't know where . . .'

'I don't. All I'm saying is, we're part of the

Alliance, we will be invited – maybe the . . . uh, invitation hasn't arrived yet.'

'Invitation?' Mo looked incredulous. 'You think they send out invitations, like it was someone's birthday party or something?'

He had no idea what they did. All he knew was that there was a very important meeting about to take place, and as yet he hadn't been invited. He shrugged. 'Relax,' he said, 'they'll be in touch. How're they going to hold an Alliance meeting without us?'

Mo gave him a look that said, 'Quite easily,' but she didn't actually say anything.

They walked back to Eddie's apartment. They took a very long and circuitous route in order to avoid Bacon or Bap or any other of Captain Black's foot soldiers and arrived without incident. Eddie was relieved to find that Scuttles was at work. His mum was busy in the kitchen. She said, 'Hello, Mo.'

'Hi.'

She had never really warmed to Mo. He supposed it was because she looked so odd. And because her father had recently been in prison. And she probably blamed her for getting Eddie into so much trouble, because he'd never been in trouble before they moved to the city and it was only since he'd been hanging about with her that all this nonsense about gangs had started.

'Good day at school?' his mum asked. Eddie nodded. 'And what about you?' She smiled at Mo. Mo shrugged. Mo hadn't been to school for as long as Eddie had known her, and his mum knew it as well, and didn't like it one bit.

'Any post for me, Mum?'

His mum's head jerked towards him, and her cheeks flushed. She was already shaking her head before she remembered something and said, 'Oh – yes, of course – there was something. It's on the mantelpiece.'

Eddie gave her a perplexed look, then turned back into the living room. He hesitated in the doorway for a moment, his heart pounding; there, on the shelf just above the electric storage heater sat an envelope, long and thin. Mo gave him a little push from behind and Eddie stepped somewhat nervously forward.

From the kitchen, his mother called: 'It's an invitation to a birthday party.'

Eddie lifted the envelope and turned it over in his hands – it had clearly already been opened.

'You opened my post?' Eddie shouted back.

'Sorry, misread the front of it, thought it was for me.'

Eddie turned the envelope over again. It said 'Eddie Malone' in very big black capital letters. How could she possibly misread that?

'I'll have to see about getting glasses,' his mum called.

Eddie shook his head. He glanced at Mo. She nodded. He pulled up the tattered flap and slipped out a green card. There was a picture on the front which on one level was quite innocent: a young family enjoying a picnic on a beach. But if you looked a little more closely you could see that instead of happy smiling faces, they looked quite scared, and what was scaring them was the flock of birds flapping around them.

Seagulls.

One was ripping a sandwich from a little girl's hands. Another had landed on the picnic blanket itself and was tearing at it with its beak. Beside him, Mo tutted. Eddie nodded, then opened the card; inside in the same big black capitals it said: EDDIE MALONE (and <u>one</u> guest) is invited to AL LIANCE'S BIRTHDAY BASH, SATURDAY, 23 OCTOBER, DUNDONALD ICE BOWL, 11.55 pm.

From the kitchen, his mum called again: 'The Ice

Bowl, that'll be fun! But I think they made a mistake on the time! Eleven fifty-five pm! That's nearly midnight! Honestly, kids today, can't even tell the time!'

Eddie shook his head, then passed the card to Mo. 'Well,' he said, 'it looks like we're going to a party.'

Six

Eddie couldn't sleep that night – partly because of the upcoming party, but mostly because of something else, and he just couldn't put his finger on what it was. Something had disturbed him, something was nagging at him, but the more he tried to pin it down, the more elusive it became. He tossed and turned and tossed and turned, but still it wouldn't come to him, and neither would sleep. Eventually he got up and padded into the living room. He made himself some Frosties, then turned the TV on and flipped through the channels, hardly paying attention. He glanced at his watch: 4 am. Three hours before he usually got up for school. Around him, the entire block of flats vibrated gently to the sound of his mother's snores. Scuttles, who stayed about three nights of the week, had gone home shortly before midnight.

When he finished his early breakfast, or late supper, depending on your point of view, he took the dish into the kitchen, washed it and set it on the rack. Then his eyes fell on the invitation and torn envelope sitting on the kitchen table. *Al Liance*, indeed. Very clever. *Dundonald Ice Bowl*. Smack in the middle of territory controlled by the Lords of Dundonald, a fancy name for what he knew to be quite a small gang. But evidently it was considered a safe place to hold this emergency meeting of the Alliance. And there was certainly no mistake about the time: just before midnight. Suitably dark, suitably mysterious. While everyone else was settling down for the night, Belfast's gangland warlords would clearly be gathering to decide on what to do about the Seagulls.

What would he do? What would he say?

He had no real idea.

He didn't know enough about them to say one way or another. He knew that people disliked them – both adults and their gangster children. Quite possibly they feared them as well. Certainly the sight of the Seagulls, storming through the city centre that day, had struck the fear of God into him. But just because they were scary, didn't mean that they were necessarily bad. They were strangers in a strange land, and possibly they had just banded together to protect themselves.

Crush.

Perhaps that was the difference between boys

like Eddie and the Seagulls. They were drug addicts, and wherever there were drugs, trouble was sure to follow. He might not read the newspapers or watch serious programmes on television, but even Eddie knew that much. His mum was right, he supposed, warning him to stay away from . . .

Mum.

That was it. That's what was troubling him.

The way she had looked when he asked her about the post. Embarrassed. Flustered. Perhaps, even, *guilty* of something? And she had opened the letter, even though a blind man in a coal mine could have read the name on the envelope. What was she looking for? And more importantly, what had she found? Had there been something else in the envelope? Some other information? She was always warning him about getting into trouble again – perhaps this was her way of making sure, or of protecting him. So she intercepted his letters and fished out anything that might lead him astray. But what else could there have been?

Eddie sat down at the kitchen table and tried to puzzle it out. An invitation – a date, a time, a place, and a strong suggestion of what the meeting would be about, without actually spelling it out. But what else was he missing – or was he misreading his mother's reaction completely? He studied the picture on the front again: a happy family on one level, and on another, a family under attack. It was what his English teacher would call a metaphor. Using one thing to illustrate another. But was there another, less obvious message? The Seagulls. The family. The sand. The waves. He couldn't think of one – and if he couldn't, how could his mother have worked it out? So, no, it surely wasn't the illustration. He studied the envelope again. Although it had been somewhat carelessly torn open there was no other indication that anything else might have fitted inside. Eddie slipped the invitation back into it. Almost a perfect fit. If there had been anything else it would have had to be very thin – paper thin, in fact. So possibly another sheet of paper. What might that contain? Instructions on how to get there? Possibly. A list of the gangs attending? Probably not, that would give the game away to any parents who happened to open their children's mail.

Then he thought about getting there. Whatever way you approached Dundonald Ice Bowl you had to pass through territories belonging to at least six other gangs. So could that be it perhaps –

passwords? To allow you safe passage through enemy territory? Because even though they were nearly all signed up to the Alliance it didn't make them friends; it was just a way of reducing fighting between the different gangs. The more Eddie thought about it, the more it made sense. And if his mum recognised the passwords for what they were, she could conceivably guess that her removal of them would prevent him travelling to the 'party'. That was why she'd looked so shifty when he asked about the post.

So if there were passwords – what had she done with them?

Eddie checked the pedal bin in the kitchen first: nothing but empty Jaffa Cake boxes. Some things never changed.

Next he searched the black bin bag in the hall which Scuttles kept forgetting to take down to the communal rubbish skips downstairs. More Jaffa Cake boxes, junk mail, scrapings from breakfast and dinner, newspapers. But no passwords.

So she hadn't thrown it out. She was keeping it. But where? Eddie opened the drawer in the kitchen where she kept the household bills. Not there. He opened the cupboard in the hall where she kept important family documents in a cardboard box –

birth certificates, passports, his school reports. Nope.

Eddie walked down the hall to his mother's bedroom. In there, under the bed, she kept her jewellery in a small metal cash box. Not that she had much in the way of jewellery; or that what she did have was particularly valuable; or that under the bed wasn't the first place a burglar would look; or that the tiny little padlock would stop anyone above the size of a garden gnome from cracking it open; but still, that was where she kept her most precious things. It was the only other place Eddie could think of. He opened the door a fraction and immediately winced at the volume of her snoring. He padded softly into the room – although he really didn't need to. A herd of elephants could have stampeded through and still not have been heard over her snoring. He got down on his knees, then flattened himself out and crawled under the bed. He located the cash box and withdrew it. Next he moved around in the half light trying to locate her handbag, which is where she kept the key to the padlock. He knew this because she had told him once. Eddie found the bag sitting on her dressing table. He lifted it and the cash box and withdrew.

Back in the kitchen he set the cash box on the

table, and rummaged through the handbag until he found the key. And a packet of Jaffa Cakes. He shook his head. He wondered if there was an organisation for people who were addicted to Jaffa Cakes, in the same way that people who drank too much or gambled too often could seek out the support of fellow devotees. He put the biscuits back in the bag and slipped the key into the tiny padlock. He turned it once and it clicked open. His mother wasn't half as smart as she thought she was. And the chances were she would never find out about his early morning raid; he would copy down the passwords, then lock them back into the cash box and return it to her bedroom.

Eddie lifted the lid. Inside he saw several silver rings, a necklace, and a dozen or more earrings – some in pairs, some obviously missing their partners. But no list of passwords. He stood, disappointed, for several moments; then he reached into the box and felt along the sides of it for some hidden compartment, but there was nothing. Then he pressed down on the base, and was rewarded with a kind of springiness which suggested that there was something hidden below. So he pushed down harder on one side of the base, which lifted up the opposite side enough for him to slip his fingers underneath and pull up the entire base.

Ah.

A single sheet of white paper, and some other envelopes beneath.

Eddie unfolded the sheet. There was a list of innocent-looking initial letters written in the same style as the envelope and invitation, and which might easily have stood for the names of the supposed birthday party guests, but which Eddie recognised as standing for the names of the gangs that controlled the territories surrounding Dundonald Ice Bowl. Beside each set of initials there was a single word – Scrooge, Tiny Tim, Uriah Heep, Micawber, Copperfield and half a dozen others – which could have been nicknames for the boys whose initials they were beside, but which Eddie was now certain were passwords. He found a pen in one of the kitchen drawers, and quickly noted the gang names and the passwords on a page from the notebook which his mum kept by the kitchen phone. Then he tore it out and slipped it into his pyjama pocket. Eddie allowed himself a little smile. At last, a small victory over his mum. He knew she was just trying to protect him, but he was big enough and smart enough now to look after himself. He was no longer the fresh-faced kid who'd arrived in Belfast just a year before. He was a gangster, and soon he would be sitting down with his fellow gangsters to decide the fate of the Seagulls.

Eddie folded the piece of paper exactly as he had found it, and lifted the base of the cash box again to slip it back inside. It was only now that his eyes happened to glance over the front of the other envelopes in the base of the box. He was looking down at them, and they were upside down, but something about the handwriting seemed familiar. He tried to lift the top envelope out, but when it wouldn't come he saw that there was an elastic band holding it tight against the other ones below. So he lifted them all out together – and was surprised to find how many there were. The base of the cash box was deeper than it looked. He guessed there had to be about fifty of them. He turned the tightly bound package around so that he could read the name and address on the top envelope properly.

It said: Eddie Malone, Snow Cottage, Groomsport, Northern Ireland.

And so did the second, the third, the fourth and all of the others.

Eddie felt the colour drain from his cheeks.

It wasn't the fact that each and every envelope bore his name and his former address. It was the fact that each and every one of them had been addressed to him by his father.

Seven

Eddie exploded through the door to his mother's bedroom.

It was exactly forty-five minutes after he had discovered the letters from his father. His father, who had disappeared so completely from his life. His father who had apparently wanted nothing to do with him, who had run off with another woman, who hadn't once tried to contact him or call him. His father who had, in fact, written to him every week, without fail, to tell him about his new life, his new job, how happy he was with Spaghetti Legs and, most importantly, as far as Eddie was concerned, how much he missed his son. Eddie hadn't read all of the letters yet – he read the first four or five entirely, then skipped towards the later ones. All the time he was growing angrier, and angrier, and angrier and angrier. His father hadn't forgotten him at all, he loved him dearly, but he believed Eddie wasn't writing back to him because *he* was angry about him leaving home with Spaghetti Legs. His dad had written that he understood this, that of course Eddie was angry, but that perhaps one day he would understand.

Eddie understood, all right.

He understood that his father had written to him once a week for the past year – and that his mum had hidden the letters.

The bedroom door cracked off the wall with enough force and noise to cut through his mother's snores, and she came roaring up out of the bed as if a bomb had gone off beneath her.

'Wooooaaahhhwhaaa!' she screamed into the semi-darkness, her eyes suddenly wide, her nostrils flared, her hair standing at mad angles.

'*You . . .*' Eddie began.

'Eddie . . . ?' his mother spluttered, starting to recover herself.

'*You . . .*'

'Eddie, what's wrong?'

'*You . . .*'

'Eddie . . . have you hurt yourself?'

'*You . . .*'

'Eddie, have you had a nightmare?' Her hand was clutched to her chest. She was breathing hard.

'You stupid, fat, moron!'

'*Eddie?*'

'You unbelievably dense rat-bag!'

'Eddie?'

'You stinking, putrid brain-dead old cow!'

'Eddie, I don't know what exactly the problem—'

'This is the problem!'

Eddie held up the envelopes.

His mum squinted at them for a moment, and then her mouth dropped open a little. 'Oh,' she said.

'Oh?' said Eddie. 'Is that it, *oh*?'

'Oh my God.'

'Oh my God? Too bloody right!'

Eddie came further into the room, and then hurled the letters at his mother. She ducked down instinctively, but they merely rained harmlessly down over the bed.

'How could you?' Eddie yelled. 'How could you!'

His mum raised her head cautiously. 'Eddie, I—'

'How could you, Mum?

'I thought it was for the best.'

'The best? All this time I thought he'd disappeared or was in prison or was hurt or just didn't bloody care, but now I find out he's been writing to me every bloody week!'

'Eddie, I'm sorry!'

'You will be!'

Eddie stormed out of the bedroom. He stomped down the hall. He stared out of the front window. He returned to the kitchen. He slumped down at the table and buried his head in his hands.

His dad was OK. He was fine. He still loved him. He was sorry about running away with Spaghetti Legs and he desperately wanted Eddie to come and visit him. All the months and months of worry, all the sleepless nights when Eddie had somehow managed to blame himself for his father's decision to leave home. But it wasn't his fault at all! It had never been his fault. He didn't know if that meant it was his mother's fault entirely, but right there and then, sitting in that kitchen, he was prepared to believe that it was. That she had driven his dad away from home, and then when his dad had tried to maintain contact with him she'd hidden away his letters on purpose.

He heard footsteps behind him, but didn't turn.

His mother tried to put her arm around him, but he shrugged it off. She pulled out the other chair and sat opposite.

'Eddie,' she said, 'I'm sorry.' He ignored her. He kept his eyes closed behind his hands. She reached out and put a hand on his arm. He pushed it away with his elbow. 'Eddie, please, talk to me.'

No way.

'I'm really, really sorry, Eddie. I thought I was doing the right thing.'

Eddie's hands snapped down, and he glared at her. 'The right thing?' he shouted. 'Chasing my dad away, then hiding his letters? Yeah right, you old witch.'

She winced a little at the name, but she forced herself to remain calm. 'Eddie – it wasn't like that. You know it wasn't. Your dad did the running off with Spaghetti Legs.'

'Because he couldn't stand you!'

'Yes – maybe. But I loved him, and he said he loved me. So I was the one with a broken heart when he ran off. Why he did that – well, you'll have to ask him.'

'And how could I ever have done that? You hid his letters!'

'I didn't . . . I mean, I did, but I didn't mean to, Eddie . . . it just happened.'

'Yeah, right.'

'It did, honestly. Eddie, we moved from Groomsport very quickly, so quickly that we forgot to tell the Post Office where to forward our mail. So all the time your father was writing to you they were still going to the old address. Eventually they tracked us down, but it was about a month after we'd moved – there were five or six letters addressed to you, but you were right in the middle of all that stuff with the babies, and I didn't want to upset you any further and . . . well, I was still very angry with your dad. I wanted it just to be me and you, I didn't want him to cause us any more heartbreak. So I didn't give you the letters, and then when more started to arrive I kept them from you as well. I'm sorry, Eddie, I shouldn't have. I really shouldn't have.'

Eddie shook his head. 'No you bloody shouldn't.'

'It's only because I love you, son. I was just trying to protect you.'

'From what?'

She looked helplessly at him. She had no idea how to respond.

'Can I get you some Frosties?' she asked, eventually.

'No you bloody can't!'

Eddie stormed off into his room and slammed the door shut.

About an hour and a half later she knocked gently on his door and said, 'Eddie, are you ready for school?'

GALWAY COUNTY LIBRARIES

'No! I'm not going!'

'Eddie . . .'

'Get lost!'

'Well, you can't stay in there all day.'

'Watch me!'

'Eddie, we have to be grown up about this!'

'Yeah. Right. Hiding letters, that's grown up!'

'Eddie, please, you need to go to school!'

'I need to bash your head in!'

A while later he heard her talking on the phone. Scuttles. Then she was back at the door: 'Bernard says—'

'I don't give a flying farmyard what Bernard says!'

'He says you're quite right to be angry and that I've been very stupid.'

'Woah!' Eddie shouted through the door. 'There's a world first – me and Fat Slob agree on something at last!'

'Eddie, I've said I'm sorry!'

'I don't care!'

It went silent on both sides of the door for another few minutes. Then his mother said his name quietly.

'What?' he snapped back.

'I was reading some of his letters.'

'Well they're none of your business!'

'I know, I . . . well, he's left his phone number. If you want to call him, that's all right.'

Eddie was about to shout back, 'Too right I'm going to call him!' but he hesitated. He felt strange. He was still wild and angry, but he was also growing more and more confused. Despite his bad temper, he kind of understood why his mum had hidden the letters from him. Understood, but didn't agree with. And though he had prayed and prayed to hear from his dad, now that he had the chance to talk to him on the phone, he wasn't quite sure what it was he wanted to say, or hear.

Whatever way you looked at it, his dad had run off without him. Left him behind.

OK – he'd sent letters.

But . . . so what? The electricity people sent letters, it didn't mean they cared for him.

The milkman left milk, it didn't mean he worried about his mental health.

His dad sent some letters. How hard was that? Ten minutes' work, then he could forget about his son for another week.

Eddie sighed. His head was sore.

His mum tapped on the door again. 'Do you want to call him, Eddie?'

'Not when you're around,' Eddie hissed.

'Well, maybe I should go out for a while, and you can do it then.'

'Maybe you should go out for good.'

'Oh, Eddie.'

He knew how mean he was being. He just couldn't help himself. She left him alone for another half hour. Then she came back and tapped again on the door. 'Eddie,' she said quietly, 'will you forgive me?'

'Sure,' said Eddie.

'Thank you, son.'

'When you're about ninety-nine years old and you have no hair and you can't walk and you're in a wheelchair and I'll push you over the edge of a cliff.'

'Oh,' said his mother.

She rested her head against the door. It was going to be a very long day.

Eight

Saturday, 23 October was one of the longest days in Eddie's life. Not because he was still at war with his mum, and it being a Saturday he had to spend more or less the whole day with her, not because Scuttles was giving him a hard time because he wouldn't forgive her, not even because little Paddy seemed to be aware that something was up between his mother and his brother and cried even more incessantly than usual. It was the longest day because not until the very end of it would he have to attend the grand meeting of the heads of Belfast's leading gangs. It was now three o'clock in the afternoon; shortly before midnight Eddie and Mo would enter Dundonald Ice Bowl. Eddie was determined to make an impact, to show the rest of the city's young outlaws that his gang was every bit as rough and tough and bright and daring as the rest of them; he would show Captain Black, who would undoubtedly be there, that he wasn't the slightest bit scared of him; he would seek to make friends with the other leaders, forge alliances with some of the smaller gangs so that they in turn could unite together in times of shared trouble. And he would speak eloquently on the subject of the Seagulls. He would argue that . . . well, what exactly would he argue? He didn't know enough about them. So instead, he would listen, and give an opinion if and when he was asked for it. He would be wise and calm and responsible and respectful.

'Eddie! That funny little muppet is at the door for you!'

Scuttles. Eddie glanced at his watch. It was a little after five o'clock. Scuttles was back in his chair, leaving the front door lying open. Eddie pulled his jacket on. On the way past he said, 'See ya later, fat chops.'

Scuttles growled something back, but Eddie was already at the front door. Just as he stepped through it his mum appeared in the kitchen doorway.

'Eddie?'

He stopped, but didn't look back. 'What?' he said flatly. Mo was standing in front of him.

'Where are you going?'

'Out.'

'When will you be back?'

'When I come through the door.'

'Eddie, I don't want you going to this thing.'

'And I don't want you hiding my mail.'

He stepped out of the apartment, and slammed the door shut behind him. He walked away down the hall so quickly that Mo had to break into a run to catch up with him.

'I take it you've not made peace with her yet,' she said.

'Nope,' said Eddie.

'Do you not think maybe you should?'

'Nope.'

They took the lift down to the ground floor. When they got there, Eddie saw that Gary Gilmore was waiting for them.

'What're you doing here?' Eddie snapped. He gave Mo an accusing look. 'Did you bring him? The invitation said I could bring one guest, not two.'

'No, Eddie, I didn't bring him,' Mo spat angrily back. 'But so what if I had? He's entitled to come just as much as you or me!'

'Oh really?' said Eddie.

'Yes, really.'

'It's only fair,' said Gary. 'We're all in this together. Besides, I've brought some bombs – we can blow things up if we get into trouble and have to escape in a hurry.'

Eddie rolled his eyes. 'See?' he said, and pointed a finger at Mo. 'This is precisely why I didn't invite him! This is supposed to be a meeting of gang leaders – everyone's going to be nervous enough without him turning up with bombs! We're bound to be searched on the way in, if they find bombs on us they'll throw us out.'

'You don't know that, Eddie,' said Mo. 'They'll probably all have weapons.'

'What would you know about it?'

Mo's eyes blazed with anger. Eddie turned and walked away. He stood by the entrance to the apartments and rubbed at his head. Mo left him for a full minute before coming over. Then she stood before him with her arms folded. She gave him a long and searching look.

'What?' Eddie asked eventually.

'I'm waiting,' said Mo.

'What for? A bus?'

'No, Eddie. An apology.'

'Well, I hope you've a lot of time to waste.'

Now she tapped her foot impatiently on the footpath. She gave him an even harder look.

'What now?' said Eddie.

'I'm still waiting.'

'What for? A train?'

Mo's eyes narrowed. She looked across at Gary, who was watching with interest. She sighed, then held her hand out to Eddie. 'OK, Eddie, you're the boss. Let's just all be friends – it's going to be a long night.'

Eddie nodded. Good. He had made it absolutely clear who was in charge. He grasped her hand. 'OK,' he said. 'Gary, you can come, but you'll have to lose the bombs, and if they say you can't come in then you'll have to— aaaaaaaah!'

Eddie let out a scream as Mo suddenly twisted his arm up and around behind his back, then jarred it up harder still; the pain was immense. Mo pushed his arm again, then kicked out at the backs of his legs, which forced him down on to his knees.

'Mo . . . ! What're you— aaaah!'

She twisted his arm, hard. She bent down and hissed into his ear: 'Let's get one thing straight, buddy-boy. We're all in this together – that means we all have to get on, we all have to be nice to each other. Now I know you're having a hard time with your mum, I know it can't be a barrel of laughs having Scuttles around the place, and maybe the baby does cry all night – we've all got our own problems. But the moment we step outside our front doors we leave them behind. Because it's hard

81

enough and dangerous enough out here already, we don't need a hard time from you as well. Do you understand?'

'I don't know!' Eddie yelled. 'I can't think! You're breaking my arm!'

'And I'll snap it right off unless you apologise for being such an arse!'

'I'm sorry! I'm sorry!'

'What for?'

'For whatever you think I've done!'

'That's not good enough!'

'What do you want, blood?'

'I want you to say sorry and mean it!'

'I mean it! God Almighty, I mean it!'

She let go of his arm. Eddie staggered to his feet, rubbing at his arm, desperately trying to quell the pain and force some life back into it. 'Jesus,' he said, 'there was no need for that.'

'There was every need for it, Eddie. We're all in this together. We don't need anyone acting the arse, not with such a big night ahead of us.'

Eddie was feeling braver now that he was standing square in front of her and she couldn't take him by surprise again. Maybe if she ganged up with Gary they'd be able to beat him, but Gary was standing grinning stupidly, with his arms folded, enjoying the show. He wasn't about to get involved.

Eddie sighed. He blew air out of his cheeks. 'OK. Really. I am sorry. I know I've been . . . well, you know. Let's just forget about it, OK?'

'OK,' said Mo.

'Friends?' Eddie asked. He held out his hand.

Mo managed a sarcastic grin. 'How stupid do you think I am? You'll twist it!'

Eddie retained a straight face. 'Mo? It's over. Let's be friends.' He kept his hand out. She grasped it somewhat reluctantly. Eddie smiled. Then suddenly he twisted it up and around her back. She let out a scream. He moved around behind her, forcing her arm up further, but just as he began to repeat her earlier move, kicking the legs from beneath her, her foot shot backwards and smacked him right in the willy.

Eddie saw stars, felt a lot of pain, and collapsed to the ground. He rolled around in agony for three minutes and twenty-three seconds – Gary Gilmore timed it – then fell silent, his eyes closed, his hands covering his private parts.

Eventually Mo stood over him and said, 'Eddie – are you OK?'

'Yes,' Eddie managed to whisper, 'but I may

not pee for another thirty years.'

Mo shook her head. 'Don't be silly, Eddie, you'd burst.'

'I'd prefer to burst,' said Eddie, 'rather than pee. Too . . . much . . . pain.'

Eventually, eventually, he felt better and they made their peace. Mo even apologised. She said she was worried, nervous, and tense about the Alliance meeting, and she was sorry for kicking him in the willy.

'That's OK,' said Eddie, 'but one day I'll get you back.'

'I don't have a willy,' said Mo.

'I'm not so sure about that,' said Eddie, and she and Gary laughed, and they were all friends again.

Mo surprised Eddie by taking out a fiver and saying, 'We'll go by bus.' She'd stolen it from her dad's wallet. So they got one bus into the city centre, and then another one out to Dundonald. Of course this meant that they arrived two hours before the meeting was due to begin, and had a lot of time to kill. So they decided to hang out in a McDonalds, which sat opposite the Ulster Hospital, which was extremely modern compared to the hospital Eddie's mum worked in.

'Good job we're so close,' said Gary, nodding across at it. 'Just in case things go wrong.'

'You mean if one of your bombs go off?' Mo asked.

'No, in case there's a fight at the meeting. You put so many gang leaders in one room, gang leaders who dislike and distrust each other, there's bound to be trouble.'

Eddie had to admit he had a point. Despite the fact that they were all signed up to the Alliance, there was always trouble going on between the gangs, and it was more a question of luck than planning that the whole city hadn't erupted into serious violence.

They ate burgers and fries and talked about the Seagulls and crush. Mo knew a number of kids who were addicted to it; Gary didn't. Eddie wondered if anyone at Brown's Academy had ever tried it. Somehow he doubted it. He would know. As the hour grew later, their conversation died. They were all nervous now. It was dark and they were in a strange territory. They had already had to use their passwords three times, once to get through Reservoir Pups country to get to the bus stop, once when they got off the bus in Dundonald, and again when they'd crossed the road to get to the McDonalds. The Ice Bowl was another twenty minutes' walk away. They would set out soon. The minutes ticked by. Soon. Soon. They were all reluctant to move. Here, in the fast food restaurant, they felt reasonably safe, but outside was a different matter. It was eleven o'clock. McDonalds was closing. Traffic was almost non-existent on the road outside the hospital.

Eddie took a deep breath. 'It's time to go,' he said.

He nodded at Mo. She nodded back.

'Gary? You ready?'

'I was thinking about waiting here.'

'Gary . . .'

'You said I wasn't invited. You might have a point.'

'Gary . . .'

'No, seriously. I'm going to wait here until you come back.'

'It's closing, Gary.'

'I'll wait outside.'

'Gary.'

'Really. I'll be fine.'

There was no persuading him. Gary stood by the McDonalds window, which was now in darkness, and waved them off. He shivered. Mo shivered. Eddie shivered. As they walked along the road away from the restaurant, following Tourist Board signs towards Dundonald Ice Bowl, Eddie said, 'Did you ever think this might be one big trap, masterminded by Captain Black?'

Mo nodded.

'So what are we doing here?'

'I have no idea,' said Mo.

'Good,' said Eddie, 'I have no idea either.'

Having agreed upon that, they kept on walking.

Nine

Dundonald Ice Bowl was in complete darkness. It covered a vast area and was made up of more than just an ice rink – there were shops, a restaurant, an adventure playground. Eddie had half hoped that these would all be open and busy and that that would have provided some measure of protection, but everything was closed down, and even the huge neon signs above the main buildings were switched off. If it wasn't for the streetlights, you wouldn't even have known that the place was there. There was a boy standing by the gates to the car park, which were closed and locked. As they drew closer, Eddie was distressed to find that it was Bacon, one of Captain Black's right-hand men.

'Well look who it is,' Bacon sneered. 'Curly and his girlfriend.'

Eddie had never quite worked out how Bacon, or his mate Bap, had ever come up with Curly as a nickname for him, because his hair was straight; but right now it didn't matter. He had to stay calm.

Mo was about to snap something back, but Eddie put a hand on her arm.

'We're here for the meeting,' Eddie said.

'Well, I didn't think you were here for your ice-dancing lesson, girly-boy,' Bacon hissed. 'Password?'

'Cat in the hat.'

'Cat in the hat it is.' Bacon pushed his foot against the wire to one side of the gate, bending it back enough for Eddie and Mo to duck through. 'Catch you later,' said Bacon. They didn't respond. As they walked towards the main entrance Mo whispered, 'One day I'm going to get that little . . .'

'Me too,' said Eddie.

The main entrance was just as dark as the rest of the building. They tried the door, but it was locked – then they heard a low whistle and turned to see a torch being flashed at them from a dozen metres away along the main wall. They moved towards it, and then followed the beam towards a Fire Exit sign. When they reached it they saw that Bacon's mate, Bap, was holding the torch. 'In here, Curly,' he said, pulling the fire exit door open.

They ignored him, and stepped inside. They stood for a moment, getting used as best they could to the even more intense darkness. 'Do you ever get the impression,' Eddie whispered, 'that the Pups might be running this show?'

Mo didn't respond. She didn't really need to. It was obvious.

As their eyes adjusted, Mo touched Eddie's arm and pointed into the distance. 'There,' she said. He followed her gaze, and saw a flickering light, and then another, and another. Candles. Leading their way.

Eddie took another deep breath. 'OK,' he said, 'let's go.'

They followed the candles, one after the other. There were about thirty in all, and they led them through several sets of swing doors into the main arena. As soon as they set foot in it, Eddie could feel the cold coming off the ice. Chairs had been set out right in the middle – about forty of them, he guessed. There were candles everywhere, and the smoke from them hung over the whole arena, a dark, foreboding cloud.

A voice behind them said, 'You're early.'

Eddie turned to find Billy Cobb beside them, with a clipboard in his hand.

'Well . . . you . . . you know,' Eddie stammered, 'early bird gets the . . . worm.'

He had no idea what he was saying. Luckily

Cobb ignored it; instead he made a note on his clip-board, then directed Eddie and Mo to their seats. 'Make yourselves comfortable,' he said, 'it's going to be a long night.'

And so they arrived, two by two, the kids who ruled the city. Eddie knew from the password list that had come with the invitation that there were twenty-three gangs attending: most of their names he could work out from their initials, gangs like the Ramsey Street Wheelers, the Churchill Regulars, the Malone Marauders; others he could guess from their attire as they entered: the two with the skull and crossbones on their jackets had to be the Ormeau Pirates, the pair with webs tattooed on to their foreheads had to be the Ballysillan Spidermen. Some he had no idea about at all: there were two lads who looked like they'd just come from church, two others were wearing army uniforms.

There wasn't much in the way of talking: some spoke to Eddie or Mo as they took their seats, others ignored them but said hello to others; for every friendly nod exchanged around the arena, there were a couple of filthy looks. Some complained about their seats, some demanded to be moved, others refused to move. Billy Cobb moved between them all, calm, efficient, trying to smooth everything out. Beside Eddie a big fella with a skinhead nodded down at Mo. 'Don't have to ask who you are,' he said. 'Andytown Albinos.'

'Used to be,' said Mo. 'I'm with him now.'

'Oh yeah? And who're you?'

Eddie cleared his throat. 'We don't have a name.'

The skinhead nodded. 'Oh yeah. I've heard about you lot, the Gang With No Name.'

'No . . . no . . .' Eddie began, 'it's not . . . we don't actually have a . . .'

Mo dug him in the ribs. 'Leave it,' she hissed.

'Good little outfit, I hear,' the skinhead said.

'Cheers,' said Eddie.

'But keep off our turf, or we'll kill you.'

The skinhead sat down. Eddie sat down. He glanced at Mo; she was doing her best to suppress a grin. He was just about to say something to her when his eyes fell upon Bacon and Bap emerging from the candlelit corridor into the main arena. Behind them rolled Captain Black, leader of the Reservoir Pups. He was, as usual, sitting in a wheelchair, but it was no ordinary wheelchair. Eddie, living next door to a hospital, thought he'd seen every kind of wheelchair known to man, but this was something else. It wasn't quite jet propelled, but it wasn't far from it. It rolled into the arena under its own power, gleaming in the shimmering light; its tyres were thick and thickly tracked, almost like a tank, so that it could move over the most difficult terrains; the engine at the rear and the entire frame was heavily armoured and there was an array of controls and a joystick set into each arm rest. Eddie could only guess what kind of manoeuvre they allowed the wheelchair to perform or what weapons they were connected to. Quite possibly, it could fire missiles. It was a very impressive piece of work.

Captain Black stared straight ahead, refusing to recognise anyone, and those who hadn't yet taken their seats were forced to jump out of the way. Of course, Black didn't need a seat himself, so he took up a position on the far side at the front of the semicircle of seats, and when he was in place, with Bacon and Bap standing at his shoulders, an uncomfortable silence fell on the arena. Everyone but Captain Black exchanged glances, and there was a palpable tension in the air, mixed in with an unhealthy dose of suspicion. Billy Cobb finished making notes on his clipboard, then moved to the centre of the arena.

'Well, here we go,' Eddie whispered.

Billy Cobb, leader of an East Belfast outfit known as Cobb's Commandos, was a small fella with short blond hair, a sharp nose and an easy smile. His gang wasn't one of the biggest or the most feared, but was universally regarded as tough but fair. He had been one of the gang leaders most responsible for organising the Alliance and worked hard to make sure its agreements were observed. He said, 'Thanks for coming, folks, and thanks to the Lords of Dundonald for organising this venue – I hope you didn't have to pay too much for it.'

Laughter echoed around the arena at the very concept of paying for something.

Cobb smiled and nodded around the gathered gang leaders, then raised his hands for silence. 'As you know, membership of the Alliance gives any member the right at any time to call a special meeting, and tonight's meeting has been called by Rollie Hayes of the Duncrue Detonators.' All eyes turned towards a heavily muscled boy sitting a little to the right of Captain Black. Eddie knew the Detonators worked very closely with the Reservoir Pups. He was virtually certain it was Black who had actually called the meeting; Rollie Hayes was just his front man. 'Rollie,' said Cobb, 'I think we all pretty much know what this is about, but perhaps you'd like to get things rolling.'

Hayes got to his feet. He cleared his throat. A lot of people cleared their throats: the air was thick with candle smoke mixed with the thin mist coming off the ice. To Eddie it looked like something out of the Dark Ages: a gathering of Satanists or a coven of witches on a frozen lake.

'This is about the Seagulls, and what we're going to do about them.' The gangsters nodded around him and murmured supportively. 'They're breeding like flies – every day you look there's more of them, and I hear there's more on the way.'

Several of the gangsters booed.

'Do we actually know there's more on the way?' Billy Cobb asked.

Captain Black raised his hand. Cobb nodded towards him. 'We tapped into the government computers, Billy – another two thousand of them are coming this way.'

This drew gasps of astonishment from around the arena.

'Two thousand!' someone shouted. 'That's madness!'

'That army camp will never support another two thousand!' said another.

95

'It's not supposed to!' shouted Rollie Hayes. 'I'm told they're going to close the camp down, they're going to move them out into houses, into our territories!' More shouts and yells filled the air. 'They're going to get a foothold in every one of our territories!'

'No!'

'We have to stop them!'

'We have to drive them back to the sea!'

Captain Black raised his hand again. He was being very polite. None of the others were bothering. Cobb nodded for him to speak again. 'At this moment we estimate that the Seagulls have about one hundred and fifty to two hundred members. If another two thousand refugees come across the water, that could easily double or triple the number of gang members. We're just about holding them at bay now, but if they get any stronger they'll be able to put us all out of business; they'll control this city.'

All around the arena, gang leaders stamped their feet on the floor in support, throwing up slivers of ice. Even Eddie and Mo found themselves joining in. *If we really were on a frozen lake*, Eddie was thinking, even as he pounded the ice at his feet, *we'd fall right through and drown.*

Hayes shook his fist in the air. 'Not only will they control the city,' he shouted, 'they'll bring chaos and disease, and worst of all, they'll bring crush. We've already seen what it's doing to them, and now it's starting to creep into our gangs. Soon it'll be all of us, our members, our friends, our relatives, even our parents ... they'll all be destroyed by it!'

Applause rolled around the cavernous arena.

Somewhere at the back – Eddie could hardly see because of the semi-darkness – one of the gangsters began to chant, 'Seagulls out! Seagulls out!' and soon they were all joining in, punching the air with their fists, stamping the ice with their feet. It was like being at a football match – but it was tinged with a threat of violence which Eddie found unsettling. Through the raised fists he caught glimpses of Captain Black, sitting smugly at the front, nodding his head in time to the chanting, but not taking part. 'Seagulls out! Seagulls out! Seagulls out!'

Eventually Billy Cobb raised his hands to quieten things down, although it still took a couple of minutes. Eddie glanced at Mo; it was always difficult to tell what she was thinking, because she couldn't go any whiter, to show fear, and never,

ever, went red, to suggest anger. Although Eddie had felt compelled to join in the chanting, he had noted out of the corner of his eye that Mo had not. He gave her a little nudge. 'Are you all right?' he whispered.

She shook her head slowly. 'This . . . is . . . *horrible . . .*' she whispered back.

'I know . . .'

'Then why are you joining in?'

'Because there's seventy-five of them, and two of us.'

'That doesn't make it right, Eddie.'

'What do you expect—' but then his eyes fell on the skinhead behind him, who was clearly listening. Eddie abruptly stopped talking, and shook his head at Mo. She tutted, then turned her attention back to Billy Cobb at the front.

'Well, now that we all seem in agreement, the question is, what do we do about it?' His eyes surfed around the gathering. 'How do we stop this invasion? How do we fight back? How do we show them we're not prepared to lie down and take it?'

'Take what, exactly?'

It was a small voice, but it cut the atmosphere like a knife. Billy Cobb scanned the seats as an angry murmur grew. 'Who said that?' he shouted.

It was a girl's voice. A familiar one, at that. There were two other female gangster leaders in the room. But the one who had spoken was standing beside Eddie. Mo. Mo had risen to her feet.

Eddie could, and should, have stood with her. But he was frozen to his seat. Everyone was looking at them. And none of them looked very happy.

'I said it,' said Mo, 'and I'll say it again. What exactly is it that they've done?'

There was some laughter, some shouting. Eddie whispered harshly: 'Sit down, Mo! Sit down, this isn't the—'

But she wasn't having any of it. Her voice rose in pitch. 'I don't want a war to start for the wrong reason. They're strangers in our country. They've lost everything. They're probably scared, and they're quite right to be suspicious. It doesn't mean they're against us. Has anyone actually approached them? Asked them about their plans? Offered to sit down and discuss territories? Has anyone actually asked what they can contribute, how they can help *us*?'

'Help us!' roared Hayes, and his laughter was joined by nearly all of the others. 'Help us! We're going to help *them* – right back into the sea!' That was met with wild applause. Encouraged, he stepped it up another gear. 'They're the scum of the earth! We work ourselves into the ground to make a living, and they get everything given to them by the government! And what they do get, they spend on crush, and they kill themselves doing it! And not content with that, they try to sell it on to us, so that they can watch us kill ourselves as well!'

Mo was looking down at Eddie. 'Eddie – aren't you going to say anything?' she whispered desperately.

Eddie swallowed. He pushed himself nervously to his feet. A silence packed with anticipation filled the arena. They knew exactly who Eddie was – stories about his Babysnatching exploits and his fight to return the head of Oliver Plunkett were well known in gangland circles – but even better known was the hatred Captain Black held for him. They were all very interested in what he had to say and whether he would once again take on the leader of the Reservoir Pups.

Eddie took a deep breath. He had absolutely no idea what he was going to say: half of him was caught up in the excitement of the meeting and demanded that he support his new-found friends and allies; half of him wanted to support Mo and her voice of reason; and half of him wanted to say nothing, to go away and think it through. And that meant there were three halves to satisfy, which was an impossibility.

He glanced nervously down at Mo. She gave him an encouraging nod. He could see that her fingers were crossed, all of them.

He looked across at Captain Black, who had a cool, confident expression on his face, with just a hint of a sneer.

He looked around all of their expectant faces, or as many as he could make out in the half-light.

'Well . . .' he began, 'this is obviously a very important—'

But before he could go any further, the swing doors at the end of the arena burst open and a boy he had not seen before came charging through.

'The Seagulls!' he yelled. 'The Seagulls have set fire to the building! Get out! Get out while you can!'

The meeting erupted. Gang leaders leapt from their chairs. None of them had any idea how long the Ice Bowl had been on fire – the smell of the candles and the roar of the voices had covered up any tell-tale signs. But as they piled into the corridor it was suddenly clear to them how serious the fire was: the air was thick with smoke, a black, acrid smoke that caught in their throats and chests. The ceiling was beginning to crack with the intense heat and they could see licks of orange flame through it. They began to panic. They pushed and pulled and punched and kicked in their bid to escape the burning building and eventually they burst back out into the car park through the fire exit, coughing and spluttering and gagging.

Captain Black coughed along with them. Bacon and Bap stood by his side – together with four other Reservoir Pups. His own personal bodyguard.

Eddie knelt down to where Mo was on her hands and knees, trying to be sick. He patted her back. Behind them, Eddie heard Billy Cobb shouting questions over the hubbub of noise at the boy who'd broken the news of the fire. 'What did you see? What did you see!'

'I saw two of them, they were Seagulls all right – one guy, one girl – I saw them sneak in, they went around the back, I went to follow – but I go around the corner and the whole place is up in flames. It was them, I tell you!'

Cobb hurried across to Captain Black, while

those who were fit enough turned their attention to the car park and the landscaped gardens which surrounded the Ice Bowl. The glow from the burning building illuminated everything around them – but there was no sign of any Seagulls. Then, above the crackle and spit of the fire, they began to hear fire engines.

Mo struggled to her feet. 'We have to get out of here . . .'

'I know . . .' Eddie managed to say. He rubbed at his throat. It felt like he'd gargled with the contents of an ash tray.

Billy Cobb straightened beside Captain Black, and shouted above the noise. 'Listen up, everyone – the last thing we want is to get caught here, so make your way home via minor roads, back lanes, gardens – stay out of the public eye! Captain Black and I agree – this attack by the Seagulls means war!'

Everyone agreed. Even Mo nodded.

'Tomorrow morning there'll be a meeting of the War Council in the Pups' HQ, and we'll decide then how to deal with this!'

And with that Captain Black and his men turned and zipped off towards a gap in the fence at the back of the Ice Bowl, and the remaining gang leaders scattered in different directions, scurrying towards and then clambering over fences and gradually disappearing into the darkness. Eddie and Mo scaled the fence easily enough, then hid in a garden about half a mile away; they climbed a tree and watched as four fire engines battled to save the building.

'I have a feeling,' Eddie said, 'that things are about to get a whole hell of a lot worse.'

'You can say that again,' said Mo.

So he did.

Ten

The next morning, a Sunday, Eddie was quite happily in the land of Nod when his mum shook him awake. She said, 'Wake up, Eddie – there's someone at the door for you.'

Eddie was still sleepily confused, so he forgot for a moment that he still wasn't speaking to her. 'What . . . who . . . who is it?' he asked, stifling a yawn.

'Well how should I know?' She bent to pick up his clothes where he'd dropped them in a heap at the foot of the bed. She only meant to straighten them out, but she caught a whiff of something and quickly pressed them to her nose. Then she gave Eddie a hard look. 'Have you been smoking?' she snapped.

'No,' said Eddie.

'Eddie – don't lie to me, these clothes stink of smoke!'

'Don't lie to me?' This time he gave her an accusing look. 'Uhuh.'

She wagged a finger at him. 'Eddie, we might

not be getting on right now, and you might feel you've every reason not to like me, and I accept that, but I absolutely draw the line at you smoking. That hospital is full up with people dying because they smoke, I'm not having you go that way.'

'I wasn't smoking.'

'Well how come . . . ?' she asked, raising the clothes as irrefutable evidence.

'I was at a secret gangland meeting last night, and the building got burned down and I escaped by the skin of my teeth.'

She shook her head. 'Eddie . . .' she began, then sighed. 'Please, promise me, you won't smoke any more.'

'OK,' said Eddie. 'I won't smoke any more.'

She managed a faint smile, then turned with the clothes to leave the room. As she reached the door Eddie added, 'Or any less.' Then gave her a sarcastic smile; she hesitated for a moment, on the verge of snapping something back, but then walked on. Eddie closed his eyes again. He didn't like being mean to his mum. But he was doing it with distressing ease. What if he was slowly turning into all the things that Scuttles had always accused him of? Mean and vindictive and sarcastic and a gutter rat and a troublemaker? Eddie yawned again. No – he really wasn't any of those things, he decided. He was pretending to be because of what his mum had done with his dad's letters; soon he would decide she'd had enough punishment and he'd go back to being his usual self. An angelic little choirboy. Or something like that.

Eddie was just nestling back into his pillows when Scuttles hammered on the door and barked: 'Eddie! The door!'

Eddie bounded out of bed, fighting another yawn, and yanked the door open. 'All right, all right!'

Scuttles was already back in the kitchen. He scowled across as Eddie tramped past. Eddie ignored him. His legs felt heavy, his throat was still sore from the smoke, and as he reached up to open the front door he noticed that his hands were filthy, black from the smoke, green from climbing trees. He was exhausted. Sundays were for doing nothing. It was nine o'clock in the morning. What sort of a moron called for someone at that time on a Sunday?

As he was opening the door, he was already saying, 'Mo, what time do you . . . ?' when he saw that it wasn't Mo. It was Bacon. One of Captain Black's top soldiers.

'Oh,' said Eddie.

'Morning, Girly,' said Bacon.

'What?' said Eddie, somewhat groggily.

'Like the pyjamas, Girly,' said Bacon, nodding down at his nightwear. 'Nice little teddy bears.'

Eddie looked at his pyjamas, suddenly horror-struck. There *were* teddy bears emblazoned all over them. Little brown fluffy teddy bears. Smiling, little fluffy brown teddy bears. His normal pyjamas were . . . well, normal, but these – he hadn't worn them in years and he kept telling his mum to throw them out because they were so childish but she never did and sometimes he had to wear them when his usual ones were in the wash. He'd put them on last night in the dark, too tired to even think about what he was wearing. But of all the times to be caught out wearing teddy-bear pyjamas!

'They're . . . they're not mine . . .' Eddie stammered, 'they're . . . my sister's.'

Eddie wasn't quite sure how that was supposed to help matters.

'You don't have a sister,' said Bacon.

Eddie's face could scarcely go any redder. So his hands did. And his arms and his legs and he began to sweat through his . . . well, teddy-bear pyjamas. 'What exactly is it you want?' he asked weakly.

'You've to come to HQ.'

'HQ?'

'Headquarters.'

'Yes I know what HQ means. But what . . . where?'

'Pups HQ. The War Council is in session. They want you there.'

'Me? Why?'

'You'll find out.'

'Well . . . well . . . well . . . I can't just—'

'Yes you can. It's not an invitation. It's an order.'

This was a step too far. Eddie, who'd been slumping forward somewhat, now stood erect and defiant, and was pleased to note that in the preceding months he'd gained more than an inch on Bacon. He curled his lip up and hissed, 'Black doesn't order me around, all right?'

Bacon responded with a sarcastic laugh. 'It's not the Captain ordering you, it's the War Council. You want me to tell them you're saying no? It's no skin off my nose, Girly.'

'I didn't mean . . . I mean, if it's from the War Council, then of course . . .'

'Right. Then let's go.'

'Now? I can't just . . .'

'I'm to escort you there. We need to go now.' Bacon glanced at his watch. He shook his head. 'I'll give you two minutes to lose the pyjamas.'

Eddie took a deep breath, then nodded. He started to turn away from the door, then hesitated. 'I have to let my second in command—'

'The albino? Don't worry about her, Girly, Bap's getting her. You'll see her there.'

Twenty minutes later, Eddie and Bacon were hurrying towards the vast and sprawling housing estate called the Rivers, which was home to the Reservoir Pups' brand spanking new headquarters. Brand spanking new because Eddie's comrade Gary Gilmore had burned down their previous headquarters. Naturally, Eddie hesitated at the entrance. There was at least a dozen Reservoir Pups standing on guard; they carried baseball bats and bamboo canes and there were bottles and piles of stones sitting by the side of the road.

'How do I know I'm not walking into a trap?' Eddie asked.

'You don't,' said Bacon, and gave him a thump in the back. Eddie staggered forward. 'Sorry,' said Bacon, 'I must have slipped.'

'Yeah, right,' said Eddie.

'Course I did. Wouldn't I be a terrible fool to smack the leader of such a powerful gang?' Bacon gave him a sarcastic smile, then strode ahead of him into the Rivers. 'Come on, Girly,' he called back.

Eddie stood fuming for several moments, and then reluctantly followed Bacon into the Rivers. He really had no choice.

The new headquarters of the Reservoir Pups had once been a primary school, but had lain empty for several years. With the insurance money Captain Black had received from the burning down of his previous headquarters he had purchased the school and had it totally refurbished: there were now security cameras and floodlights outside, and inside there were banks of computer equipment, electronic maps showing the Reservoir Pups' operations throughout the city; other maps keeping track of what rival gangs were up to. The computers were operated by squads of keen, efficient and ruthless young Pups recruited almost exclusively from the tough streets of the Rivers.

These were boys and girls who did not shine at school – on the few days when they managed to turn up there – but who shone brightly under the tutelage of Captain Black. They were computer experts who could tap into any facility in the city – into government computers, police computers, hospital computers, importers, exporters, suppliers, banks, airports; they could steal information, products, money; they could cause havoc, shut down systems, spread viruses. But it wasn't only about computers. That was but one field where they excelled. They also excelled at threatening people with violence – they had hundreds of troops who terrorised and blackmailed and attacked and bullied and destroyed everything and anything. They had a grip on the city that other gangs could only dream of. And at the head of this insidious operation was fourteen-year-old Captain Black, who, although confined to a wheelchair, nevertheless bestrode the city like a colossus.

The War Council of the Alliance, now gathered in a large boardroom at the top of the former primary school, were talking amongst themselves as Eddie was ushered in. He nervously approached the long wooden table they were gathered around. There were six of them, including Captain Black himself and Billy Cobb. Eddie became aware of movement to his left, and was relieved to see Mo rising from a chair along the far wall. She hurried up to him.

'What's going on?' Eddie whispered.

Mo shook her head. 'I don't know. They just came for me.'

'They?'

'Bap and half a dozen others. I think they were worried I would make a fight of it.'

She smiled defiantly.

But why had they sent seven to get Mo, and only Bacon to get him? Did they really think he was so weak that even if he put up any resistance, Bacon by himself was enough to subdue him? Or did they think that Mo was really the leader of their gang? Perhaps it was both. She had, after all, once terrorised parts of the city as the leader of the Andytown Albinos. The fact that they had never actually existed, and that she had caused so much trouble all by herself, was her main claim to fame. Eddie decided not to let it worry him. Captain Black surely knew better than to underestimate him. Hadn't he outwitted him over the babies? And the head of Oliver Plunkett? So – perhaps Black was making a point. Playing a mind game. Showing Eddie no respect. And by showing respect to Mo he was hoping it would drive a wedge between Eddie and his second in command.

I don't think so.

Bacon was now bending over Captain Black's shoulder and whispering something. Black's head jerked towards Eddie, and his cool, dark eyes locked on his. They stared at each other, unblinking. Eddie felt a deep, deep dread in the pit of his stomach, and his muscles ached with tension – but he would not blink. It seemed to last for ever, but it could only have been a matter of seconds. The spell was broken by Billy Cobb banging the table; the tiniest smile crept on to Captain Black's face and then he turned towards Cobb. Eddie kept looking at Black and only tore his eyes away when Cobb began speaking.

'Eddie', said Cobb, 'thank you for coming at such short notice.'

'No problem,' said Eddie. *As if I had any choice.*

'As you know, since their unprovoked attack on our Alliance last night, we have declared war on the Seagulls. Any war, Eddie, should not be undertaken lightly. It takes time to plan a war, it takes patience, it is never good to rush into battle. However, we feel it is essential that we show the Seagulls that they cannot strike us at will without facing the consequences. So, while we work on the master plan for a full-scale war, Captain Black has suggested, and we have agreed, that your gang . . .' and Cobb picked up a piece of paper sitting before him, his eyes briefly flitting over it, 'your Gang With No Name, be allowed to undertake an attack on the Seagulls. The ways and means of the attack will be left entirely up to you, with the proviso that real physical damage be caused to their headquarters. Let me see . . .' and his eyes scanned the sheet again. 'According to your application for membership of the Alliance, you have thirty active members in your gang.'

Eddie swallowed. He felt Mo stiffen beside him. He was aware also of Captain Black's eyes upon him. 'Thirty-two, now,' said Eddie.

He heard Mo exhale quietly beside him.

Of course there weren't thirty or even thirty-two members. There was him and Mo and sometimes Gary Gilmore, but they would never have let his gang into the Alliance with three members. So he had lied on the application form. What did they expect? They were all gangs engaged in various levels of illegal activity. Did any of them really tell the truth? Thirty members he had said, and somewhere, somehow, he would have to find thirty members to mount an assault on the headquarters of the Seagulls.

'Thirty-two,' said Billy Cobb. 'Even better. And do you accept this task, as laid down by the War Council of the Alliance?'

Eddie cleared his throat. Mo's eyes were burning into him. But this was exactly the kind of opportunity he'd been waiting for, the chance to show everyone what he was made of.

'I do,' he said.

'Then so shall it be,' said Billy Cobb. He banged his hand down on the table. All around, the other leaders of the War Council banged theirs as well. Even Captain Black. 'Let's go to war!' shouted Billy Cobb.

Eleven

They were escorted out of the Rivers by Bacon and Bap and more than a dozen of their comrades. Nothing was said: Bacon and Bap walked directly behind them, the others trailed further behind in case there was trouble. Even though they didn't say anything, Eddie knew they knew about the true membership of his gang. Of *course* they knew. Because Captain Black knew everything; he was a master at gathering and using information. Now he was using it to strike back against them by sending them into danger.

But what choice did they have?

If Eddie admitted that there were only three members of his gang, he would be thrown out of the Alliance, and once outside the organisation he would almost literally have nowhere to turn in the entire city. He would never be able to leave his apartment again! Captain Black knew that, and that was why he had proposed that Eddie lead the attack on the Seagulls.

What was he going to do? Eddie had dreamed

about leading a huge gang, a huge network of gangs, world domination; but despite his previous adventures, what experience did he actually have of battle? Of leading an army? None. More to the point, where was he going to find thirty people to join his gang? Eddie didn't even *know* thirty people.

As they approached the exit from the Rivers, Eddie chanced a quick glance at Mo. *Uh-oh*. The same steely, angry, determined look she'd been wearing since the very instant that he had claimed to have thirty-two members. Since then she had walked stiffly at his side, far to mad to even look at him.

At the end of the road, where it met the dual carriageway, Bacon and Bap said their goodbyes. This consisted of yelling abuse after them. It had to do with teddy bears and pyjamas and girlies, but Eddie was too concerned about Mo to pay any attention. He hadn't been honest with her. He hadn't lied, exactly, to her, but neither had he told her the whole truth. They walked for about a hundred metres further on, until they were out of sight of the Rivers and the Pups standing guard at its entrance, then Mo stopped suddenly and stamped her foot on the ground and yelled: 'What the hell were you thinking of?'

Eddie shrugged. 'It seemed like a good idea at the time, Mo.'

'Good idea? Good idea? *Good idea?*'

'Although, perhaps, on reflection . . .'

'Eddie – they want us to attack the Seagulls. That's you and me, attacking the Seagulls!'

'Plus Gary.'

'Gary! Great! That makes it all OK then!'

'I know, I'm sorry, but—'

'But nothing!'

This time Eddie stamped his foot. 'Now just you wait one minute! Aren't you forgetting something? Weren't you the leader of the Andytown Albinos? Wasn't your gang supposed to be the most dangerous in the city? Didn't you pretend you had hundreds of members? How is it OK for you to lie, and not for me?'

She put her hands on her hips. 'Because, Eddie, I never claimed to have hundreds of members. People just presumed I had because I was so successful.'

Eddie rolled his eyes. 'That's rubbish, Mo, you were always talking about the Albinos and command posts and supply depots like you had your own private army.'

'Well . . .' and for a moment she looked lost for

words, 'maybe I did a little bit, but it was all talk – I never lied to the Alliance, I never agreed to go to war on their behalf. I used it to scare off other gangs; I never tried to attack anyone with an army which doesn't exist.'

'Well,' said Eddie.

'Well,' said Mo.

They stared at the ground for a long minute. Traffic roared past beside them. Spits of rain began to fall.

'Last night,' said Eddie, 'you were all for making peace with the Seagulls.'

'That was before they tried to burn us alive.'

'Fair point.' He scuffed one of his shoes on the ground and looked rather sheepishly up at her. 'What are we going to do?'

'You're asking me?'

'I'm asking you.'

'I have no idea.'

'Neither have I.'

'Well at least we're agreed on something. We have no idea.'

Eddie sighed. 'Well, we better find an idea. And soon.'

They walked on. After a full minute Mo said, 'Well, have you thought of one yet?'

'No,' said Eddie.

'Neither have I.'

'Maybe we should call Gary,' said Eddie.

'That would strengthen our numbers by . . . oh, one.'

'One's better than none,' Eddie said rather weakly.

'Just about. And considering it's Gary, maybe not even that.'

They walked on. When they reached the car park outside Eddie's apartment block, Scuttles was just emerging from the main doors, pushing Paddy. Scuttles scowled at them as they drew closer, but he stopped nevertheless, and Mo immediately craned her neck into the pram to get a proper look at the baby. She started *ooing* and *aahing*.

'You'll wake him up,' Scuttles complained. But then he too looked in at the baby and started making gurgling noises. Eddie smiled in at Paddy as well.

'He's just like his daddy,' Eddie said softly.

'Do you think?' Scuttles beamed.

Eddie nodded. 'Sure I do. He's as fat as a pig and he smells like a toilet.'

Eddie ducked as Scuttles tried to slap him, then ran off laughing. Mo followed, laughing as well;

Scuttles stood for a moment, shaking his fist back at them and shouting all kinds of threats before pushing the pram on out of the car park. They could almost see the steam coming out of his ears. Eddie and Mo smiled at each other, then took the lift to the apartment. Mo leant against the back wall.

'You know,' she said, 'Scuttles was no match for us. The Babysnatchers were no match for us, and we sorted out Oliver Plunkett's head. If we put *our* heads to it, there's no reason why we shouldn't be able to deal with a few lousy Seagulls.'

Eddie grinned. 'I knew you'd see it my way,' he said.

Twelve

The Palace Barracks Army Camp on the outskirts of Belfast had been deserted for nearly two years before the first of the refugees from Ruritania were sent there. If you think of how quickly a banana goes off, left to its own devices, turning from a gorgeously firm yellow to a mushy black in a matter of a few days, imagine how much an entire housing estate might deteriorate over the course of two years of neglect. You might think there is little connection between rotting food and brick houses, but you would be wrong. Both are, in their own way, living organisms. The banana, removed from its tree, is dying from the moment its life support system is removed; the army camp, with its hundreds of houses for the soldiers and their families, began to die as soon as the last soldier saluted it goodbye. It started with the gardens and open spaces, where grass and weeds were soon growing wild, providing cover for the rats which were soon gnawing their way into the houses. Storm damage was never repaired, leaving many

GALWAY COUNTY LIBRARIES

houses with roof slates missing, which allowed in the rain so that the houses grew damp; windows were smashed by passing vandals, who also destroyed or stole anything they could lay their hands on. The Rivers, home of the Reservoir Pups, was widely regarded as having some of the worst housing in Europe. But Palace Barracks made the Rivers look like a holiday camp.

It wasn't a very nice place at all.

Eddie realised this just a few moments after driving into it. Not only did the houses look badly in need of repair – the people living in them didn't look so hot either. There were hundreds of them, perhaps thousands, and they seemed to be everywhere: standing around with nothing to do, dressed in a ragbag of mismatched clothes. Dozens and dozens of kids were kicking a misshaped ball on a tarmac quadrangle, seemingly unaware of the shards of shattered glass which glinted all around them.

Eddie was sitting in the front of an ambulance, feeling nervous, scared and rather excited at being transported like this into the very heart of the enemy camp. He had always thought that he was a magnet for bad luck – his life had been largely a catalogue of disasters since the day his father had left home. But he also had to admit that he had had his share of good luck – being helped by the very bizarre-looking test-tube teenagers called the Forgotten while facing certain death from Alison Beech in her cavernous headquarters under the Mourne Mountains; being helped to escape from Scuttles in the hospital and saved from the Reservoir Pups outside Botanic Station by the body washer and lollipop man Barney; and now being given easy access to the army camp where the Seagulls were based – all because of a chance remark by his mother.

Eddie and Mo had spent several days trying to work out how to strike back against the Seagulls with their tiny gang, but without success. Gary Gilmore had turned up for their weekly meeting, but once he'd heard what they had to do he had suddenly remembered a dental appointment and left. They didn't have a plan – and they'd just lost one third of their fighting strength.

'He's just a big chicken,' Eddie said, watching Gary hurry away across the car park.

Mo shrugged. 'He's just being sensible.'

'A sensible chicken,' said Eddie.

'And he didn't even leave us any eggs.'

'What're we going to do?'

Mo shrugged. They had already taken a trip to survey the camp – it covered about a square mile, and it was completely surrounded by a high fence, topped with barbed wire; there were security cameras and watch towers, although it wasn't clear whether this was to keep people out or keep an eye on those who lived within. Police patrols continuously circled the perimeter. At the entrance itself they saw groups of adults armed with clubs and sticks standing guard. Whenever they left the camp – adults or gang members – they always moved in large groups. Eddie and Mo walked the full length of the perimeter fence, but could find no obvious way in. Two or three times Seagulls shouted at them from the walls, or from overhanging trees, warning them in broken English to stay away.

'Maybe if we went back to the Alliance and explained—'

'We can't do that,' Eddie said quickly, 'you know we can't . . . Captain Black would . . .'

'It doesn't have to be Black – we could tell Billy Cobb, say you're being sent away by your mum or pretend that I have some sort of disease . . .'

'No, Mo. Even if we could fool Cobb, Black would know. He knows everything. He set this up expecting us to fail, that's why we have to do it.'

Mo knew he was right. But what else were they—

'Eddie . . . !' His mum was calling from the kitchen. 'I'm making the dinner. Does Mo want to stay?'

'Why don't you ask her?' He wasn't exactly being cheeky – he was just trying to get them to talk to each other. He thought his mum was slowly warming to Mo, but she was still quite wary of her. She thought she got her golden boy into trouble. When of course it was only Eddie who got Eddie into trouble.

His mum appeared in the kitchen doorway. 'Would you like to stay? It's just burgers.'

'That would be great, Mrs Malone.'

His mum smiled and began to turn back into the kitchen, then stopped and looked back at her son. 'Oh Eddie – while I remember. I won't be home for tea tomorrow, and Bernard's taking Paddy round to meet some of his relatives, so you'll have to sort yourself out.'

Eddie shrugged. He was well used to it.

'All right,' his mum said, 'so don't ask me what I'm doing.'

Eddie wasn't the slightest bit interested, and was

in fact looking forward to some time to himself away from Paddy's crying and Scuttles' complaining. He sighed and said, 'What are you doing?' in a very bored voice.

'Well. I've volunteered to help with a clinic the hospital's set up for the Seagulls.' And then she tutted and quickly corrected herself. 'Oh dear – I shouldn't really call them that, should I? But that's what I'm doing.'

Eddie glanced at Mo. She gave him a nod of encouragement. 'The Seagulls? You mean the gang or the grown-ups?'

'Well – both, I suppose. I don't really know. I'm quite nervous about it actually – I've never been into the . . . you know, the camp where they live.'

'You're going into the camp?'

His mum looked quite surprised by his reaction, and immediately mistook it for concern. 'Don't worry, son, I'll be quite safe. They send guards in with us.'

Eddie's brain was racing. His mum was going into the camp! It was almost too good to be true . . .

'Mum . . . Mum . . .' Eddie stammered, rising from his chair by the window. 'I . . . have to go with you . . .' He crossed the room to her.

His mum smiled down at him. 'Eddie – I'll be perfectly safe.'

'No, no . . . I know you will. But I have to go . . . my school project . . . this is perfect . . .'

'Your school project?'

'Yes, Mum! Remember? I told you!'

She looked confused. 'Yes, of course . . .' she said rather vaguely.

'Mum, I told you I was doing something on the Seagulls . . . about how they've settled and how they— how their health is . . . but I haven't been able to find out anything about them. And it has to be . . . finished by Friday. And I'll get a bad report and maybe they'll throw me out and I've been doing so well lately and you're always saying if there's anything you can do to help me . . . and this would really, really help me and—'

'Eddie – I can't take you into the camp, it wouldn't be allowed.'

'Yes it would, Mum – please . . .'

'It's not safe . . .'

'I'll stay right with you, I just want to watch . . .'

'No, Eddie . . .'

'You *owe* me, Mum.'

They had been getting on somewhat better in

the past few days, but they still weren't back to the way they used to be.

His mum looked a little sad and said, 'That's not fair, Eddie.'

'Life's not fair, that's what you're always saying. I need to go in there, Mum.'

'Well.' She rubbed her hands together. 'I suppose I could ask Bernard.'

'What do you have to ask that fa— him for?' Eddie snapped.

'Because he's going too – he's organising the guards. But he's bound to say no, Eddie.'

'Oh.' Eddie summoned up his most disappointed look. 'If he's involved – well . . . I know he won't let me go, that's for sure.' He gave a slight shake of his head, then tramped unhappily back to Mo, who'd listened silently to the whole exchange. As he sat back down opposite her he said, 'It would have been great, but you know what Bernard's like.' His mum couldn't see his face – couldn't see the big smile or wink he gave Mo. His mum stood thoughtfully in the doorway for a moment, then said, 'Just give me a moment.'

She walked off down the hall, and a few moments later they heard her talking in hushed tones on the phone in the bedroom. Five minutes later she came back into the room with a broad smile on her face.

'Eddie – Bernard said no . . . at *first*. . . but I've talked him into letting you go – as long as you swear to God you'll be on your best behaviour.'

Bingo! Eddie knew he could rely on Scuttles to get him in – the fat oaf still detested him, but Eddie knew he would do anything to show Eddie's mum he was trying to get on with him.

'Oh thanks, Mum!'

He ran up and gave her a hug. She was quite surprised by this, given their recent history. She hugged him back. Then held him at arm's length and said, 'This clinic is very important to me, Eddie. You won't get yourself into any trouble, will you?'

He kissed her cheek. 'Mum – it's for a school project! What sort of trouble am I going to get into?'

She smiled down at him again. 'I know, son, I know, I know you'll be good.' She even smiled across at Mo. 'He is a good boy, you know.'

'I know,' said Mo.

'All right then – I'll get those burgers ready.'

She turned back into the kitchen.

Eddie immediately lifted Mo's jacket from the back of the chair and handed it to her. 'Time you were on your way,' he said.

'What?' Mo asked, surprised. 'I thought I was—'

'There isn't time, Mo – you've got to go to Gary's right now.'

'Gary's? But why?'

'Mo! Don't you listen? I'm going into the Seagulls' camp tomorrow!'

'Yes – I'm not stupid, Eddie. But what on earth has that got to do with Gary?'

'Mo – use your head. The Seagulls' headquarters! I need Gary to build me a bomb!'

And so he found himself travelling into the lair of the enemy late the following afternoon. He rode up front, squashed in beside Scuttles, whose uniform was so heavy with gold braid and decorations that he looked more like a conquering emperor than the head of security at a busy hospital. There was a driver beside Scuttles, and in the back of the ambulance there were three nurses and two doctors plus lots of equipment and medicines.

They pulled up in front of a long, rusting metal hut which was being used as a community centre. There was a queue of about a hundred people waiting for them already. Scuttles jumped down from the ambulance and began to oversee the transfer of the equipment and supplies from the ambulance into the centre. Several women came forward to help them carry it, but Scuttles shooed them away, worried that they were more interested in stealing than assisting.

Eddie's mum was in charge of the nurses, leading them in their crisp blue uniforms across the dusty forecourt into the community centre. Eddie followed behind, feeling quite self-conscious – he was wearing his very loud and very disgustingly purple school uniform (his mum had insisted) and carrying a large notebook. His schoolbag was draped lazily over one shoulder. Inside it he carried a bomb.

Mo had met him after school and transferred it into his schoolbag. She told him quickly how to prime it and set the timer. He said, 'It looks very small.'

'It is small, Eddie. But it will do a hell of a lot of damage.' She gave him a hard look and said, 'And that's all we want, Eddie, isn't it? Damage?'

'What do you mean?'

'We don't want to be hurting anyone, do we?'

'Don't we?'

'Eddie?'

He smiled at her. 'Of course we don't. We're just

going to show them we're not to be messed with.'

She nodded, then gave him a hug and wished him good luck. Part of him wanted to say, *Will you stop hugging me!* And the other part wanted to say, *Give me another one!* He hadn't quite worked out what he felt about her. She was his best friend, though, without a doubt.

The clinic in the rusting hut was soon underway. Eddie sat on a hard wooden chair and watched for a while. The nurses dealt with the more minor cases: there were eye infections, head lice, cuts and sprains and coughs; and everyone had the sniffles. Even though the Ruritanians' skin was much darker than Eddie's, many of them still managed to look quite pale. The doctors dealt with more serious cases behind a makeshift curtain. Eddie knew this wasn't a great place to live, that these people had travelled hundreds of miles to get here only to find a cold, inhospitable climate and people who spoke a different language and offered little in the way of welcome. Eddie knew in some small way how they must feel – even if his journey had only been twenty miles up the road from Groomsport. He knew they'd had a hard time – but he still couldn't bring himself to warm to them. Maybe it was because they'd brought crush into the country, or maybe it was because they'd tried to burn the Alliance alive in Dundonald Ice Bowl.

Eddie was just thinking about this when he saw the girl from the hospital, standing in the treatment queue. Her name was ... her name was ... Rotavia? She was wearing her black Seagull uniform, but she'd rolled up the left sleeve and was holding her arm gingerly. She was obviously in some kind of pain, but she looked an awful lot better than on either of the previous two occasions he'd seen her – being carried through the streets of Belfast by her fellow Seagulls, and then lying wired up in the hospital. As he looked at her, her eyes met his, and he looked away quickly. When he looked back she was still looking at him; he felt his face going red. He opened his notebook and pretended to write something.

The queue of patients was shuffling past him quite quickly now that the nurses had gotten into the swing of things, bringing Rotavia closer and closer. He wanted to get up and walk away, because he felt uncomfortable under her continuing gaze, but he couldn't quite bring himself to move. He tried to keep his eyes on his notebook, but occasionally he couldn't help but glance up at the patients being treated right in front of him. One man, who looked to be about seventy-five years old, was having his ears syringed; another woman of around his mother's age was having stitches inserted in a wound on her forehead. 'A brick . . .' she was saying in a thick accent, 'someone throw a brick.' The nurse tutted, but didn't say anything.

Rotavia was right beside him now. 'I know you.'

Eddie looked up. She was slightly shorter than he was; her hair was black and cut short above elfin ears, her nose small and slightly turned up at the bottom; her eyes were brown. He took all of this in in the brief moment before he stammered, 'Wh-at?'

'I know you.'

Eddie's face was already crimson. 'I don't think so,' he spluttered.

'I see you at hospital.'

Eddie shrugged.

'You come to my bed with white girl and read my chart.'

'No I . . . well yes we . . . it wasn't my idea, she—'

'She say about crush . . . you think I asleep, but I awake . . . I hear.'

'We . . . she was . . . she was just curious.'

'You should . . . how you say – mind own business.'

Eddie didn't know how to respond to that one. He gave another little shrug of his shoulders.

'Well? You say nothing?'

Eddie cleared his throat. 'We didn't mean anything.'

She gave him a hard look, but was then ushered forward for treatment before she could say anything else. It was only when she took her place before the nurse and turned her arm up towards her that Eddie saw the state of her arm: the skin, from the wrist right up to the elbow, was pink, bubbled, and enflamed and looked very, very painful.

'Well, dearie,' the nurse said, 'and what happened to you?'

'Accident,' said Rotavia. 'I burn it.'

The nurse nodded, and began to examine the wound.

A burn.

A burn which has clearly gone untreated for a while.

Hadn't the Pup on guard at the Ice Bowl said that one of the Seagulls who'd set fire to the building was a girl?

And here was Rotavia, right before him, with a burn on her arm.

It made perfect sense. This then was surely one of the Seagulls who'd tried to kill him.

It immediately served to harden Eddie's resolve. He'd been looking at the lines of poor sick Seagulls and thinking about what a hard life they had and how difficult it must be coming to a foreign country where you weren't welcome. But if you went around selling drugs and trying to burn people to death of course you weren't going to be made welcome. They had to be shown that they couldn't get away with that kind of behaviour. And Eddie, lifting his schoolbag with the bomb inside it, was exactly the right person to show them.

Thirteen

Eddie emerged into the late afternoon sun – the schoolbag-a-bomb carefully hitched over one shoulder – and surveyed his surroundings. There was still quite a lengthy queue of Seagulls waiting to see the medical team; beyond them he could see dozens of kids still playing football on the dusty quadrangle. The houses, with their broken roofs, boarded-up windows and flaking paint, were mainly set into a smallish hill which rose gently behind the clinic. He didn't fancy getting much closer to these houses – most of their occupants, who clearly didn't have jobs to go to, were sitting or standing around their front doors enjoying a rare glimpse of good Northern Irish weather. So instead, Eddie walked down a slight incline towards a series of long, narrow huts similar to the one the clinic was based in. One had been turned into a small shop; he caught a whiff of strong spices as he walked casually past. Another seemed to function as a café. A third had been converted into a church and he spotted several adults inside, sitting on benches, praying. There was a large cross attached to the far wall and a minister, or priest, or whatever they called him, was reading from what Eddie supposed was a Bible. He wasn't reading in English – and it didn't sound like the language he'd heard so far. Perhaps it was Latin. The fourth hut was much larger, but divided into sections for use by various different groups within the camp – he saw a small class being taught English by a nervous-looking young man; there was a crèche where half a dozen babies – orphans, his mum told him later, whose parents 'didn't make it' – slept in battered-looking cots; a workshop where household appliances like washing machines and fridges were being repaired; and then he came to the final section of the final hut, and saw that there were two young Seagulls in their black military style uniforms sitting by the door, keeping guard while within – well, there were twenty or thirty more of them. They were marching up and down in formation.

My God, Eddie thought, *they* are *an army*.

Eddie hurried past, aware that he was now being watched with increased interest by the Seagulls on guard. When he turned the corner he realised that the huts were set in such a way as to create a rectangle of space within them – yet they were close enough together to prevent anyone from easily seeing what might be inside that rectangle. Doubtless there were doors on the other side of the huts which gave access to it, but he could hardly go marching through them to find out. So he walked nearly the whole way round again, looking for some kind of access, but without success. Then he realised that the huts were actually propped up on columns of bricks, designed to keep them off the ground and therefore, theoretically, dryer. Eddie glanced around to make sure he wasn't being watched, and then dropped to one knee and pretended to tie his shoelaces. He was low enough now to peer under the huts. He could see grass on the other side – and unlike in the rest of the camp, this grass was perfectly maintained. A lawn, in fact. And there was something sitting in the very centre of it – some kind of sculpture or statue he thought, but it was difficult to be sure, as he could only see the bottom third of it from his prone position.

Eddie checked again, saw that the coast was still clear, then quickly darted to one side, dipped down and slipped under the hut. He crawled through weeds and stones until he reached the far side. He touched the edge of the manicured lawn with his fingertips, then bent his head to try and get a better look at the object. Yes, it was definitely a statue. But it was facing away from him. He thought at first that it might be something left over from when this place was an army camp – a statue of a leading general or of Queen Victoria, perhaps. But why would the Seagulls let the rest of the camp go to rack and ruin while creating such perfect surroundings for a statue which had nothing to do with them? No, it didn't make sense. It had to be something of theirs which was precious to them, which they had brought with them from Ruritania.

It was exactly what he was looking for.

Something which he could destroy without actually physically harming any of them. It would send a warning: *This is what we're capable of, watch out*.

Eddie quickly surveyed the sides of the huts which formed three sides of the rectangle. Luckily there were only a few windows which looked out over the lawn, and all of them, he was pleased to see, appeared to be empty. That left the one side directly above him. Eddie crawled cautiously forward, then twisted his head up to see if he could be observed from any of its windows. But no – there was just one window, and a blind had been pulled down over it.

Excellent!

Eddie jumped to his feet and darted across the grass. As he ran he swung the schoolbag round from his shoulder, and was already reaching inside for the bomb when he came to a sudden halt beside the statue.

'Oh,' he said.

There was a small, bald, elderly man sitting on a concrete step at the foot of the statue – he'd been completely invisible from where Eddie had been lying. He was wearing a short black tunic and black trousers – he might have been one of the Seagulls, if he hadn't been about seventy years too old.

'I'm . . . sorry . . .' said Eddie. 'I didn't realise. I was just . . . I mean . . . I'm doing a school project – and I saw . . . and . . .' And then he stopped for a moment, suddenly realising that he was grasping for explanations when he didn't need to. He said, 'You don't speak English, do you?' As if to emphasise the point he added, 'You old duffer.'

The old man's eyes crinkled slightly and he said, 'On the contrary, my English is perfectly adequate.'

Eddie went a little pale. 'Wh-wh-wh-wh-wh . . .' he stammered.

'But what, please, is *duffer*?'

'It's . . . it's an old Irish word. For . . . garden – gardener,' Eddie lied.

The old man nodded. 'Well. That is what I am. A gardener. A duffer. And yes, I am old. So I am – an *old duffer*, yes?'

Eddie nodded. Sweat was beginning to stream down his brow. The man struggled to his feet, then turned and looked up at the statue. 'You from school – interested in General Killster?'

Eddie followed the old man's gaze. General Killster was certainly an imposing figure. He was resplendent in armour, beneath which bulging muscles were just visible. He carried a massive sword and shield and wore a spiked helmet. His eyes were wide and staring and his teeth were bared in anger. It was possibly the most fearsome statue Eddie had ever seen. Although, truthfully, he hadn't seen that many. Nevertheless, he nodded enthusiastically.

'General Killster – yes.'

Beneath the statue, on a single stone column, there was a plaque with words inscribed on it, but even without bending towards them he could see that they were in a foreign language. Whatever they spoke in Ruritania.

Eddie pointed down at the plaque. 'Please,' he said, 'what does it say?'

The old man positioned himself directly in front of the stone column. He had a definite stoop to his shoulders – but now he pulled himself up stiff and erect and translated the words in a strong, confident manner. 'This statue of General Killster, First King of Ruritania, was unveiled May 2004 by his proud descendants – One People, Wherever We May Be!'

The old man nodded to himself for several moments, then turned to Eddie. 'The General looks after us,' he said simply.

Well, Eddie thought, *he doesn't look after you very well.*

Eddie reached inside his schoolbag. Instead of taking out the bomb, he removed his notebook and a pen. 'I would like to draw the statue,' he said.

The old man smiled and said, 'I will leave you in peace, young man.'

His shoulders slumped down again, and he leant forward as he walked away, as if his back was sore. Eddie waited until he had disappeared inside one of the huts, then stood in front of the statue with his notebook and pen. If anyone had been watching it would have looked like he was drawing, but he was only pretending; he was checking the windows again. He had been caught by surprise, finding the old man, but nothing else had changed. Indeed, he was more fired up than ever. General Killster! He was obviously very important to the Seagulls – destroying his statue would certainly be a pleasure. Eddie reached inside his bag again, and this time located the bomb. It was tiny, hardly bigger than an eraser. In fact, when he drew it from the bag, having set the timer, he pretended that it was an eraser, rubbing it back and forth over his non-existent drawing of the statue, before quickly darting his hand out and attaching the sticky plastic on its base – Gary had thought of everything! – to Killster's exposed armpit. There; it was in place. He checked his watch. He had thirty minutes before it went off. So he stood for another little while, pretending to draw, then made an elaborate show of putting his notebook back in his bag. He walked towards the door of one of the huts, but then quickly dived underneath it and scrambled back through the weeds to the other side. He waited for a couple of women carrying bags of rubbish to pass by, then jumped out, wiped the dust off his trousers and hurried back towards the clinic.

* * *

The last few patients were being treated. His mum had been too busy to speak to him in the two hours since they'd arrived, but now she looked across at him and smiled. 'I could just do with a nice cup of tea and a bun,' she said. Eddie smiled back. He looked at his watch. Twenty-four minutes.

The nurses were packing away their equipment. Eddie volunteered to help them carry the unused medicines back to the ambulance, but his mum said they were leaving them behind for the 'Sea—' and then she stopped herself and said, 'Ruritanians.' 'God love them,' she added, shaking her head. 'This is a dreadful place to bring up kids.'

The doctors emerged from behind their curtain, and Scuttles – who, after satisfying himself that the nurses and doctors were in no danger at all, had spent the past hour sleeping in the back of the ambulance – reappeared and began shepherding them all back into the vehicle.

Twenty minutes.

'Doctor!'

Eddie spun around to see a middle-aged man hurrying into the clinic, blood dripping from a gaping wound in his arm. 'I sorry! I sorry!' the man was crying, 'I fall on glass! I fall on glass!'

The doctors ushered the man into a chair, and

two of the nurses put down the medical files they'd been carrying to help. Eddie groaned. The arm was examined and the doctors decided that the man should go to hospital to have the wound treated. Eddie breathed a sigh of relief. But then the man refused to go, and they argued back and forth – the argument made more confusing, and much, much longer, by the fact that his English wasn't very good. Eventually they agreed to stitch the wound there and then, and hope for the best. The man was very happy with that, and the doctors and nurses were happy with that, and the only person in the whole place who wasn't happy with it was Eddie, who kept looking at his watch.

Fifteen minutes.

Ten minutes.

And still two nurses and one doctor continued to work away at the man's arm.

Five minutes.

Eddie was walking back and forth, becoming increasingly panicked. Scuttles noticed and said, 'What's wrong with you – ants in your pants?'

'Yeah, right,' said Eddie.

Four minutes.

Then finally, finally, the man was stitched up, and he was so grateful he went around hugging them all. He even tried to hug Eddie, who backed away like he had the plague or something. Eventually, the bandaged man left, and then the nurses and doctors slowly made their way back to the ambulance. Scuttles held the rear doors open for them, then locked it before sauntering around to the front where the driver had the engine started.

Two minutes.

The ambulance began to pull away from the hut. Many of the patients who'd been treated stood with their relatives in little groups and waved the medical team away. Eddie, squashed in beside Scuttles, saw Rotavia standing by herself, watching the ambulance depart, not waving, not smiling, just watching. Their eyes met, for just an instant, and then Eddie looked away. He could feel the colour in his cheeks again. They moved down the hill towards the camp gates. Again they were waved through by the men standing guard there. Finally the ambulance turned out on to the dual carriageway which led back into Belfast, and Eddie breathed a sigh of relief. He turned as much in his seat as he could so that he could glance at his watch without Scuttles noticing.

Fifteen seconds.

Ten.

The second hand seemed to take for ever.

Five.

Four.

Three.

Two.

At that precise moment the ambulance driver reached across and turned on the radio. There was an immediate blast of rock'n'roll and everyone flinched.

'Sorry,' said the driver, and turned the volume down to a more comfortable level.

Eddie's heart was racing like an express train. He put his hand to his chest to calm himself and took a deep breath. He took another look at his watch.

Three seconds past.

Eddie leant forward so that he could look in the ambulance's side mirror. At first all he could see were the cars following behind. But then he noticed a button which allowed him to alter the angle of the mirror. He pressed it and the mirror slowly tilted upwards, giving him a perfect view of the increasingly distant Palace Barracks Army Camp, and the pall of black smoke now hanging over it.

Fourteen

It was all over the news that evening, and late at night, and the next morning, and for most of the day: how racists or terrorists or both had broken into the army camp and destroyed a statue dedicated to the memory of the Ruritanians' founding father. Not only that, three people had been injured by flying glass, and the building used as a church had collapsed due to the force of the blast. It was very lucky that nobody had been killed, a reporter said. All sorts of important people, like the Mayor of Belfast, the Prime Minister, even the Prime Minister of distant and much troubled Ruritania condemned the bomb attack. Many people who, in private, disliked and distrusted 'those Seagulls', made different noises in public, about how we should all learn to live together and respect each other. Nobody even hinted that the bomb might have anything to do with the war which was brewing between the Alliance and the Seagulls.

Eddie's mum watched the news in disbelief. 'We

were just there! We could have been hurt! You could have been . . . oh, Eddie!' And she gave him a hug and dug out one of her hidden packets of Jaffa Cakes and gave him three and told him how much she loved him.

Mo, who didn't go to school, but was nevertheless just about the most intelligent person Eddie knew – apart from himself, of course – was waiting for him when he set out for the train to school the next morning.

'I was glued to the TV all night!' she said as she ran up. 'It was fantastic! We taught them a lesson all right – and the great thing was, nobody was hurt, not really.'

Eddie nodded – although inside, he didn't feel quite right. From the moment he'd met Rotavia's eyes on the way out of the camp, he'd had an uneasy feeling about what he was doing, and now about what he had done. Planting a bomb! He'd gotten into all kinds of trouble before, but nothing quite as life-threatening – not for him, but for other people. What if the old man had gone back to the statue? Or Rotavia? Or a mother had walked her small baby into the garden to enjoy the sun? That would be *murder*. That it had all worked all right was down to luck rather than design. Why hadn't he thought it through properly? Weren't there other ways for him to attack the Seagulls? Indeed, why had he lied to the Alliance at all?

'What's wrong?' Mo asked when he didn't respond.

'Nothing.'

'You should be pleased!'

'I know.'

He managed a smile. She punched his arm playfully. 'It's done. You won't have to do anything like that again.'

He took a deep breath. 'Hope so.'

The streets they were approaching, and which he had to pass through to get to Botanic Station, were now completely controlled by the Reservoir Pups; and for the past few weeks he had either had to make a mad dash through them or take the long way round, which meant a twenty-five-minute detour. Eddie could see three boys he recognised as Pups waiting just at the edge of their territory. The moment he tried to enter he would be considered fair game for a beating. Eddie stopped.

Mo saw what he saw, and said: 'We can out-run them, or we can fight them. They don't look that tough.'

But Eddie wasn't in the mood for confrontation,

or for running. He was still thinking about the bomb.

'No,' he said, 'let's just take the long way round.'

She looked at him in surprise. 'You really aren't on good form, are you, Eddie?'

He shook his head. They were just turning to their right, when there was a shout.

'Hey!'

'Just keep walking,' Eddie whispered.

'We can take them, Eddie . . .'

'No, not today, let's just—'

'Hey! Eddie!'

This time Eddie stopped and looked back at the boys, who were now hurrying towards them. Beside him Mo tensed, ready to fight. She glanced at Eddie, and was mystified to find that he was smiling.

'Eddie?'

'It's all right. They never call me Eddie.'

And he was right. They usually hurled abuse and disgusting nicknames. But these boys came right up, and instead of throwing punches, clapped Eddie on the back and said, 'Well done!'

'You showed those bloody Seagulls!'

'They know who they're messin' with now!'

'We'll chase them right back into the sea, bloody Seagulls!'

Eddie shrugged. 'It was nothing, I just . . .'

'You blew up their king!'

'Well, I . . .'

'He's like their god or something!'

'Well, we should get moving . . .' Eddie gave Mo a nudge, but as they moved to continue on their circuitous route to the train one of the boys said, 'Hey – you're going to the train, right? This way's quicker!'

And he turned and pointed directly through Reservoir Pups territory.

'But . . .' Eddie began.

'Anyone who takes on the Seagulls in their own back yard, he's a friend of ours. You won't get any more hassle through here, Eddie Malone.'

They clapped him on the back once more, and then Eddie, with Mo beside him, stepped somewhat nervously into Reservoir Pups territory.

As they walked Mo hissed, 'Do you think it's a trap?'

'I don't know . . .'

They kept their eyes on the alleyways and shop doorways and junctions, expecting at any moment to be attacked by a vicious pack of Pups, but nothing happened, nothing at all.

When they saw the sign for Botanic Station in

the distance, Eddie finally breathed a sigh of relief. Beside him, Mo smiled widely. 'That was ... amazing,' she said.

'I know, I can't quite believe it. The Pups and us, best of mates!'

'Do you think it came from Black himself?'

'What, the order to let us through?'

'Yeah – or was it those boys just showing their own personal thanks?'

'I don't know, Mo. But I'll tell you one thing – I'm not going to call Black to find out.'

She laughed at that. She walked him to the train and waited with him until it came. He almost wanted her to climb on board with him, but then when the carriage pulled to a stop he saw the familiar purple uniforms of his classmates pressed against the windows. They were looking at him, and they were smiling and pointing and giving him the thumbs up.

My God, Eddie thought, *everybody knows*.

The doors opened.

And there was cheering and clapping and Eddie beamed.

The Pups love me.

My classmates love me.

They all think I'm a hero!

All thoughts about what might have happened with the bomb were suddenly banished. He had taken a calculated risk, and it had worked out. He had been brave. A warrior. He had led by example. He alone out of all the members of all the gangs, had taken the war to the Seagulls, and he had triumphed.

I am a hero!

Eddie stepped on to the train, and was quickly surrounded by his new admirers. As the doors closed behind him, he didn't even think of Mo standing there, looking surprised, a little shocked and very hurt that he had so completely and so quickly forgotten her.

Fifteen

'Well – is she going or isn't she?' his mother was asking, standing in the bathroom doorway, her dressing gown loosely tied about her and her hair dripping.

'I don't know,' said Eddie. 'I've been trying to call her.'

His mum tutted. 'Honestly,' she said, 'she is the strangest little girl.'

Eddie was inclined to agree. Mo looked strange, she acted strange, she *was* strange. His new little brother was getting baptised in three hours' time, and Mo had been invited weeks ago. She'd said then that she'd love to come, but Eddie hadn't heard from her in days. Ever since she'd walked him to the train station the day after the destruction of General Killster's statue. What on earth was wrong with her? Maybe her dad was keeping her in, and away from the phone. Or perhaps he'd spirited her off to Scotland, like he had one time before.

Eddie briefly considered the possibility that she

might be slightly jealous of his success. After all, he'd pulled off an extremely brave act of war, without any help from her at all. And now, everywhere he went he was being hailed as a hero. Whether it was on the streets or at school, boys and girls alike were always coming up and saying well done, or offering him sweets or drinks or asking him to go to this party or that. He'd lost track of the number of times kids had asked about joining his gang. He'd played it pretty cool – he took a note of their names and phone numbers and then said they would be considered by the 'Committee'. There was, of course, no committee, there was just him and Mo and Gary, but now he couldn't get in touch with Mo at all. And Gary – well, he didn't seem very interested in the gang any more either. Every time he called, Gary said he was busy with experiments or homework, or both. But Mo, jealous? He didn't think so. They were friends, mates – his success was their success. He couldn't have done it without her.

Well – yes, he could.

But she didn't need to know that.

He was now fabulously successful, the most popular guy in town – but he wanted to share it with Mo.

Except, no show Mo.

Paddy was crying in the lounge – Scuttles had bought him a ridiculous tiny little navy suit for him to wear to the christening, and the baby, showing very good taste indeed, obviously didn't approve. He was twisting this way and that in his cot and his face had gone slightly purple with the effort of screaming his lungs out.

Eddie's mum reappeared in the bedroom doorway, a hairdryer in her hand. 'Eddie, I need to get ready!'

'What's that got to do with me?'

'That crying is driving me mad! Just take him out, take him out for a walk somewhere! Anything for some peace and quiet!'

'Och, Mum . . .' Eddie began.

'I'll take him,' said Scuttles.

'You stay exactly where you are. I have to get *you* ready next.'

'Me?' Scuttles was wearing a smart-looking suit and he'd had his hair cropped and his shoes polished. 'I *am* ready.'

Eddie's mum rolled her eyes. 'Yeah. *Right*,' she said. 'Eddie – please, just get Paddy some fresh air.'

Eddie sighed. He lifted Paddy out of his cot and

into the pram. Immediately his little brother stopped crying, and began gurgling happily.

'See?' Eddie's mum beamed as he pushed the pram towards the door. Eddie smiled bashfully. 'Don't be long, son,' she said.

'Be careful,' Scuttles growled as Eddie opened the door.

'Don't worry,' said Eddie. 'Oh, and by the way – make sure you get Mummy to comb your hair, you big baby.'

He gave Scuttles a sarcastic smile and pushed Paddy out of the apartment before he could reply.

How long was 'don't be long'? Ten minutes? An hour? Eddie glanced at his watch. It was two and a half hours before the christening. Say they had to leave for the church in two hours. That was plenty of time to walk over to Mo's, find out what her problem was, and get back. A few days ago it would have been a different matter – he would have had to negotiate various back streets and roundabout ways to get to her house in order to avoid the Pups, but now that he was a real hero he could get there in half the time.

He set off, whistling happily. Paddy smiled up at him. Before long they were chatting away, although it was of course something of a one-sided conversation. He told him what football team to support – Liverpool – he told him what books to read and films to see and which PlayStation games were the best, he told him to be sure to watch out for Scuttles and then laid out his own plans for world domination, and described in painstaking detail how he'd defeated the Babysnatchers and returned the head of Oliver Plunkett.

'One day, when you're older, you'll have your own gang, Paddy, your own territory. I'll be living somewhere else by then – you know, New York, or Paris – but I want you to know, if you need any help or advice, you need something sorted out, you only have to call and I'll be right there. Or I'll send some of my people. Or money. Or both. You probably won't need either – one mention of my name, it'll be enough to scare away whoever's giving you trouble. You understand?'

It was difficult to tell whether Paddy understood. There was a slightly higher pitched gurgle, which might indicate his appreciation, or just the fact that he had just unloaded a huge and sticky poo into his Huggies.

'That's one for Scuttles,' Eddie said to himself, and pushed on towards Mo's house.

Mo's dad, who had not long been released from prison, and was, as far as Eddie was concerned, every bit as unpleasant and nasty as Scuttles, yanked the door open and spat out an ignorant, 'What?'

Eddie blinked up at him. 'I was looking for Mo.'

'Well keep looking.' He began to close the door.

Last time Eddie had called for Mo her dad had also tried to close the door on him. Eddie had foolishly put his foot out to try and stop him – and had nearly broken his foot in the process. This time he didn't do anything so rash. He shouted, 'Wait!' loud enough for Mo's dad to hesitate.

'Wait for what?' he snapped.

'I . . . I just really need to talk to her. She's supposed to be coming to the christening . . .' He nodded down at the pram. Mo's dad looked down at Paddy, and his nose crinkled in disgust. 'Jeez. . .' he said, 'that's stinkin'.'

Mo's dad didn't exactly smell like a bed of roses himself, but Eddie ignored that for the moment. 'I know – I know – sorry. . .' he said. 'I just really need to speak to—'

'Well she's not here.'

'Oh.' Her dad went to close the door again. 'It's just . . .'

'Just what?'

'Well last time I called for her you said she wasn't here and that she'd gone off to Scotland to stay with her relatives, but then it turned out she was here all the time . . .'

'You calling me a liar?'

'No – no – you were . . . just trying to protect her . . . honestly . . . but I'm her friend and she's supposed to be going to the christening but I'm starting to get worried because she . . . well, I just need to know if she really isn't here or she's hiding upstairs pretending not to be here.'

'You *are* calling me a liar.'

'I—'

'She's not here! So bugger off! And take that bag of crap with you!'

Mo's dad finally slammed the door. Eddie stood there, embarrassed and angry. Paddy started to cry. He gave the pram a gentle shake. 'It's OK, it's OK,' he purred, 'you're not really a bag of crap. Although, admittedly, you do smell like one.'

Eddie sighed. Mo's dad really was a bit of a monster. Although she did seem inexplicably fond of him. 'His bark's worse than his bite,' she had once told him. Eddie wasn't sure about that. He stepped back and looked at the upstairs window in the vain hope that he might catch a glimpse of Mo peeking out, but he saw nothing but grimy windows and behind them unmoving curtains stained yellow by sunlight.

Eddie pushed the pram away up the street, quietly fuming. Who did she think she was anyway? She was what his mum called a fair-weather friend. Friends when it suited her, and when it didn't she just cut him off without so much as a word. Well, two could play at that game. Next time she turned up for a gang meeting the door would be locked, and would stay locked. She could form her own bloody gang. *Do I need her? No I do not. I blew up the Seagulls all by myself! What do I need with an albino?*

When he reached the top of the road Eddie spotted a newsagent's shop. He checked his pockets – good, he had enough for a Twix and a can of Coke. Or as it was known around his house, 'breakfast'. He parked the pram outside, made sure the brake was on, and then peered in at his little brother. He gave him a big smile and said, 'Try not to cause any trouble, I'll only be a minute.' Paddy's eyes twinkled in response.

Eddie hurried into the shop. He took a can from the fridge and a Twix from a display beside the cash desk. An elderly man took a pound off him – and then held the coin up to the light and turned it over in his hands.

'Sorry – have to check,' he said. 'We have kids in here all the time trying to pass fake ones.'

Eddie shrugged. Apparently satisfied, the man opened his till and gave Eddie ten pence change. Eddie held the 10p up to the light and examined it. 'Sorry,' he said, 'shops are always trying to rip me off.'

Plenty of shopkeepers would have yelled at him for being cheeky, but the man laughed and said, 'Fair enough.'

Eddie left the shop, smiling to himself. He slipped the can into his pocket, kicked off the brake and began to push the pram away with one hand. He lifted the Twix to his mouth with the other and tore at the wrapper.

He spat out the torn end, and took his first bite. Then as a joke he held it out for Paddy. 'You ain't got no teeth, but Mum tells me you've got a mighty suck . . .' and then he stopped and he gave a kind of half laugh as he looked down at the pram.

The *empty* pram.

He said, 'Paddy?'

And even though it was blindingly obvious that the pram was indeed empty, he tore at the blankets as if the baby might have somehow managed to shrink to fluffy-toy size and hide himself in the folds, but the pram was empty, empty, empty.

Eddie straightened, a sick feeling already churning in his stomach.

He looked beneath the pram.

He looked back at the shop.

He looked at the doors and the windows of the surrounding houses. Nobody was watching; nobody was giggling. There was no one there, and more importantly, there was no baby.

His throat was suddenly as dry as a desert.

'This isn't funny,' he croaked, looking about him in desperation. He shouted it: 'This isn't funny!'

Nothing.

'This isn't funny!'

A few metres away a front door opened and for a moment Eddie was filled with hope, but it was just an old woman. She gave him an odd look, and then sank to her knees and began to rub at her front step with a damp cloth.

Eddie was feeling dizzy. Sick, dry throat, dizzy.

He glared at the woman. 'Where is he?' he demanded. 'Where is he?'

The woman stared back.

'Where is he!' Eddie yelled. The woman scurried back into her house and closed the door.

Eddie wheeled the pram around and raced it back to the newsagent's. He left it outside and burst through the door. The newsagent looked shocked, and was already reaching for an alarm button, thinking he was about to be robbed, when Eddie shouted: 'Where is he? What have you done with him!'

'What have I done with—?' the newsagent began.

'The baby! Where's the baby?' Eddie raced forward and peered over the counter. 'Where is he? Paddy! Paddy! It's all right! I'm coming!'

The newsagent quickly locked his cash drawer and removed the key. He moved back away from the counter. 'I don't know what you're talking about!'

He was used to local kids coming into the shop and causing trouble, stealing stuff or shouting abuse, but he could see this was different. As Eddie turned and raced back out of the shop, the newsagent reached for the phone, and called the police.

Outside Eddie yelled at the top of his voice. 'OK! Enough! This isn't funny!'

He ran to one end of the street, and looked both ways. Nothing! He ran to the other end. Still nothing!

'Mo! This isn't funny!'

Up and down the street, more doors were now opening. Old women, men, kids were venturing cautiously out, many in vests, or bare feet, or clutching half eaten rounds of toast.

'Where is he?' Eddie yelled. 'Please!'

He heard a baby cry, and for a fleeting moment his heart soared as he spun towards – a woman holding a baby in her arms! Eddie charged towards her and she backed away, fear etched on her face. 'Patrick! Patrick!' Eddie bellowed. But even as he approached he could see that the baby was dressed in pink and had a full head of reddish hair. It wasn't his little brother. The woman jumped back into her house and slammed the door.

Eddie hammered on it nevertheless. 'Where's my brother?' he yelled.

Tears sprang from his eyes. He spun on his heels and saw that twenty or thirty people had now come out of their houses. The newsagent stood in his doorway, shaking his head.

GALWAY COUNTY LIBRARIES

'Where is he?' Eddie screamed, his voice breaking. 'Please! Just give him back to me! You must have seen something!'

But they said nothing because they had seen nothing. They stared at him, this frightened boy slowly sinking to his knees, his whole body shuddering.

I've lost my brother, I've lost my brother, I've lost my brother . . .

The thought went round and round and round in an endless, horrific loop.

I've lost my brother, I've lost my brother, I've lost my brother . . .

Sixteen

Eddie sat, absolutely dejected, in the back of a police car. His face was pale and tear stained; he had sweated through his clothes; his stomach felt like it had been ripped apart with knives. He'd been sitting there for half an hour. Every few minutes another police car arrived – if he'd been interested in counting them, he would have counted eight in all. Police officers had cordoned off the area with yellow and black coloured crime scene tape; those people who lived in the street and the newsagent were being interviewed, one by one, about what they had or had not seen. On the other side of the tape, at either end of the street, a crowd of onlookers . . . onlooked. Reporters and photographers, cameramen and soundmen jostled for position. The pram, sitting outside the newsagent's, was being dusted for fingerprints and minutely examined for forensic evidence. Eddie was fingerprinted; fibres from his jumper and trousers were snipped off and taken away for examination. Every once in a while a female police officer came up and asked Eddie if he was OK, but he couldn't even manage a nod, he just stared straight ahead.

Then he heard something of a commotion and he glanced up, hoping against hope that it was good news, that somehow little Paddy had been found nearby, that some kids had taken him just for a bit of fun and hadn't realised what trouble they would cause – but then he saw his mum, her eyes red, her hair ruffled, hurrying towards him, and beside her Scuttles in his best Sunday suit, looking like thunder.

His mum came up to the car and opened the door and sank to her knees. 'Oh, Eddie, Eddie, what happened, what happened?'

'Mum . . .'

'You little monster!' Scuttles yelled. 'What have you done with my son!'

'I didn't—'

'Eddie,' his mum cried, 'how could you lose my baby . . . ?'

'Mum, I just—'

'You're sick!' Scuttles screamed. 'You're evil! You're the child of the Devil!'

Scuttles burst into tears. He pounded his fists on the roof of the police car and let out an agonising wail. 'No . . . ! No . . . ! Not my baby!' A policewoman came up and helped him away towards a waiting ambulance.

'Eddie,' his mum pleaded weakly, 'you have to tell me . . .'

'Mum – I just went into the shop, I was only a few seconds . . . please, Mum, you have to believe me . . .'

'Eddie, Eddie . . . I want to, I really want to. But you've got yourself in so much trouble before—'

'Mum! I would never . . . !'

'Well, what am I supposed to think? You take my baby out for a walk and he just disappears!'

'Somebody took him!'

'Please son,' said his mum, taking hold of his hand and squeezing it, 'please son, this isn't a joke, just tell me what you've done with him.'

'Mum . . .'

'If it's one of your little schemes, please, just bring him back and we'll forget all about his—'

'Mum . . .'

'Please, Eddie! He's my little baby! I know . . . I know I mightn't have given you as much attention since he came – but that'll change, that'll change – I love you, Eddie, I'll always love you, but you can't just do something like this . . .'

'I haven't done anything!'

'You've taken my baby away from me!'

His mum turned away, and now she began to cry hysterically. Eddie tried to get out of the car to comfort her, but his way was blocked by a police officer.

'Best if you wait in the car, son.'

Eddie tried to get past him, but was then firmly pushed back inside.

'And that's an order.'

'But I have to tell her . . .'

'Your mum's upset, son. Anything you think would help find that little baby, you tell us, eh?'

'I've told you everything!'

The policeman nodded down at him. 'Well,' he said, 'we'll see about that.'

Then they drove him to the police station.

They don't believe me.

At first he didn't quite believe it, but the longer it went on, the more he came to realise that was exactly what the problem was.

They think I'm responsible for Paddy's disappearance.

They think I've kidnapped him, or sold him, or . . . killed him.

The police didn't come right out and say it, but

174

the kind of questions they asked made it absolutely clear. They hardly seemed bothered whether he had seen anything suspicious – he hadn't, of course – but were much more interested in where he had been, who he had talked to, why he had taken such and such a route, why he had decided to leave the baby alone outside the shop. He told them he'd been at Mo's house – and half an hour later he heard Mo's angry voice in the corridor outside the interview room, and then her dad's voice, just as upset, and he knew that the police had raided her house as well. He guessed that, just as before. Mo had been hiding upstairs when he'd called, and now the police supposed that she was part of the plot to kidnap Paddy as well.

Eddie didn't even bother to ask if he could speak to Mo – he knew he wouldn't be allowed.

He asked to see his mum, but was told that she was too upset right now.

He asked to see his dad, and the police officers exchanged glances and said they didn't think it was a good idea, as Mr Scuttles would probably tear Eddie's head off if he saw him, he was so angry; but Eddie said no, my real dad, my dad in Liverpool. But no, he couldn't remember the address or the phone number so, no, he couldn't see his dad.

They questioned him for hours. They brought him hamburger and chips from the station canteen but he couldn't eat. How could he eat? When the police had asked as many questions as they could think of a woman in a white coat and wearing a name badge that said Dr Coates came in and explained that she was a child psychologist and that she had some of her own questions. They weren't much different at first, but then she started asking him about whether he'd ever had a pet, and when he said he'd had a hamster once she asked if he'd ever hurt it on purpose. Then she asked whether he liked destroying things or getting people into trouble. Eddie knew what she was doing.

'You want to find out whether I'm mad or not. Barking. Mental. Isn't that right?' he asked.

She began to give him a rather complicated answer, then cut herself short and said, 'Well, yes.'

'Do you think I'm mad?'

'I think you're upset.'

'Do you think I stole Paddy?'

'I really don't know.'

'I didn't, I swear to God, why would I do something like that?'

'I don't know, Eddie.'

'I would never do anything like that.'

'Although you once stole twelve babies.'

'I was stealing them *back*.'

'Ah. You were a hero.'

'Yes!'

'Do you miss being a hero?'

'Well sometimes I— what do you mean?'

'I mean, if you were to somehow find your little brother again, then you'd be a hero all over again – is that what you want?'

'Yes . . . no! I mean, I want to find him, but I don't want to be a hero . . . that's sick. I just want my little brother.'

'Although he's not really your little brother, is he?'

'What do you mean?'

'He's more like your step-brother, isn't he?'

'He's my brother.'

'But you must resent him being there, getting all the attention—'

'No!'

'And do you get on with his father?'

'Scuttles.'

'Scuttles.'

'Yes. Fine.'

'Yet you don't call him Dad. Or Bernard.'

'No.'

'Because you don't like him.'

Eddie sighed. 'All right. So I don't like him.'

'You hate him, in fact.'

'Yes, I hate him. What does that prove?'

'It means you might have a reason to want to get back at him, to harm him, or harm something that belongs to him . . .'

'Not Paddy! I wouldn't! Not in a million years!'

Dr Coates made a note in her book. 'Eddie – Patrick is a defenceless little baby. By hurting him, you're not getting back at anyone.'

'I didn't hurt him! Good God Almighty! How many different ways can I say it? Patrick's my brother! Whoever stole him is out there with him! Instead of wasting your time talking to me you should be out there trying to find him! Do you hear me? Do you hear me!'

Before he quite realised what he was doing Eddie angrily reached across the table and ripped Dr Coates' notebook from her hand. He didn't even bother reading what she'd written down – he tore the pages out and scrunched them up. 'You're making bloody notes while my brother is all alone out there!' He flung the notes at her – they were just little balls of paper, but she ducked down like he was throwing hand grenades – and then she made a dash for the door and yanked it open.

'It's not safe to be alone with him!' she cried as she jumped out into the corridor. Immediately a heavy-set police officer glowered in at Eddie, then pulled the door closed and bolted it.

Eddie slumped back down at the table and buried his head in his hands.

He had experienced many dreadful things since he had moved to Belfast – but this was by far and away the worst. His brother was *missing*. He could even be *dead*. And even though he was entirely innocent of anything beyond a little carelessness, he was being blamed for the worst crime imaginable. It was so completely and utterly wrong – but entirely in keeping with the way his luck usually ran.

Nobody believes me.

Nobody ever believes me.

Not Mum, not Scuttles, not the police or the child psychologist.

But I AM NOT GUILTY.

I have done nothing wrong.

One moment I'm a hero, next a villain.

A hero?

He had been feeling so great for the past few days, ever since he'd destroyed General Killster's statue . . .

That was how he needed to feel now.

Feel like a hero – *act* like a hero.

Somebody had stolen his little brother. And everyone believed he had done it. So he had to prove them wrong. He had to get out there, find his brother, and make sure whoever really had taken him was arrested and thrown in prison. He would do it! He had to. He had no other option – but more than that, he would do it because he was Eddie Malone, he was a gang leader, he was the conqueror of the Seagulls and a hero to kids all over the city. Whoever it was had better be scared, because he was coming for them, he would save his brother and he *would have* his revenge.

Seventeen

Of course, first of all, before taking revenge, etc., etc., Eddie had to face up to the fact that he couldn't go home.

The police came to him and said, 'Son, we're going to release you.'

Eddie said, 'You believe me!'

'No, son, we just haven't got enough evidence to charge you – yet.'

Eddie's face dropped. 'But I . . .'

'Save it,' the police officer snapped. 'We're releasing you – but you can't go home. We're sending you to a children's home where you'll be kept under close supervision.'

'You're – you're – you're . . .'

'Face it, sunshine – if you're a killer, and we're pretty sure you are, we're not just going to let you out on to the streets so that you can kill again, are we? Besides, your mum's in an awful state, why would she want you at home reminding her all the time of what's happened? Even if you didn't do something to the baby, it was your fault for leaving him alone. And Mr Scuttles, a fine and upstanding man, would string you up if he could just get his hands on you. So we're going to put you somewhere where you can be kept nice and safe until we can nail you. It's the children's home for you.' He wagged a warning finger at Eddie. 'And let me give you a word of advice – you try stepping out of line in there, you'll live to regret it. Perhaps.'

Eddie didn't quite know what to say. He had thought that things could not possibly have gotten any worse, that he had the entire world on his shoulders already, but now they'd gone and added the Moon, Mars and possibly Venus as well.

A children's home?

'She's waiting outside for you.'

Eddie looked up hopefully. 'My mum?'

'Dr Coates. She will escort you there. And don't try anything funny with her either. She's got a black belt in karate and she wrestled at the Olympics for Botswana.'

'Botswana?'

'Yes. It's a long story. But you've been warned.'

Eddie was marched out of the police station. He looked in vain for some sign of his mum or Mo, but all he saw were reporters and camera crews and photographers. Thank goodness he was too young to have his picture taken, but it didn't stop the reporters shouting their questions. 'What did you do with the baby?' 'Where's he hidden?' 'Did you steal your own brother?'

He wanted to shout back at them, but the two police officers escorting him pushed his head down and forced him forwards, then more or less threw him into the back seat of a police car. As it took off at speed reporters ran after it, still bawling out their questions.

There was a policeman beside him, and another one driving. Dr Coates glanced back at him from the front passenger seat. 'This won't take long,' she said, 'it's only down the road.'

'I don't want to go there, wherever it is,' said Eddie.

'It's for your own protection. And everyone else's.'

'I haven't done anything wrong. Please. I need – I need a solicitor. A lawyer.'

'If you haven't done anything wrong, why do you need a lawyer?'

Eddie slumped back in his seat. 'I don't know,' he said vaguely.

The doctor smiled sympathetically at him. 'You could make this a lot easier on yourself, Eddie.'

'How?'

'Just tell us where Patrick is.'

'I don't know!' Eddie exploded.

Dr Coates' face hardened again; she turned to the front and folded her arms. 'Have it your way,' she snapped.

The Melody Hill Centre for Trouble Makers was a very dull, very grey, very dilapidated building on the outskirts of the city. It had badly needed a lick of paint for more than eighty years. In that respect it was very similar to its two neighbouring buildings: the Purdy Home for the Very Strange and the Silent Valley Crematorium. These three buildings had nothing in common but for the fact that they looked the same, sat side by side in vast, barren, unkempt grounds, dealt with a clientele nobody else wanted to deal with, and were all connected by a network of underground tunnels. They also shared a management committee made up of twelve austere gentlemen who had not smiled in very many years. So, in fact, the buildings had a lot in common. They dealt with the bad, the mad and the dead. It was said that if you stayed in Melody Hill long enough, you ended up in the Purdy Home, and that if you stayed in there for a few months you eventually went up in smoke, courtesy of the Silent Valley.

Eddie, having lived a quiet, innocent life in Groomsport, was not aware of the tales of horror which came out of these three buildings. In particular, he knew nothing of the Melody Hill Centre for Trouble Makers: of the boys who went in full of anger and violence and came out meek and religious (not a dreadful thing, in itself, of course, but there was something about their sudden conversion from mad as a brush to saint and scholar that was deeply disturbing); he knew nothing of the boys who went in screaming about revenge, and emerged dull eyed, barely able to talk or tie their shoelaces, or of the boys who went in – and were never seen again. Most of the 'troublemakers' were there because they had no relatives to take them in hand, or because they'd been rejected by their parents after getting into mischief once too often, so there was nobody to cause a fuss when they simply disappeared. On that rare occasion when a relative had a change of heart and enquired after their, say, missing cousin, they would be told that the boy had run away, or had left of his own accord and had gone off to England to work. And the relative would accept that story, because you tend to accept explanations given by people in positions of authority; so they would drive away, quite content that they had done their duty, not even thinking to look in their mirrors – where they might perhaps have spotted their loved one's outstretched hands pleading with them from behind the bars of the mental home before being savagely beaten back. Or perhaps they might even have noticed the puff of smoke above the crematorium, all that was left of little Johnny, another life extinguished by fires that were hotter than hell.

At least, this is what Jimmy McCabe told Eddie as he lay on his bunk, that first night in Melody Hill.

'How do I know you're not talking a lot of crap?' Eddie asked.

'You'll see,' said Jimmy.

Jimmy was fourteen, he had a skinhead and a limp. The skinhead he'd volunteered for, the limp came courtesy of the Reservoir Pups. Jimmy said they'd picked on him for no reason, beating him with baseball bats, breaking his leg so badly that it had never healed properly. Eddie knew that the Pups were well capable of such violence, but there was something about Jimmy that suggested he wasn't exactly an angel himself. Eddie had been taught not to judge a book by its cover: but he had learned that sometimes you could; that if a boy looked tough and dangerous, he quite often was. Jimmy looked tough and dangerous, so it was no particular surprise when within three minutes of Eddie's arrival in the dorm he pulled a knife and ordered Eddie to hand over his money.

'I don't have any money,' said Eddie.

'Your mobile phone.'

'Don't have one.'

'Well what do you have?'

'Nothing.'

'Well that's no use to me.'

'Sorry. I could write you an IOU. But I don't have a pen. Or paper.'

Jimmy put his knife away and sat on his bunk. 'Welcome to Melody Hill,' he said. 'I had to try.'

Eddie shrugged. He looked around the dorm; there were sixty beds – but all the others were empty.

'Where is everyone?'

'They're having dinner.'

'Oh right. Excellent. I'm starving.' He hadn't eaten all day, and although he felt miserable about what had happened, both to Paddy and himself, at least his appetite was starting to come back. He needed to eat. To maintain his strength. For what he had to do.

Jimmy glanced at his watch. 'You're too late, mate,' he said. 'Anyone who arrives after six has to wait until breakfast.'

'Breakfast?'

Jimmy lay back on his bed. 'Them's the rules,' he said.

'But I haven't eaten all day.'

Jimmy moved his hands, pretending to play the violin. 'Tough,' he said. He glanced across at Eddie. 'So, mate, what're you in for?'

Eddie shrugged.

'Please yourself,' said Jimmy. He rolled over and appeared to go to sleep. Eddie walked around the dorm, checking for escape routes, but all the doors were bolted shut from the outside. He sat on his bed for a while and prayed to God that Patrick was safe, that there had been some kind of horrible mix-up, that his brother and himself would soon be at home together.

After about half an hour the other boys were marched in by a stern-looking guard with weeping sores on a face which sat at the foot of a dome-like skull, which was itself scantily covered with tufts of greasy hair. Eddie's mum would have described him as 'no oil painting'. But then she was in love with Scuttles, so she was clearly no great judge of what was or wasn't a great oil painting.

The boys stood by their beds until they were ordered to get changed into their pyjamas, which were all exactly the same colour – blue striped – and size. That is, they boasted a universal fitting size, which suited nobody. Too big for the little ones, too little for the big ones; they clung or they hung. Even for those of decidedly average proportions they seemed to conspire to be exactly the opposite of what was required. The guard, who was wearing a perfectly-fitted black uniform with a red arm band, seemed to notice Eddie for the first time – and the fact that he was neither standing to attention nor getting changed into the ill-fitting pyjamas he didn't yet possess. He hurried over, his eyes wide and angry. Eddie got up off his bed.

'You!' the guard bellowed. 'What's your name?'

'Eddie,' said Eddie.

'Eddie? Eddie what?'

'Eddie Malone.'

'Eddie Malone what?'

Eddie blinked at him, somewhat confused. The guard's face was wide and pink and his nostrils were slightly turned up; he looked like a pig with a moustache. Although, admittedly, Eddie had seen few pigs with moustaches. Unless you counted Scuttles. 'I'm sorry, I—'

'Eddie Malone what?' the guard screamed.

'Just Eddie . . . Malone . . .' He was sick and tired of people shouting at him. It seemed like they'd been doing it for ever – first at the scene of Paddy's disappearance, then at the police station, now . . .

'EDDIE MALONE WHAT?'

Eddie's eyes darted about – the other boys had paused in their changing to watch.

'I'm sorry I—'

The guard's fleshy face zoomed into his, until they were only a few centimetres apart. 'Sir! Sir!' he yelled, spraying Eddie's face with flecks of spit. 'It's Sir! Do you hear me, boy?'

Eddie nodded.

'OK! So for the last time – what's your name?'

'Sir Eddie Malone. At your service.' He stood to attention and gave a little salute.

Surprised giggles rolled around the dorm; Eddie couldn't help but grin himself.

And then the guard slapped him hard across the face, wiping off the grin and silencing the giggles. Eddie tumbled backwards on to his bed. His face stung like hell. Tears threatened to spring forth of their own accord, but he fought them back. The guard loomed over him.

'You're a funny one, eh?' snarled the guard. 'Sir Eddie Malone. That's a great joke. Very funny.' He turned then and addressed the other boys. 'You know who this clown is, don't you?' The boys either shook their heads, or looked away. 'Well, why would you? Idiots like you lot don't watch the news. So I'll tell you. You boys, you're all in here for a good reason – you've stolen stuff, you've destroyed things, you've caused trouble, trouble, nothing but trouble. You all know what you've done, and you accept your punishment. You're what we call good honest criminals. This boy, though – you know what he's done? He's done something to his baby brother. Little baby has disappeared. Maybe he killed him. Maybe he hurt him. Maybe he sold him. His own brother.'

The guard turned back to Eddie, who was still lying on the bed, nursing his now swelling cheek. 'We all hate people who mess with little kids, Sir Eddie.' He wagged a warning finger down at him. 'You, boy, you aren't going to last more than a couple of days in here.'

He turned and strode out of the dorm. Eddie

pulled himself up into a sitting position. All of the other boys were now staring at him. 'I haven't done anything wrong,' he said. 'Someone's kidnapped my brother.' They continued to stare at him. 'Honestly,' said Eddie.

The lights went out, suddenly – clearly they were controlled from outside the room – plunging the dorm into complete and utter blackness. There were no windows to allow in any light, and even if there had been, the nearest streetlights were half a mile away beyond towering walls. There were no bedside lights, not even the dull glow of an Emergency Exit sign. Eddie felt for the edge of his blankets, then eased them back and crawled beneath them. He was hungry, and frightened. He lay for five minutes, surprised and terrified by the complete silence that seemed to hang over the dorm like an invisible death mask.

Eighteen

Three days passed, during which Eddie ate hardly any food at all. It wasn't for the want of trying. When he queued up in the canteen the servers either deliberately spilled his food or point blank refused to serve him. They muttered 'killer' under their breath. Eddie thought he was in luck when one of the supervisors finally helped with the serving, and gave him a generous helping, only for another to trip him as he turned to find a table. He went sprawling across the tiled floor, his plate clattering off the tiles and echoing around the packed but otherwise silent room. Then they screamed at him to clean it up.

So he didn't eat any meals, but he did manage to slip an apple inside his jacket without anyone seeing, and later, half a banana, and then half a can of flat Coke that someone had abandoned. So he didn't starve, but it wasn't enough to keep a growing boy going, or, indeed, a growing gerbil.

After having breakfast – or after not having breakfast, as the case was – Eddie was called up before the headmaster, or 'The Governor' as the boys called him. The guard who'd slapped his face, whose nickname was Slaterbake, marched him up, and poked him in the back the whole way. Slaterbake knocked on the Governor's door, then pushed it open without waiting for a response. He positioned Eddie in front of the Governor's desk and told him to stand to attention. The Governor continued to examine some paperwork for several minutes, and then eventually his hooded eyes flicked up and briefly examined him.

'So,' he said, evidently satisfied with his inspection, 'this is the boy who done in his brother.'

'I didn't—'

'Silence!'

Slaterbake cracked him across the back of the head. Eddie cowered down for a moment, then gradually straightened again. The Governor gave no indication of either approving of or disapproving of the violence. He simply didn't react at all. Instead he clasped his hands together and informed Eddie that the police, who had interviewed him three times a day since his arrival, were satisfied that they had gotten as much information out of him as they were going to get, and that they were now deciding whether or not to charge him with the kidnap and/or murder of his baby brother. 'If they don't charge you, it doesn't mean you're not guilty, it just means they haven't enough evidence to charge you – yet.'

'But I'm innocent,' said Eddie.

The Governor shook his head. 'That's what they all say.'

He was a small man, very small in fact. He sat on several cushions to make himself appear more imposing behind his desk. In fact, it made him look like a small man sitting on several cushions. He wore thick glasses which made his eyeballs appear unusually large. Like a frog. Like a small frog sitting on several cushions, wearing glasses.

'What about my mum?' Eddie asked. 'Is she not coming to see me?'

'I think, Eddie, that actions speak louder than words.'

'What's that supposed to mean?'

'It means, well, she's not here, is she? And there's nothing stopping her. We encourage family visits, Eddie, and I would say that your mother's nonappearance speaks volumes.'

'Can I phone her?'

'No.'

'No?'

'Eddie, why don't you just admit what you've done. It'll be a lot easier for you in the long run.'

'But I haven't done anything, and as soon as I get out of here I'll prove that I . . .' He stopped, because the Governor was smiling. 'What?' he asked.

'Sorry, I know it's not funny.'

'What's not funny?'

'What you just said. But I can't help myself sometimes.' This time he actually giggled. And when Eddie glanced around, Slaterbake was laughing as well.

Eddie couldn't think of anything he'd said that was remotely funny. 'I don't understand – what did I . . . ?'

'Of course – sorry, Eddie, perhaps you're not aware . . . You said, "as soon as I get out of here." The point is, unless you admit your guilt or give some indication of what happened to your little brother, well, you won't be getting out of here. Not ever.'

'Ever?'

'Well, until you're eighteen at least, and when you're your age, that might as well be for ever.'

'But – but – you can't just . . . *keep* me here!'

The Governor smiled pleasantly. 'Of course we

can. Until you're eighteen your parents call the shots. Both your mother and father feel it would be better for you to stay here, where we can keep you out of trouble.'

'They what . . . ?'

The Governor nodded. 'It's right here in front of me.' He lifted a sheet of paper, examined it briefly, then set it down and spun it round so that Eddie could see what was written on it.

Eddie leant forward. 'No,' he began to say, 'my mum wouldn't . . .' It was a long letter, beginning with *'Dear Governor, It is with a heavy heart that I write to ask you to look after Eddie for the foreseeable . . .'* 'No! She wouldn't . . .' He found his eyes skipping on down, picking out words almost at random. *'gang'*, *'theft'*, *'Plunkett'*, *'burning school'*, and it was only when he found himself stuck on one of the words – it looked like *'warhead'* but might as easily have been *'warthog'* – that Eddie realised that this wasn't his mother's handwriting at all. The words filled one side of the page, and then continued on the other, but as Eddie reached out to turn it over, Slaterbake reached across and slapped his hand away.

'Don't touch!' he snapped.

'But it's not my mum's handwriting . . .' He

reached out for it again, but this time the Governor whipped it away, and then held his hand out to stop Slaterbake from striking Eddie again. Slaterbake gave a disappointed shrug. The Governor turned the letter over in his hand. 'You're quite right, son, it's not from your mother. It's from your father.' Eddie's heart was in his mouth. His dad. His dad had written requesting that he be kept in this hell-hole for ever. His dad, who had written him so many letters which Eddie hadn't even known about, and now here was one he did know about, and it was basically condemning him to a life sentence. Eddie felt his knees begin to give way. He was going to faint. Faint like a girl. Not only his mum, but his one and only hope, his dad, had betrayed him as well. Eddie forced himself to remain standing. He would not faint. He *would not*.

The Governor smiled up at him. 'Yes, son, your father knows exactly what kind of a troublemaker you are. He's a good man your dad, a fine judge of character. I've known him for many years. In fact, I would consider Bernard to be one of my very best friends.'

Eddie's mouth dropped open.

Bernard.

BERNARD!

Eddie stepped forward. 'No – no – you've got it wrong . . . Bernard – hah! Scuttles, he's not my father, he's not my dad, he's got no right to—'

But then he felt a hand on the back of his jumper, and Slaterbake was pulling him backwards.

Without thinking Eddie threw his arm out, and the back of his hand caught Slaterbake on the side of the jaw.

The guard staggered back. He looked genuinely shocked for a moment, then he quickly reached into his pocket and withdrew a whistle, which he immediately blew.

Eddie jumped forward again. He gripped the side of the desk. 'Scuttles isn't my da!' he shouted. The Governor pushed himself backwards on his wheeled leather chair. Some of the pink-pigginess colour had drained from his cheeks and he looked genuinely frightened as Eddie, his face a mask of anger and confusion, screamed again. 'He's not my da! You have to believe me!'

The Governor cowered down as Slaterbake grabbed hold of Eddie again. Behind them the door to the office burst open and five more guards charged in and immediately joined in, jumped on him and forced him to the floor.

In a matter of moments he was handcuffed, his

legs were bound and Slaterbake had sprayed some kind of gas into his eyes which burned like hot pokers. But he still yelled, 'He's not my dad! He's not my dad!'

They lifted him between them, and carried him out of the office. The Governor put a hand to his chest to steady his racing heart, then lifted a glass of water and took a long drink. The *nerve* of the boy, causing such a scene in his own office. The *anger*, the *violence*. But then, what else could you expect from a boy who would do something like *that* to his own brother?

The Governor lifted the letter and walked across to the window where he stood for several minutes admiring the view across Melody Hill's overgrown gardens. He glanced at Scuttles' letter again, then folded it into his inside pocket, and patted it. Then he leant forward a little so that he could appreciate the side view of the Purdy Home for the Very Strange and next to it the ash-speckled frontage of the Silent Valley Crematorium. If the police didn't charge the boy, then he'd let things settle down for a while before he ordered Slaterbake – and even the Governor called him that, although never to his horrible face – to walk the little troublemaker along one of the underground tunnels into either

Purdy or the Silent Valley. Left or right. It really didn't matter which. Either way, just as he had with all the other little troublemakers, he'd announce that the boy had escaped, and then he would never be heard from again.

Nineteen

That evening, after the lights went out, Eddie
was lying in bed, massaging his stomach. He had
hardly eaten a scrap since arriving at the Melody
Hill Centre for Trouble Makers and now he felt
weak and tired and his head hurt. But more than
just his head – his very soul seemed to ache.
His little brother had been stolen. That was bad
enough. But what if he was dead? It was a wicked,
wicked world. Eddie sometimes played along
with the idea that his gang was wicked – evil,
even. But it wasn't really – it *got up* to things, it
annoyed people, it ran schemes, pulled moves,
caused mischief, it aggravated, sometimes it even
ran amok, but it wasn't *evil*.

Or was it?

Now, as he lay starving in bed, he began to see
that a pattern was emerging. Where once his gang
had become involved, almost by accident, in
fantastic adventures for all the right reasons, like
saving babies or rescuing a sacred head, now it –
and by *it* he included himself and Mo and Gary –

was becoming increasingly involved in things that were less clearly for the common good and which, if seen from the point of view of a parent or guardian or headmaster or the police might be perceived as purely evil. The burning of the Reservoir Pups' HQ by Gary? Was that not evil? It was pure chance that the Pups had escaped the fire which raged through their building. What if dozens of them had been killed? And what about the bombing of the statue of General Killster? What if the old man he'd met or some baby Seagulls had been passing when it exploded? Wasn't *that* evil?

What's happening to me?

Have I become so obsessed with building a gang, with impressing the other gangs, with showing that I'm rough and tough, that I'm starting to turn into . . . Captain Black?

All I ever wanted to do was have friends, and have fun.

And now look where I am!

He was in Melody Hill because he was a danger to society. Even his own family didn't trust him. Scuttles had written the letter that was keeping him here, but who could blame him?

His son has disappeared, and I'm the only real suspect. Of course he wants me locked up.

Eddie closed his eyes tight against the pain in his head. *Concentrate, concentrate . . .*

Paddy's been stolen – but who would steal a defenceless little baby? And why?

Eddie decided that there were two possibilities:

One – some sick individual who liked to steal children.

Two – the Seagulls.

What if they discovered I was responsible for the destruction of General Killster's statue, and this is how they've taken their revenge? He hadn't exactly kept quiet about his attack on the statue – and news of it had spread like wildfire. He'd loved being hailed as a great hero for doing it. But the Seagulls were hardly going to see it that way.

If it was a madman who'd taken Paddy, then there was nothing he could do about that. But if it was the Seagulls – well, if he could just get out of Melody Hill, then at least he knew where to start looking. The army camp. He had managed to sneak in once before; he could do it again.

But how was he going to get out of Melody Hill? The police had described it as a children's home – but it was more like a prison camp.

'Eddie. You awake?'

Eddie recognised Jimmy McCabe's voice, whispering in the darkness.

'Jimmy?'

'We have something for you.'

Eddie tensed. *My God*, he thought, *they're going to attack me.*

Slaterbake had warned him that the boys would give him a hard time, and now they were coming to punish him for what he'd done to a helpless little baby.

A beam of a flashlight was suddenly in his face, almost blinding him. He could just see dark figures approaching his bed – from all sides.

Lie down and take it – or fight for your life.

Eddie's fingers curled into fists.

If they beat me up – so be it. But I'm going to hurt some of them in the process. Otherwise they'll think they can pick on me any time they like. I have to show them. I have to . . .

The beam dropped from his face on to his bedclothes; it reflected up again off the white top sheet to show that almost the whole dorm was now gathered around his bed. Jimmy was closest. He seemed to be in charge – so maybe if he took him out first, they wouldn't be quite so enthusiastic.

Eddie took a deep breath. One. His fist tightened

further. Two. Hit him under the chin. Thr—

'Here,' said Jimmy. He held out . . . a sandwich.

'Here,' said another boy. Another sandwich.

'Have this,' said a third, and cautiously placed a Mars Bar on the edge of Eddie's bed. Boy after boy after boy followed suit – and in a few moments the top sheet was peppered with different items of food. Apples, bananas, Twix, cans of Coke, a bottle of Lilt, a packet of Jaffa Cakes, several rolled up slices of cooked ham . . . Eddie looked at it, confused – but also very hungry.

'I don't understand . . .'

'You haven't eaten for days,' said Jimmy.

'I know, but . . .'

'We heard you attacked the Seagulls,' said another boy.

'You're Eddie Malone – you're the one captured the Babysnatchers single-handed.'

'I . . .'

'And you got back the head of Oliver Plunkett by killing Scarface Cutler.'

'Well, I . . .'

'We were scared to approach you before,' said yet another one, 'but then we heard you smacked Slaterbake in the chops – so we know you're one of us.'

'Well that's . . .'

'So we saved this food for you,' said Jimmy. 'You must be starving.'

Eddie looked around at them. He didn't know whether to laugh or cry.

But, seeing as they seemed to think he was some kind of hero, he decided it was better not to cry. He looked at the food, and his stomach rumbled happily. But he didn't tuck in – not right away. This was the time to show what he was made of, that he really was one of them . . .

He nodded around the circle of prisoners. 'Thank you for this,' he said, 'but we're all in this together – so this food's for all of us. We share it out evenly.'

'We get enough,' said Jimmy. 'You haven't—'

'Evenly,' Eddie said firmly, 'or I eat nothing.'

The boys exchanged glances, then nodded. Eddie lifted one of the sandwiches and two of the Jaffa Cakes and a can of Coke. Then he nodded, and eager hands darted out to remove the rest of the food from his bed.

Eddie unwrapped the sandwich. Ham and cheese. Not his favourite exactly, but it was food, and he felt dizzy just looking at it. But he didn't devour it immediately. He didn't want to look too desperate. What had the boys said – that they'd been too scared to approach him? And the awe with which they'd spoken of his exploits with the Babysnatchers and Plunkett and the Seagulls? None of them had started to eat either. They were waiting for him.

So he bit into his sandwich, and they followed suit. He chewed slowly, methodically. They did the same.

He smiled around at them, they smiled back.

'So,' one ventured, 'what was it like smacking Slaterbake in the mouth?'

'I heard you split his lip,' said another.

'I heard there was blood everywhere.'

Eddie shrugged modestly. The fact was that he had struck Slaterbake by accident, but there was no need for them to know that. 'It just kind of happened,' he said. The boys nudged each other, as if to say, *It just kind of happened – who's he kidding? He attacked Slaterbake!*

Eddie took another small bite. What he actually wanted to do was swallow the entire sandwich without chewing, he was that hungry. Suddenly ham and cheese tasted like the most beautiful meal in the history of the world. And as for the Jaffa Cakes – he wanted to slip one up each nostril and sniff them up into his brain. He was as close to

heaven as he could imagine, and for a moment the
weight of the world on his shoulders felt a little
lighter.

'How long have you lot been in here?' he asked.

'Eight months,' said Jimmy.

'Two years,' said one boy.

'Three years,' said another.

They all stated how long they'd been locked up
in Melody Hill.

'And how long have you got to go?' Eddie asked.

They looked at each other and shrugged.

'Till they let us out,' said Jimmy.

'You mean there's no set time?' Eddie asked.

One of the boys, a sturdy-looking lad with a
pudding-bowl haircut and a pair of glasses with
one cracked lens, shook his head. 'Whenever they
decide we're better, that we won't get into trouble
again.'

'That's not right,' Eddie said bluntly. 'Don't your
parents complain?'

'It's them that sends us here in the first place,'
said a skinny fella with lots of freckles. 'They don't
care.'

There was more nodding, all around the group.
Eddie looked at Jimmy. 'When I first came here,
you said that some boys just disappeared – I

thought you were just trying to scare me.'

Jimmy, and most of the other boys, shook their heads.

'There's lots,' said one, 'lots who just disappear from their beds in the middle of the night, and we never see them again.'

'How do you know they haven't been released . . . or maybe escaped?'

'Because no one is ever released,' said the freckled boy.

'And no one has ever escaped,' said the sturdy boy with the pudding-bowl haircut.

'But *how* do you know it?' Eddie asked.

They exchanged glances.

'Because – they're never heard from again,' said Jimmy, 'and one day . . .' He hesitated for a moment, looking for support from his companions. Several of them nodded. Many of them stared at the floor. All of them stopped chewing. 'One day there was a cave-in.'

'A cave-in?'

'Aye – there's tunnels under here, they run across to the mental asylum and the crematorium . . . right through the gardens outside. And one day there was a storm and the grounds flooded and . . . well I don't really know how it happened, but the roof of one of the tunnels collapsed while we were outside working in the gardens and some of us fell in and we were covered in mud and water and . . .' He glanced up at the others, and they nodded their encouragement, '. . . and *bones*.'

'Bones?'

'Bones.'

'Kids' bones,' the freckle-faced boy added grimly.

'But – but . . .' Eddie began, 'what if they'd been there for say, hundreds of years or something?'

'Not just bones,' said Jimmy, 'entire skeletons – and some of them wearing clothes. Modern clothes. Trainers. A Swatch watch. They come from here, Eddie, right here, and nobody will believe us.'

'But you believe us, don't you?' asked one of the boys.

Eddie nodded. Of course he did. He had already experienced plenty of evil in his short life. He knew it existed, whether it manifested itself in the theft of a dozen babies or the kidnapping of an old head.

'Do you . . . do you think they're all in it together?' Eddie asked. 'The Governor, Slaterbake . . . all the guards?'

'They have to be,' said Jimmy.

'And the thing is,' said yet another boy, this one

with his head shaved and the tattoo of a spider on his forehead, 'we never know who's going to be next. That's why we all behave, that's why we never step out of line – we don't want to end up like, like . . .' and he trailed off, unable to finish.

Jimmy moved closer to Eddie now. He sat on the edge of the bed. 'We've been scared, Eddie, we don't mind saying it, but now that you're here . . . you can help us, can't you? You've shown that you're not frightened of them – you have to get us out of here!'

Eddie blinked at Jimmy, and then slowly looked around at the rest of them.

This was indeed a hellish place, but he was as much a prisoner here as the others. What was he supposed to do? He'd already incurred the wrath of Slaterbake and the Governor – how much longer before he became just another pile of bones in the tunnels beneath Melody Hill? The boys stared back at him, their eyes full of hope and desperation. Eddie had no idea what he was doing, but he nodded his head and said, 'Of course I'll get you out of here.'

Twenty

Eddie spent the next few days familiarising himself with as much of Melody Hill as he could manage. Where they could, the boys helped him by causing diversions, drawing the guards away from stairs and corridors. He walked the perimeter wall, he watched the gates and counted the guards and timed the security cameras in their long sweeps across the overgrown gardens. He checked for holes in fences, for rusty locks on the windows and doors. He scoured the workshops for weapons and the greenhouses outside for tools. At the end of it all he sat on the edge of his bed and said to himself, *I have no idea what I'm doing. There's no way out of here. We're all going to die.*

But then he saw their expectant faces again: at lunch – not that he was getting any, the supervisors saw to that – and again at night as they prepared for bed; looks which said, *How much longer?*

He saw the fearful way they looked towards the dormitory door as the lights went off and knew that everyone was thinking, *Is this the night they come for me?*

He didn't think they would come for *him* just yet. He was still quite a new arrival, and he was sure there was still a major hunt going on for Paddy outside. So they surely wouldn't try anything until all that fuss died down. But the fact was: they would eventually come for him. It was as sure as . . . as sure as the fact that the sun would rise in the morning.

But what was he to do?

He had examined every inch of Melody Hill, within and without. It was extremely well guarded. The surrounding wall was high and smooth and topped with barbed wire; guards passed along it every few minutes. The main gates were three metres high and appeared to be made of the toughest steel. There were guards stationed there permanently. Every inch of the grounds was regularly swept by security cameras. One day, as he watched, a cat innocently strolled close to the wall – and then nearly dropped dead from fright as shrill alarms sounded and screaming guards charged towards it.

No. It seemed clear to him that there was no way out.

Eddie tossed and turned in bed, thinking about it. Even if the boys overcame their fear of Slaterbake and attempted to escape, they wouldn't get very far. They might break out of the dorm – the lock was pretty strong, but the door wasn't the sturdiest. If they were very lucky they might get downstairs; but the chances of getting out of the building, across the grounds and over the wall without being detected were extremely small – even for one boy, let alone the sixty who slept in the dorm every night.

And if they were caught – what would happen then?

The Governor, or Slaterbake, or whoever was in charge of what happened down in the tunnels – well, he couldn't kill *all* of them. At least, not all at once. But he, they, would surely make their lives even more miserable, and then, as time went by, one by one, they would begin to disappear. There would always be new arrivals, of course, but the sixty who'd taken part in the attempted escape, sooner or later, would be whittled down, and down, and down . . .

Eddie fell into a disturbed sleep. He was being led down into the tunnels. Dark, clammy, the stench of dread and fear and death. Slaterbake was pushing and prodding him. They turned this way and that, the path always leading downwards, until it seemed to Eddie they were in the very bowels of the earth . . . and then Slaterbake stopped him and pointed at a wall. There was a spade resting against the damp wall and Eddie knew instantly what it was for . . .

For digging his own grave.

In his dream he was digging, digging, digging, and there were worms and beetles and maggots crawling all over him, and then when he had finished – drenched in sweat, his limbs aching – Slaterbake came up behind him, took the spade from his hands as if to place it back against the wall; but instead raised it and then swung the steel blade down on to his . . .

'Noooooo!' Eddie shot up out of bed, blinking in the darkness, drenched in sweat, not sure whether he was safe or he really had been murdered by Slaterbake in the dank bowels of Melody Hill.

'Are you OK?' Jimmy whispered.

'Yes . . . I'm . . .' And then he stopped, for something had sparked in his mind, something important and for the moment he just couldn't put his finger on it. Dreams worked like that sometimes – you had brilliant ideas, but you had to grasp them the moment you woke up or they might escape and never be reclaimed. He reached for it, he concentrated hard, hard, hard . . .

'Eddie,' Jimmy whispered, 'have you come up with a plan yet?'

'Shhhhhh,' Eddie hissed, still trying to locate the elusive thought.

'You have to get us out of here,' said Jimmy. 'I can't stand it any longer . . .'

'I know, I know, I know . . .' Eddie said over and over, his mind reeling. *No, don't let it be gone, don't let it be . . .*

And then suddenly he had it, and it was Jimmy that had helped him pull it back.

You have to get us out of here . . .

Out.

Out.

That's where they were going wrong!

Eddie sat up in bed. His pyjamas, still far too big for him, were stuck to him; his hair lay dank on his head. 'Jimmy,' he whispered, 'I know how we're going to do it.'

Even in the darkness Eddie could see a sudden new brightness in Jimmy's eyes. His friend slipped out of bed and sat on the edge of Eddie's. 'You do?' he whispered excitedly. 'What . . .'

'Listen,' said Eddie, 'I think I've been looking at it the wrong way – I've been trying to think about ways of breaking *out*. And all of the security is designed for just that purpose. And we're never going to do it.'

Jimmy's brow crinkled in confusion. 'But . . .'

'So instead of trying to get out – we go in. Into the tunnels.'

'The tunnels?'

'Exactly. All their focus is on stopping us going over the fence or through the gates – they won't be expecting us to try and get out through the very place they know everyone's terrified of. So we use the tunnels.'

'You want us to use the tunnels *of death*?'

'The tunnels of death,' said Eddie.

Jimmy stood up. 'I'll be back in a minute,' he said.

'But – where are you . . . ?'

'I'm going to be sick,' he said. 'I really am.'

It was a daring, and very, very, very scary and dangerous plan. But it was the only one that gave them any hope of escaping. Jimmy called for a show of hands.

This was the moment that Eddie, standing with

his hand in the air, feared that not a single one of them thought that his plan was achievable; but then, one by one, their hands began to rise until there was only one boy left with his hand resolutely in his lap.

Jimmy went across and knelt beside him. His name was Seamus Brown, and he was the smallest and scrawniest of them all.

'What's wrong, Seamus – don't you want out of here?'

Seamus looked up, his eyes big and round and scared. 'Course I do,' he said, 'but I'm scared of the tunnels. All them bodies.'

Jimmy squeezed his knee. 'Of course you are, Seamus. Aren't we all? That's why we all need to go together.'

'I don't like the dark,' said Seamus.

'We'll bring torches,' said Jimmy.

'What if they go out?' said Seamus.

'They won't . . .'

'What if the dead kids get us?' said Seamus.

Seamus glanced around at Eddie, who came up and knelt beside him too.

'Seamus,' said Eddie, 'if they're dead, they can't get us.'

'But what if there's ghosts, their ghosts?'

'If there's ghosts,' said Eddie, 'then they won't scare us. If they do anything, they'll help us.'

Seamus thought about that. Then he gave the slightest nod, and raised his hand. 'I'll go then,' he said.

A quiet cheer swept around the room – and was just as suddenly cut dead as the dorm doors sprang open and they turned to find Slaterbake standing there, flanked by a team of guards.

'All right you lot!' he barked. 'Get down for your breakfast!'

They stood, as one. They hadn't even realised that daybreak had come, so engrossed where they in their planning.

'All except for you, Eddie Malone!'

Eddie froze. Everyone was suddenly looking at him.

'You think I've forgotten what happened the other morning? Assaulting me? Attacking me like a vicious animal? Well you can be bloody sure I haven't.' He glanced around at one of the guards, then put his hand out. The guard handed him a long, thin, bamboo cane. The end of it was split into a hundred sharp little strands. Slaterbake rested the cane in the palm of his hand and smiled across at Eddie. 'So I'd like you to meet Slicer.'

Eddie just stared at it. 'And Slicer is delighted to meet you too, Eddie.'

Slaterbake moved forward. 'Get downstairs, all of you!' he barked.

The boys looked at Eddie, looking for some indication of what they should do next. Even though he knew he was in for some major trauma, it made Eddie feel good. Slightly good. He was a leader. He'd always thought of himself as a leader, he just hadn't had much of a chance to demonstrate it. Now he had to act like one. Jimmy was closest. Eddie could tell by looking at him that he would only have to nod and he would stand with him, try and protect him; but he knew equally that this wasn't the time. He would have to accept his punishment, hope to survive it, and then put their plan of escape into action – when there was the least chance of being disturbed by Slaterbake and his crew. So Eddie gave Jimmy the slightest shake of his head. Jimmy nodded. He turned to the others and said, 'Let's go, boys, breakfast is out.'

The boys looked at Jimmy, slightly surprised, and then followed him out of the dorm. Two of the guards left to escort them down to breakfast. Two others came forward and grabbed Eddie. One forced his hand out. Eddie tried to keep it squeezed into a fist, but they crushed his fingers until he couldn't bear the pain any longer and slowly he released them. Then the guard held his hand out flat.

Slaterbake stood over him.

'OK Slicer,' he said, 'do your work.'

And he raised Slicer high above his head, and then whooshed him down again, and again, and again, with all the strength he could muster.

Twenty-one

For a moment he didn't know where he was; there was only the sensation of helplessness . . .

Of Paddy crying.

Of birds circling above his pram.

Seagulls!

Eddie was in the shop doorway, but somehow cemented to the ground. He couldn't move, not a centimetre; he was screaming and shouting at the birds – but not a sound would come out. They drew closer and closer to the pram, and then they were inside it, their jagged claws digging into the covers.

Then suddenly whatever had been holding him firm let him go and Eddie charged towards the pram, and now his voice was back, shrill and loud. But he was too late, he was too late . . . the biggest bird, a mass of dirty yellow feathers, its beak as sharp as a spear, had hold of Paddy and was already flapping its wings to take off. Eddie dived after it and grabbed hold of his little brother and a furious tug-of-war began. At first he thought he had a chance, but then the other birds began to dive at him. They pecked savagely at his hands, tearing and shredding until finally the pain was too much to bear and he had to let go. The bird holding Paddy squawked triumphantly and wheeled away, flying high towards the darkened clouds while Eddie tumbled back, tumbled, tumbled, tumbled towards . . .

'Eddie?'

He tried to force his eyes open, tried to focus – the Seagulls, the Seagulls, he had to – Paddy – he had to . . . but no – it was a dream, a nightmare, he was . . . his eyes opened; there was something burning, no – not burning, but *like* burning, the *pain* of burning . . . Jimmy was standing over him, looking concerned. The other boys were crowded around. He was . . . lying on his bed. He tried to sit up by putting his hands on the mattress and pushing up, and it was then that the real pain hit him – the moment his left hand touched the covers. He almost fainted. He looked at his hand. There was a towel which had clearly once been white wrapped around it; it was now half red, and even as he watched, it was growing redder.

'I – I don't under—' Eddie muttered groggily.

'It's OK,' Jimmy said, gently lifting Eddie's hand.

He carefully peeled the towel away and looked at the wound. The *wounds*. 'Oh – Christ,' said Jimmy. Eddie forced himself to look at the source of his pain – and shuddered. His hand was sliced in a hundred places. The cuts were open and bleeding and already looked poisonous. He remembered now – the first strike, the intense pain, and his determination not to cry out, then the second, the third, his determination crumbling with the fourth and the fifth and the . . . and then he couldn't remember anything.

'Did I scr— did you hear . . . ?'

Jimmy shook his head. He looked down at the wound again. 'Slaterbake – he's the one should be in bloody prison. We could hear it downstairs – every time he hit you, we could hear it. Thirty times, Eddie – thirty times. No wonder you crashed out.'

'Maybe I should . . . you know, go to the nurse or something.'

The boys exchanged worried glances.

'Eddie – sometimes, boys who go to the nurse . . . we don't see them again . . .' Jimmy shook his head. 'Slaterbake says they've been sent to the hospital, and that's the last we see of them.'

'You mean . . .'

Jimmy nodded. 'The tunnels.'

'My God,' said Eddie, 'how many do you think . . . ?'

'I don't even *want* to think about it. All I want to think about is getting out of here. You're right, Eddie, we have to do it, and we have to do it tonight.'

Eddie knew he was right. He tried to stand, but his legs gave way beneath him and his head swam and then he was lying flat out on his back again. He tried to keep his mind focussed on what they had to do, but he kept drifting away . . .

'Look at it, it's infected,' he heard someone say. 'Any fool can see that.'

'I know that – but I'm not sending him there. We need to get him out of here.'

'He can't do anything the way he is.'

'Maybe by tonight he'll be feeling better.'

They were quiet then, because looking down at him, with his deathly white skin and the blood and poison seeping from his carnaged hand, they knew how unlikely that was.

Only Jimmy seemed sure. 'He'll be OK. Don't worry. He'll be OK.'

That was the last voice he heard for a few hours. He slept. He had a vague memory of one of the supervisors poking him later in the day, ordering him to come down for dinner – even if they wouldn't give him any food, it was still required that he made an appearance – and Eddie groaned and tried to stand, before collapsing on to the floor. And then the supervisor walked away, leaving him there, and it was only some time later that the boys found him again and helped him back into his bed.

Night fell, the lights were switched off and Eddie remained in a land of bitter, angry dreams. Then some time later someone was shaking him and he dragged himself reluctantly back into the real world; reluctantly, because even though his dream-world was full of nightmares, they were somehow preferable to real life, and its dreadful, cutting pain and disappointments. He opened his eyes. Jimmy was kneeling by his bed, supporting a torch between his chin and neck, a can of Coke in one hand and holding something else out with the other.

'Here,' said Jimmy, 'take this – it'll make you feel better . . .' and he pressed a small pill into Eddie's good hand.

'What is . . . ?' Eddie whispered, his voice dry and raspy.

'It'll kill the pain,' Jimmy whispered, nodding

his encouragement, and helping Eddie up into a sitting position.

Eddie put the pill on his tongue; his mouth was as dry as a bone. He took a swig of the Coke and swallowed it down. 'Thanks,' he mumbled. He closed his eyes again. 'I just want to sleep,' he said.

Jimmy shook him again. 'You have ten minutes,' he said.

'Ten ... good,' Eddie said vaguely, already slipping back into his nightmare. He was back outside the shop again, the birds were circling around the pram. Was he doomed to live this nightmare for ever, to see his little brother stolen from him by these savage rats with wings? He remained firmly planted in the doorway. The lead bird seemed larger than ever; its beady black eyes staring across at him, daring him to challenge it; the long beak slightly curved into a mocking smile.

But then ... something curious began to happen. Instead of feeling weighed down, weak, helpless in the face of the enemy, Eddie began to feel strength powering through his veins, rising up through his body as if he was a car being filled with super-strength petrol. It was little short of miraculous. He leapt high into the air from the doorway and landed on the lead bird just as it began to rise with Paddy in its claws. He saw the look of panic and surprise in the creature's eyes as he forced it back towards the earth; it was huge and vicious, like an eagle crossed with an ostrich, but as it struggled against him he realised that he was now stronger than it. He had its mighty neck in his hands, and suddenly it didn't seem so mighty after all – he flexed his muscles once and then snapped that neck in half and the bird began to plummet to the ground, already dead. As it fell, Eddie reached down and took hold of Paddy, easing him out of the creature's claws and then . . . *get this* . . . flying up into the skies himself.

He was flying.

I'm bloody flying!

I've saved Paddy and I'm flying home to Mum and Dad!

He felt so warm and powerful and happy.

Someone was shaking him – Jimmy; and at first he resisted it, he didn't want to open his eyes, didn't want to go back to the pain of the real world – but when he eventually succumbed and blinked up at Jimmy he was astonished to find that the real world wasn't so dreadful after all. He still felt warm and good and powerful.

'I . . . feel . . . better,' said Eddie.

Better was an understatement. A wild understatement. He felt fantastic. Even his hand, which he could clearly see was infected, didn't feel half as painful. It merely throbbed, now.

'Good . . .' Jimmy muttered, 'because it's time to go.'

Jimmy turned and shone his torch around the dorm. Every boy was on his feet, fully dressed, their few possessions packed and held in small schoolbags over their shoulders. They looked nervous. But also keen. And hopeful.

Jimmy turned back and extended his hand. Eddie grasped it firmly, and he was hauled to his feet. He braced himself to fall again, but his legs felt the same way as the rest of him did. In fact they were no longer legs at all. They were mighty oak trees. Excitement and adrenalin surged through him.

'We're ready Eddie – are you ready to lead us?'

'You bet.'

Jimmy smiled, then handed him the torch. 'Let's go then, Eddie Malone.'

As Eddie approached the locked dorm doors, he was pleased to see that the boys had been busy while he slept. They had managed to unscrew the hinges on either side, so that although the door itself remained locked, it wasn't actually attached to anything. Eddie gave them a nod, and the boys carefully lifted it away. Eddie stepped out into the darkened corridor. He looked both ways, then hurried along to the stairs leading down to the main entrance hall. He peered down – but all was in darkness down there as well. He turned and waved back at Jimmy, who began to usher the boys out into the corridor.

Sixty – it was a lot of boys to sneak anywhere.

Eddie had already taken the precaution of making them remove their shoes, which they now held clasped against their chests. By the time the first of them reached the top of the stairs, Eddie was already at the bottom, scouting out the next move. In his tour of the Melody Hill complex he had been able to observe the catering staff carrying food supplies back and forth to a cool cellar. He had snuck in after them, then hidden behind one of the huge bank of fridges that were lined up against a wall. When they'd left to collect more boxes from the delivery van outside he'd discovered a padlocked wooden door at the rear of the cellar. Locked, and quite sturdy; but old enough so that the wood was split in several places. Eddie had put his eye to the cracks and tried to see what was on the other side, but it was far too dark. However, this was definitely something other than just another storage cupboard – he could feel air on his cheek; not quite a breeze, but enough to suggest that there was a large space there . . . and there was also a smell. Like . . . something dead. He'd shuddered then, and he shuddered now as he led the boys down into the cellar.

Jimmy counted them all in, sixty of them, including Eddie. Little Seamus was the last through the door, his eyes wide with fright. Jimmy gave him a reassuring punch on the arm, and winked in the half light. Then he closed the cellar door.

'All here,' he hissed across at Eddie.

Eddie nodded back. He looked down at the padlock holding the wooden door closed.

Right then.

He turned quickly and reached behind one of the fridges with his good hand; he felt about, his fingers sliding through spiders' webs; he pushed a little harder, extending his arm; and then he found it. On his earlier tour he'd found a hammer – rusting, ancient, but still a hammer – and hidden it here. He pulled it out, then turned back to the padlock.

'I can do that,' Jimmy said.

Eddie stood over the padlock. 'No, I—'

'Better with two hands.'

He had a point. Even though Eddie now felt great, he knew he wouldn't be able to get enough power or accuracy into a one-handed swing. He gave Jimmy the hammer.

Jimmy stood over the padlock. Eddie shone the torch down on it.

'This is for freedom,' said Eddie. The other boys crowded silently around to watch.

'This is for freedom,' said Jimmy, and raised the hammer above his head, then brought it down with all his strength.

Twenty-two

Five miles away, in a very nice, very modern, very *rich* house, a phone began to ring. The Governor, who slept alone – his wife detested him but liked his money, so she slept in a different bedroom on the other side of the house – rolled over and buried his head under a pillow, trying to drown out the sound, but it rang on and on and on and on . . . and then gradually he remembered who he was, and what his job was, and he knew that the call would be about some nonsense from Melody Hill. His staff had lost a key, or forgotten a phone number or killed a boy by accident and now they weren't sure what to do and they were scared of asking Slaterbake because he was likely to scream at them for being so stupid. The Governor wondered sometimes why his staff weren't as scared of him. The truth was that Slaterbake was mean and horrible and tough and dangerous and absolutely ruthless. The Governor was all of these things, but he was also a coward, because he merely gave the orders but was too squeamish to carry any of them out personally. It was hard to say which of them was the more evil.

So the Governor dragged himself across his huge bed and snapped the phone off its hook on the table and barked an angry 'What?' into the mouthpiece.

But it wasn't one of his hapless guards.

It wasn't even Slaterbake.

The voice was ... familiar. Young. Not much more than a boy.

'You know who this is?' it said.

And the Governor did know, and felt his stomach lurch. Because this voice represented an evil more deadly than his and Slaterbake's combined.

'Y-yes,' stammered the Governor.

'I didn't wake you?'

'N-no.'

'Good. I have another job for you. You have the Malone boy still?'

'Yes ... of course ... Eddie Malone?'

'Yes, Eddie Malone.'

'He's been beaten as you instructed. And starved.'

'Good. Now I want you to finish the job.'

'Finish?'

'Do I have to spell it out, Governor? The tunnels.'

The Governor swallowed. He didn't like this. Not one bit. 'It's too soon,' he said quickly, 'he's only been here a few days – his parents, someone, will be suspicious.'

'I don't care! I want it done!'

'But—'

'But nothing, Governor! Don't I pay you well? And do I have to remind you what will happen if you don't do this? Your little secret will come tumbling out, and you will go to jail for the rest of your life. Now get it done!'

'Y-yes . . . of course . . . I'm sorry – it won't be a problem, I'll get right on to it . . . but . . .'

'But what?'

The Governor wasn't quite sure why he asked. Curiosity, although he was well aware of what that did for the healthy lifespan of the cat.

'I was just wondering – why him? Why so soon . . . ?'

'*Because.*'

It was all the answer he was going to get. It was a child's answer. And not one he was going to argue with. Not that he had the chance. The line was cut. The Governor held the receiver for another moment while his heart settled down again, then he dialled a number.

'What?' Another familiar voice; gruff, displeased. He almost apologised for calling so late. Almost.

'Is that Slater— Supervisor Michael Huggins?'

A hammering sound came from the very bowels of Melody Hill. In the confines of the cellar, as Jimmy raised the hammer again, and again, and again, it sounded incredibly loud. Beyond the cellar door, it merely sounded *quite* loud. In the reception, up the stairs and along the hall, you might have dismissed it as ... well, just a noise. And outside, down towards the gates where the guards spent the night alternating between a nice warm hut and patrolling the grounds, you couldn't hear anything at all.

It had been going on for fifteen minutes, and they didn't seem to be getting any closer to breaking the lock. The boys were getting restless. They were terrified at the thought of traversing the tunnels of death. But they were as terrified of being caught by Slaterbake. They wanted to charge along the tunnel to freedom; they didn't want to be stuck in this dank, cold cellar, making such a racket.

'Maybe we should go back to bed,' said one boy, 'try another night.'

'No,' Eddie said simply. 'We'll get it.'

He looked at Jimmy. 'You want me to take over?'

Jimmy shook his head. 'I'm fine. I'm getting there. Just a few more . . .'

He brought the hammer down again, hard on the padlock; another clash of metal on metal, another spark, but still it wouldn't budge.

Outside, down at the security hut, two of the guards jumped suddenly to their feet as a familiar car raced up to the gates.

'Blimey,' one of them said, nearly choking on his chewing gum, 'it's Slaterbake! What's he doing here at this . . .'

But even at that moment Slaterbake was jumping from his car and snapping his fingers. He pointed along the security fence at two guards, just returning from patrol. 'You! You! Come with me!' Then he shouted at the guards emerging from the hut. 'Give me the keys!'

The guards tossed him the keys, and he turned and hurried towards the front doors of the Melody Hill Centre for Trouble Makers.

One of the guards left behind by the hut shook his head. 'Well,' he said, 'someone's in for it.'

Another guard, standing at his shoulder, nodded grimly.

* * *

Inside Melody Hill, Slaterbake took the stairs to the boys' dorm two at a time.

'What's going on?' one of the guards ventured.

'Never you mind!' Slaterbake hissed, then put a finger to his lips as they reached the top of the stairs. 'Shhhh now, boys, we want in and out quick – we grab Eddie Malone, no one knows, see?'

The guards nodded warily. They had heard about the night-time snatches, and the boys that were never seen again, but they'd never yet been involved like this. Slaterbake pulled the keys from his pocket as he hurried along the hall. He found the correct key, then inserted it in the lock and turned it. Before opening the door, he winked at his two companions. 'We take him downstairs, and I'll deal with him from there, right?'

'Right,' said the guards, together. Neither of them felt that it was quite 'right', but they were too scared of Slaterbake to say so.

Slaterbake slowly began to turn the door knob.

But instead of the door just opening, it opened *and* fell inwards. Both doors, in fact, fell with a great clatter that would have caused every boy in the dorm to jump panicked from his bed . . .

There was no reaction at all. Not a peep.

Slaterbake stood surprised and stunned. He

knew immediately that something was very, very wrong – doors didn't just fall off their hinges, and when they did, dangerous, troublesome boys didn't just sleep through it. The light from the hall was barely enough to illuminate anything beyond the doorway, so he quickly snapped on the main lights. Behind him the guards almost suffered heart attacks when they saw that every single bed was empty.

Slaterbake turned slowly, his eyes blazing. He was so angry, he could hardly squeeze out the words.

'Where . . . are . . . *they* . . . ?' he roared.

'I – I – I . . .' the first guard stammered.

'We – we – we – we . . .' the second added, not very helpfully.

'They were here . . . earlier . . .' the first said weakly.

'The fence is secure,' the second added, slightly more helpfully.

'The cameras are working, we haven't—'

'Then where are they?' Slaterbake demanded. 'Sixty little rats can't just . . .' And then he stopped suddenly. He held up his hand. 'Shhhhhhh . . .'

'We're really sorry—' one guard began.

'SHHHHHHH! *Listen* . . .'

They listened. They strained their ears. At first they could hear nothing beyond the urgent beating of their hearts. But then slowly, slowly, they began to hear something – a vague, distant, rhythmic hammering . . .

Jimmy wiped the sweat from his brow. His arms were aching now, his muscles screaming; he was the strongest of all of them and he had rained down thirty or maybe even forty blows on the rusting padlock, but it just would not give way. He stopped for a moment, gasping for breath.

Eddie stood helplessly beside him, willing him on, but not knowing quite what to say. The boys around him were beginning to murmur amongst themselves; where one had wanted to go back to the dorm, now nearly all of them seemed to sense that their daring escape plan was floundering before it had even got properly underway. They were, after twenty long minutes, still in Melody Hill.

Eddie felt a slight tug on his arm, and he turned to find little Seamus looking up at him. Eddie gave him an encouraging smile. 'Don't worry, Seamus, we'll find a way.'

'I was wondering . . .' Seamus began hesitantly.

Jimmy struck the padlock again. Nothing.

And again. Nothing.

'Mmmmm?' said Eddie, his attention already back on the door.

'I was just wondering . . .' Seamus said again.

'What?' said Eddie.

But Seamus was shy, and instead of speaking out loud, he raised himself on tiptoes just as Eddie bent to him, and whispered in his ear: 'I was just wondering why you don't hit the wood instead of the padlock. It doesn't look very strong.'

Eddie started to laugh. What a ridic— and then he thought suddenly, *My God, he's right*. He turned and stared at the door. *It's bloody ancient*.

Eddie let out a triumphant whoop, then grabbed Seamus by the shoulders and gave him a good shake. 'Seamus! You're a bloody star!' He turned quickly back to Jimmy. 'Jimmy – give me the hammer.'

Jimmy looked confused for a moment. 'But your hand . . .'

'Never mind my hand – give me it!'

Jimmy looked back at the padlock, shook his head despairingly, then handed Eddie the sweaty handle.

Eddie nodded his thanks; and then his attention

was drawn back to the top of the cellar. The boy keeping guard by the door turned suddenly, his face ashen. 'Slaterbake!' he hissed.

A horrified moan erupted from the boys, as if their very souls were fleeing their bodies.

'Lock the door!' Eddie shouted.

'But then we'll be trapped!' said Jimmy.

'Just do it!'

'I can't!' the boy shouted back. 'The lock's on the outside!'

Of course it is!

Eddie took a deep breath. He was their leader, he had to *lead*.

'Then barricade it! Block it! Use anything you can find!'

At the top of the stairs the boy slammed the door shut and stood with his back to it until the others, scrambling about the floor, lifted the heaviest bags of food and coal and pushed and pulled them up the steps. They piled them against the door, and had just put the third and heaviest into place when the handle was rattled and Slaterbake yelled, 'Open this bloody door!'

Almost as one the terrified boys turned to Eddie.

'He'll kill us!' one cried.

'He'll kill us all!' cried another.

Eddie knew the bags would hold Slaterbake back for only a few minutes – so it was now or never. He raised the hammer in his good hand and smashed it into the door leading to the tunnels.

It immediately cracked right down the middle. He gave it a second blow and it fell apart. Stale air wafted into the cellar as Eddie jumped back. 'Let's go!'

They didn't need a second invitation. The boys congregated around the opening, pushing and jostling for entrance. Those at the top of the steps, pushing hard against the bags of food and coal, suddenly jumped away and raced across the cold floor.

Jimmy paused for just a moment before stepping over the remnants of the shattered door. He gave Eddie a nod, then shone his torch into the darkness ahead. He glanced back at the boys crowding in behind him. 'This way!' he shouted, and began to lead them along the tunnels of the dead.

Twenty-three

It took six of Melody Hill's strongest guards just a couple of minutes to break down the cellar door, and then another few seconds to remove the food and coal the boys had piled up at the top of the stairs, and all the time Slaterbake stood at their backs screaming at them to hurry up.

Then they charged down the stairs and across the cellar floor before coming to a stop at the splintered entrance to the tunnels.

Slaterbake came charging up behind them, roaring, 'What are you waiting for?' They exchanged worried looks. They knew exactly what they were waiting for – they were waiting for bravery to arrive, because they had heard stories about what went on down in the tunnels. They were big strong men, but they were afraid of this particular darkness, and what it might hold. But they were even more frightened of Slaterbake, so in the end plunging into the tunnels was the lesser of two evils.

Each of them carried a long wooden club and a

torch. The floor of the tunnel was rough and jagged and the walls were dank and dripping. Slaterbake led them at a sharp pace – there was no need to stop and search every nook and cranny, they weren't looking for one boy; they were looking for sixty. As they ran their torch beams picked up the shining eyes of rats – rats that didn't scurry away, but stood defiantly staring back at them.

'There!'

Slaterbake pointed ahead – and in the distance, for just a few moments before they disappeared around a bend in the tunnel – they saw a glow and hurrying dark figures.

'Come on!' Jimmy shouted.

He stood to one side of the tunnel, urging the boys forward. They only had a couple of torches between them and the floor of the tunnel was rutted and pitted; more than one boy had plunged into a deep pool and had to be dragged out, covered in a thick green slime.

'Come on – we must be nearly out!'

The faster, stronger ones were racing ahead – the younger, weaker ones brought up the rear. Eddie was with them, almost at the very back. Jimmy shone his torch in his face and Eddie winced. Just a few minutes before he'd felt so fantastic, leading this daring escape, the adrenaline coursing through his veins; but now that they were in the tunnels the stress and strains of the last few days were catching up with him. His head ached, spasms of pain shot up his arm from his poisoned hand, his legs felt like jelly. He just wanted to lie down and die.

'Eddie – are you OK?'

It was one of those stupid questions. But Eddie nodded. 'Just keeping an eye on the little ones,' he said, but even the effort of saying it required him to take a deep, deep breath at the end of it. He put his good hand out and steadied himself against Jimmy for a moment, then glanced back down the tunnel. A dull orange glow. 'Here they come,' he said.

Jimmy grasped Eddie by the arm. 'Come on – you can do it.'

So they hurried on, coaxing the younger boys before them.

'How long do these tunnels go on for?' Eddie gasped.

'No idea,' said Jimmy.

'Someone must know.'

'Slaterbake. Should I stop and ask him?'

Eddie managed a grin, but then stumbled over a

rock and fell heavily. Embarrassed by his carelessness he quickly tried to jump back to his feet, but instead he let out a shout of pain. Jimmy knelt beside him and aimed his torch down. There was no blood, but he could tell from the expression on Eddie's face that something was badly wrong.

'Eddie?'

'I've twisted . . . I'm OK, I'm all right . . .'

Jimmy helped him up. 'Here, put your arm around . . .'

Eddie leant heavily on him. Jimmy led them forward again, Eddie now hopping on one foot. He glanced back down the tunnel. The same orange glow, but closer.

Up ahead, the boys had come to a sudden halt. As Jimmy supported Eddie through them he said, 'What is it – what's wrong?'

Then he could see for himself – they had come to a crossroads. One tunnel led to the left, and seemed to go slightly uphill; the other, to the right, definitely sloped downwards.

'Oh *great*,' said Jimmy.

He flashed his torch into one, and then the other. Both seemed to swallow the light equally, giving no clue to what they held further along.

Behind them they could not only see the

approaching torches now, but for the first time they could hear voices, shouts, and footsteps.

'Which way?' Jimmy asked. He was looking directly at Eddie.

Eddie examined the left strand, then the right. He could feel all of their eyes upon him. Before, not even ten minutes before, he had felt brave and strong and sure of himself, he had a gang of fifty-nine fearless boys around him and he was leading them to freedom. But now? He felt weak and tired and sore, he could hardly walk, his hand felt like it was on fire, even his eyeballs were aching. He couldn't focus his thoughts. *Left or right, left or right?*

He forced himself to think.

He tried to imagine what might be above – the expansive grounds of Melody Hill, then the Purdy Home for the Very Strange and the Silent Valley Crematorium. For sure, one tunnel led to one, and one led to the other, but which was which? The main tunnel had twisted and turned so often that he had lost any sense of direction. And even if they knew which was which, which one did they actually want to go into? Which offered the best hope of freedom?

The Purdy Home for the Very Strange – well, it

would have guards, wouldn't it, to make sure the mad people didn't escape? So if they ended up in there, they'd have to escape from it all over again.

The Silent Valley Crematorium – where they burned the bodies of dead people. But there surely wouldn't be guards there? What would they be guarding against – ghosts?

That was definitely the way to go – but which way was it? The left tunnel, sloping up? Or the right, heading down?

The lights, the shouting, were getting closer, closer, closer ... Eddie felt the sweat dripping down his brow. What if he chose the wrong one? What if they couldn't get out, if they were trapped? And what if he couldn't keep up with them, and caused them all to be captured?

Jimmy was looking at him, his eyes wide with fear. 'Which one, Eddie – which one?'

Slaterbake was a big man – but he wasn't fat, it was all muscle. He trained every day in a gym, he swam, he lifted weights, he could beat anyone in a fight, but he didn't often have to use his physical strength – it was mostly his voice and his eyes that put the fear of God into the guards he was in charge of and the boys he was responsible for.

That was his job – looking after the boys.

And he certainly looked after them.

What drives a man to such evil?

And does he think of himself as evil?

Something terrible had clearly happened to Slaterbake when he was a boy himself, something that had changed him from a normal child into the murderer he undoubtedly was today. Nobody know what that was. There have been many evil men in history – Hitler, for example, was responsible for millions and millions of deaths, but he probably never actually killed anyone himself. He never pulled the trigger. He got people just like Slaterbake to do that for him. And the thing is, most people who do dreadful things like this say they are just following orders, and that actually, they're not doing anything wrong, they're just getting rid of bad people. This is the way Slaterbake thought – that the kids he took underground and killed *deserved* to die, that *they* were evil, and that he was doing a *good* thing.

He was, obviously, *barking mad*.

As he charged along the tunnel, his men behind him, he felt a tremendous excitement – a hunter closing in for the kill, an angel of death.

His men knew of the tunnels, of course, and had

heard rumours of what went on down there, but this was the first time they'd actually entered them. And they were terrified. They had their torches and clubs, but what defence were they against . . . well against whatever kind of evil lurked in these dark, underground tunnels?

They hurried along in Slaterbake's wake, as scared to go forward now as they were scared to go back. Every rat that splashed besia spasms of horror through them. Every drip from the ceiling; every spider's web which clung to their faces. This was truly a terrible place.

Ahead of them, Slatcrbake came to a sudden halt. They saw that the tunnel was now dividing into two. Slaterbake stood, hardly even breathing hard – and looked left, then right, then left again. Then he stiffened – 'There!' he exclaimed, pointing to his left.

They followed his gaze and the very faintest glow of a torch, off to his left.

'They're going to the crematorium! But the gates will be locked! We have them now!'

Slaterbake led them off again, and seemed to be going even faster, despite the ground rising steadily around them. As they closed in on the light ahead they also began to notice other things; the smell, an acrid burning – the furnaces of the crematorium, of course – but they couldn't help but think of another burning, underground place: hell itself. And the walls were drier, flaking and crumbling here, dried out by the heat wafting down the tunnels from the crematorium. There was also evidence of repair work, where gaps in the wall had been cemented over as if to hide something . . . Despite the growing heat, the guards shivered. They had heard all about the boys who simply disappeared – was this where they ended up, cemented into the walls? Or was it merely essential repair work – and the missing boys were burned up in the furnaces somewhere ahead instead?

They drew closer and closer to the light ahead – it hardly seemed to be moving at all now. The tunnel began to widen and the smell of burning was mixed with that of oil and a distant clank of machinery.

Slaterbake, his eyes growing wild with excitement, thundered ahead – and then, suddenly, there it was, just a hundred metres in front of them: the light of the torch, illuminating one wall, and then as they drew closer they saw the torch itself – lying on the ground. They came to a sudden halt.

Slaterbake bent to the torch, briefly examined it, then turned it off and scanned the broadened tunnel suspiciously. His own torch, more powerful, naturally, than all of the others, flashed ahead and picked up a set of metal gates which marked the entrance to – or indeed, exit from – the crematorium. The gates appeared to be solidly locked. He then angled the beam down to the ground which, right here, so close to the heat of the crematorium, was extremely dry and dusty. He had expected to find footprints, dozens and dozens of them, and then to find sixty boys cowering fearfully in a corner, preparing to beg for their lives.

But there were only a few footprints scattered in the dust.

Where are they?

Where the hell are they?

Sixty boys!

There's no other way out!

Slaterbake stared at the footprints. He saw now that there were two distinct sets. One quite small, the other larger. Either set could have been there for days or weeks or months.

And then he heard the slightest movement: hardly more than dust being displaced, but it was enough to swing him round. The beam of his torch shot along the ground and up a wall and . . . there, halfway up, an alcove or small cave, just like one of the ones he often used to bury the . . .

He strode closer, plunged the torch into the breach in the wall and suddenly there appeared Eddie Malone, sitting there, caked in dust, holding his injured hand and staring out, cornered like the rat he was.

In the end, it hadn't been a difficult decision. Whichever way they decided to go it was a gamble. They could be trapped at the Silent Valley Crematorium or the Purdy Home. Eddie didn't doubt that sixty boys all together probably had the strength and brain power to work out how to escape if they did find themselves trapped. But they would need time – even if it was just a few minutes – and it was time they clearly didn't have. Slaterbake was getting closer and closer and closer.

Eddie could feel himself falling apart. Jimmy's medicine had worn off and he was in agony, mentally and physically. Even if he came to a decision about the correct tunnel, he couldn't hope to keep up with them, and if they had to slow down to help him, then they'd all be doomed.

It was one of the hardest decisions he'd ever had

to make. Sacrificing himself so that the others might have a chance of surviving – and if he was going to be caught anyway, then why not buy the others some time?

So he pointed to the right and said, 'That way – and turn off your torches.' Both torches were switched off. 'Give me one,' he said. 'Now get going, I'll be right behind you, just keep your torch off for as long as you can.'

The boys started moving, more cautiously now, because it was so dark.

'Put your hand on the shoulder of the boy in front of you!' Jimmy hissed. 'No one'll get lost!'

Seamus was the last of them to pass by. Jimmy ruffled his hair, and he hurried on. Then Jimmy said to Eddie, 'You're not coming, are you?'

'Not that way. I want to, Jimmy, believe you me. I just *can't* . . .'

The footsteps sounded even closer. They looked behind them, and saw dark shapes silhouetted in the light of half a dozen torch beams.

'Better go,' Eddie gasped.

Jimmy nodded. He grasped Eddie's shoulder and gave it a gentle squeeze. 'Thank you,' he said. 'I won't forget this.' Eddie nodded. Jimmy turned to go, then stopped. He put his hand in his pocket, then withdrew it and held something out to Eddie. 'Don't take this now, it's too soon . . . but later, if you get through this – then it'll help.' Eddie looked down. He could just about make out another of Jimmy's little round pills. Eddie nodded his thanks, then slipped it into his pocket.

Jimmy wheeled away, and in a moment had disappeared into the darkness. 'Good luck,' Eddie whispered, then turned and began to hobble along the left-hand tunnel.

And now here he was, pressing back as hard as he could against the wall of the little cave while Slaterbake screamed, 'Where are they? Where are they!'

Eddie did the one thing guaranteed to enrage Slaterbake even further – he smiled. 'Who?' he said. 'Oh, you mean the fifty-nine boys who took the other tunnel? The fifty-nine boys who are probably already home free? *Those* fifty-nine boys?'

Slaterbake let out an anguished roar; he hurled himself forward, grabbing for the boy with his bulky fingers, but Eddie forced himself back even further. Slaterbake strained, stretching his arm to its full length through the elevated cave opening. Eddie felt the rocks move slightly behind him, and for a moment he allowed himself to hope that the wall would suddenly give way and allow him to escape down some magical secret tunnel that would prove too narrow for Slaterbake and his men. But then Slaterbake gave it one final effort, and this time his fingers clawed into Eddie's jumper, took a firm grip, and then whipped him suddenly out of the cave. Slaterbake held him up in the air for a moment, then threw him hard towards the ground.

Eddie hit it hard; the wind was knocked from him; his poisoned hand sank into the dust and then buckled against a rock; a spasm of hot pain shot up from his twisted ankle.

He was not in good shape.

He lay on his back in the dust, breathing hard. Slaterbake loomed over him. The other guards gathered around. Slaterbake opened his jacket.

'You know something, Eddie Malone? Right here, right now, I don't care about the others. I'll get them soon enough. I care about *you*. I thought you'd like to meet an old friend.' He opened his jacket then, and in the eerie light of half a dozen torches, he drew out Slicer.

'What I did to your hand, Eddie-boy? That's what I'm going to do to your whole body.'

Eddie gazed up.

This is it, then.

The end.

I'm sorry, Mum.

I'm sorry, Dad, wherever you are.

And Paddy – I really am sorry for losing you.

Eddie closed his eyes. He was in so much pain already, he kind of hoped that what was about to happen could hardly make him feel any worse.

But deep down, he knew that he was completely wrong.

Twenty-four

Slaterbake's grin as he whipped Slicer through the air was as wide and terrible as anything the guards had ever seen. The first strike tore down – and kicked up dirt a centimetre from Eddie's face. He hadn't missed, exactly – he was just getting his range. The next would cut Eddie open from chin to ear. No wonder, as he raised Slicer for the second time, that one of the guards turned away. He felt sick to his stomach . . . and then a moment later even sicker.

'*Looook* . . .' he said, with enough horror and surprise to put Slaterbake off his second stroke.

Slaterbake spun towards the guard, and was about to scream abuse at him, when he saw that the guard was pointing his torch into the alcove Eddie had hidden in. The dry soil he had disturbed at the back had finally given way to reveal an even smaller cave behind. That in itself wasn't horrifying. What *was* horrifying was the arm that was hanging out of it.

The dead arm.

The bones of a dead arm.

And the white, shining finger pointing directly at them.

'Oh my God,' said one of the other guards.

'It's true,' said another, backing away, 'it's all true.'

Slaterbake laughed. 'It's only some old bones,' he said. He turned his attention back to Eddie. This time . . .

But then there came a curious kind of creaking sound, a snapping, a tumbling and then the entire wall surrounding the little cave began to give way, sliding down in a torrent of rock and soil and throwing up a choking cloud of dust.

It wasn't a *major* collapse, it wasn't as if they were all going to be buried under a billion tonnes of soil – but it was enough to expose an entire hidden corridor behind the little alcove. And there, and there, and there, and there, jutting out all the way along, were other bits of skeletons. Arms, legs, skulls. And some that weren't quite skeletons, ones that still had pieces of rotting flesh or slowly disintegrating clothes hanging on to them.

If they had wanted to count them, they might have counted thirteen bodies.

They didn't want to count them.

They wanted out of there, right *now* . . .

They backed away from the bones, and even further away from Slaterbake.

'Stay where you are!' he ordered. 'Our work's not done!'

They hesitated.

And between hesitating and deciding what to do, they heard it.

A groaning.

A long, mournful groaning, coming from out of the darkness.

Immediately they were united by one terrifying thought: *ghosts.*

Ghosts of these dead children.

The sound came again, even closer.

Even Slaterbake looked a little disturbed. He lowered Slicer. 'It's nothing,' he said. 'It's just the wind.'

'Wind?' one of the guards ventured. 'Down here?'

'The cave collapsing – it's exposed an air vent. Relax.'

But even Slaterbake wasn't relaxing. He stared into the darkness. The guards raised their torches and scanned the tunnel around them – the light reflected off the skeletons, but was otherwise quickly swallowed up.

The moan came again. There was no way to tell from which direction it came or how close it was. Sound could travel for miles in these tunnels – or for just a few metres.

Then another, smaller bank of soil and dust slipped off the wall of the tunnel.

Or . . . were the skeletons moving?

Arms, legs, tumbled to the ground.

'They're coming for us!' one of the guards wailed.

'They're going to kill us!'

That was enough for them. They all took off. They raced back down the tunnel towards the junction, then charged back towards the doorway to the cellar of the Melody Hill Centre for Trouble Makers. They didn't care about their jobs. They cared about surviving. They left their boss standing screaming after them in the dark. Then he screamed even louder as he realised that he'd handed one of the guards his torch so that he could use both hands to swing Slicer down on Eddie Malone – and now that torch was gone.

'Come back, you cowards! Come back!' Slaterbake yelled. 'It's nothing! It's nothing – it's . . .'

But then the light was gone and he was in total darkness.

Slaterbake stood still, trying to get his bearings.

The first slither of fear was beginning to claw at him. He was deep underground, without light. He had traversed these tunnels a hundred times to carry out his evil deeds, always just him and his victim, but he had always had light. But he had a pretty good memory of their layout and a fair sense of direction. Plus he knew where the crematorium fence was – directly behind him. He could wait there, or shout for help – eventually, eventually some crematorium employee was sure to hear him.

But Slaterbake wasn't the type to wait. He had a job to do, and he was going to finish it.

Kill the boy, Eddie Malone, and then find his way out.

But where exactly was the boy? He had been right there in front of him, then he had turned to shout at his cowardly colleagues – and now, when he stuck out a foot to prod Eddie's body, he couldn't find it. He didn't think it had moved – it was just so damned dark – he must have strayed further from it than he had thought as he screamed at his men to come back.

Slaterbake moved to his left a metre or so and tried again, then to his right, then . . . and then he tried to remember where the fence was, and which way the tunnel went; he waved his hand in front of his face but couldn't even see the outline of his fingers.

Light, I need light.

The boy's torch! He had held it only a few minutes before, then set it down. *It must be close, it must be close.* He dropped to his hands and knees and began scampering about the tunnel floor, trying to locate it. He moved in a gradually widening circle, feeling for it, feeling for it . . . *come on, come on, it must be here . . .*

Then the moan came again, and his blood chilled.

This time there was no doubt about it: it was really close.

He could almost *feel* a presence.

A shuffling sound.

A smell of death.

Right there, far underground in the unholy blackness, Slaterbake for the first time in his awful life, began to realise the error of his ways. Images of the children he had killed, the terror and horror he had caused, flashed through his mind. He knew that some terrible creature had been sent to take revenge for his evil deeds.

He stared, but could see nothing.

But he smelled it.

He felt its hot breath.

And then two giant hands were brought down on his shoulders.

For the first and last time in his life, Slaterbake screamed in terror.

Then he dropped stone dead.

Twenty-five

Eddie wasn't sure whether he was alive or dead, asleep or awake. It was so dark he couldn't tell. Then he thought, *If I'm dead, then surely I wouldn't still be feeling such pain. But if I'm alive, where is everyone?* He tried to recall his last memory – lying on the tunnel floor, waiting for Slicer to slice, Slaterbake standing over him, the guards grouped around.

He must have blacked out. His mind had closed down. A way of protecting him.

And now they were all gone.

Perhaps Slaterbake had changed his mind, and instead of killing him outright, had left him to die an agonising death of starvation and madness, far underground. Or he'd decided not to waste time on one boy when fifty-nine others were fleeing in the opposite direction. Eddie had led them on a wild goose chase which had neither been wild nor much of a chase; it had only delayed Slaterbake and his men by a few useless minutes.

The pain in his hand had, if anything, grown

worse. His leg throbbed and felt badly swollen. He closed his eyes again. He just wanted it all to end now. He'd had enough. In his head, he'd already said goodbye to his mum and dad and the baby he'd lost. Now, lying in the dust, bloody and battered, he began to think about the Babysnatchers and how he'd met Mo. She was tough, and funny, and sensible. He wished she was here now. She would know what to do. Or she would help him to die. Whatever was best. He tried to think of the last time they'd spoken – he had a vague memory of her walking him to the train one morning, but had they agreed to meet again? He couldn't recall.

He wondered then if Slaterbake had caught up with Jimmy and the rest of the boys. He had sent them off down the right-hand tunnel on nothing more than a hunch. What if it was a dead end? Or if, before they switched their torches on again, they fell into a huge abyss and were never heard of again. He prayed that they were OK. Jimmy was a good guy. A natural leader himself. He thought of their farewell at the break in the tunnel, and wished to God he could have gone with them. And then he remembered the painkilling pill Jimmy had given him. He knew it was strong stuff and Jimmy had warned him about taking another one so soon – but as he'd been unconscious there was no way of telling how long had passed. A few minutes, or several hours? Eddie felt around in his pocket and found the pill. He had no hope of escaping the tunnel. But if he could just feel a little better, even for just a short period, wasn't it worth taking the risk?

Or even half a risk.

Eddie put the pill between his teeth and cracked down on it. It split jaggedly in two. He took one half out and slipped it back into his pocket then tried to swallow the second half, but his mouth and throat were so dry and clogged up with dust that it was nearly impossible to swallow. Instead he chewed it slowly and methodically. Eventually it was gone. He lay still, willing it to work. He thought again about Mo. It seemed to him that they had not parted on good terms, but he couldn't quite work out why. He wished he could see her, just one last time. He would say sorry for whatever it was he had done. She would be his friend again and they would sit and recall their great adventures. For they had been great. Scary and dangerous, but definitely great. He thought about Patrick. What had the Seagulls done with him?

Killed him outright? Or starved him slowly? Or was he hidden in some dark place, just like this tunnel? Or what if they'd sold him off to slave traders or some rich couple who couldn't have their own kid? Maybe Paddy was living in a palace, getting the best of everything. He would go to the finest schools. Enjoy sun-kissed holidays in distant lands. Eddie imagined himself on a beach, running into shimmering water with Mo at his side, diving into the waves . . .

He was aware now of a warmth beginning to course through his veins. His hand didn't feel quite so sore either. He gently prodded his ankle – yes, it was swollen badly, but it was no longer really painful. Thank God for Jimmy's pill. He gave it another five minutes, then pushed himself up into a sitting position. His senses, already acute from the pain he'd been in, seemed to be even further enhanced. There was *heat* coming from somewhere to his left, vague and distant, but that's what it was. The crematorium – of course! How far could it be? Was there any way in the world that he could make it that far in such utter darkness?

And then he too remembered – the torch.

He'd left it shining on the ground while he

sought a hiding place in the little cave. Slaterbake had picked it up, then switched it off. But what had he done with it? Had he taken it with him, or had he thrown it down again? Slaterbake had found him in the cave, pulled him out and thrown him across the tunnel. What if he had landed close to the torch? What if it was lying nearby? If he had light, then he had hope, surely?

Eddie felt around him.

As the warmth from the pill flooded into him he began to move in a slowly widening circle, his one good hand stretched out before him, combing the tunnel floor.

It must be here, it must be here, it must . . .

Then he heard it – a low moaning sound.

It was impossible to tell how close or how far away it was.

There it was again.

Definitely closer.

He became aware of a weird kind of shuffling sound, and a smell of . . . he couldn't quite place it, but it was somehow familiar – horrible, sickening, yes – but definitely familiar.

A longer moan.

He was beginning to panic now. Yes, he was feeling better thanks to the pill, but what good was that if some subterranean monster was about to pounce?

His good hand, still feeling desperately around for the torch, suddenly came to rest on something. At first he didn't realise what it was – it felt solid, long, and clad in some kind of material. He felt his way up it, then jumped as his fingers touched . . . something cold, yet quite soft. Eddie steeled himself, then bent to it again . . . it was *flesh*. He traced the outline – a nose – eyes – hair . . . it was a dead body, but whose? And what did it have to do with the moaning, which suddenly sounded again, this time directly to his right – no more than a couple of metres away.

Eddie scrambled backwards, in a crab-like motion. The creature must have sensed the movement because he heard it scuff through the dust of the tunnel floor after him. But then Eddie collided with the tunnel wall. He put his hand down to stop himself falling, and it landed directly on something short and hard and rubbery – the torch!

The creature was almost upon him. Its rancid smell enveloped him.

But he would not give up.

He would not die in the dark.

Whatever kind of a monster it was, it must have been in the dark for a long time. If he could just blind it for a few moments with the torch, then perhaps he could still make a break for it.

It was his only hope.

Eddie pushed the switch, and the beam exploded around him.

The creature seemed to recoil, but he couldn't be sure, because he was half blinded himself. All he saw was a vague outline of a huge figure, and then he rolled to his right. He quickly switched the torch off, plunging them back into total darkness, then scampered along on his hands and knees for a few metres until he felt he was out of range of the creature's grasp. Then he sprang to his feet and began to limp away.

He was perhaps thirty metres along the tunnel when he heard a most surprising thing.

A very worried, very frightened voice saying, 'Excuse me?'

Eddie kept running. Some sort of trick. Or was he imagining it? Was it the pill playing tricks with his mind?

But then it came again. 'Please . . . don't leave me down here!'

There was something so weak and pathetic about

it – and yet also quite familiar. The voice . . . the smell . . .

Eddie stopped.

'I've . . . been wandering around for hours, lost in the dark . . . please . . .'

My God, Eddie thought, *I know that voice.*

He turned. He switched the torch back on and began to walk back, and the closer he got the more certain he became that he was right. He *did* recognise the voice, and the smell only confirmed it.

The smell of death.

Not of monster or creature or ghost or even some stumbling zombie. But the smell of a person who had once worked day-in, day-out with dead bodies, washing corpses, preparing them for burial.

Eddie raised his torch and shined it into the creature's face.

'Barney?' he said. 'What the hell are you doing down here?'

Twenty-six

'Eddie?'

Barney was every bit as stunned as his young friend was. 'Barney?'

'*Eddie?*'

'Barney?'

'Eddie?'

'*Barney?*'

'Eddie?'

Eddie laughed. 'Barney, we'd better agree who we are before we both starve to death.'

'But ... but ... but ... but ...'

'But, but, but,' said Eddie, who was suddenly feeling *fantastic*. He was saved! Well – he wasn't exactly saved, but he had company, he had a torch, and the medicine was doing its work. Things were no longer bleak. They were bright, as bright as his torch. 'What are you doing down here, Barney? Last time I saw you you were a lollipop man.'

Barney rolled his eyes. 'Lollipop man? More like Lollipop Warrior. The trouble I had with those kids chasing me! They wouldn't leave me alone –

stones, bricks, knives – they threw everything at me. I had enough. I like things quiet. I like things . . .'

'Dead?' ventured Eddie. Barney nodded. 'You're working in the crematorium.'

Barney smiled. 'Yeah. It's great.' He was a big guy, muscular, with a large forehead and a drooping kind of a walk. If you didn't know him, you certainly wouldn't want to meet him in the dark. Only Eddie seemed to know what he was really like. If he had a family, he never mentioned it. If he had friends, Eddie hadn't heard of them. As far as Eddie was aware, he was his only friend – and he'd only met him twice. Barney put both of his hands on Eddie's shoulders and gave him a friendly shake. 'I am *so* glad to see you.'

'Likewise,' Eddie laughed. 'But what are you doing down here? And why the moaning and wandering around in the dark?'

'Moaning?' Barney looked perplexed for a moment. Then he shrugged sheepishly. 'Suppose . . . just something I do when I'm – y'know – scared. It's part of my job to come down here once a week and check out the tunnels – they can get flooded, and if the water rises as high as the furnaces, then we can't burn the bodies properly.' Eddie shuddered at the thought. 'I came down here tonight as usual, but then I dropped my torch and it broke and rolled away somewhere. I tried to retrace my footsteps back to the crematorium gates, but I just seemed to get more and more lost. I didn't think I was ever going to get out . . . then I nearly had a heart attack because I had my hands out in front of me, trying to feel my way, and next thing I knew I put them on . . . well, something that *moved*. I ran away and that made me even *more* lost. But now I've found you.'

Eddie smiled. He flashed the torch back up the tunnel – and the locked gates of the crematorium were suddenly illuminated. 'You were nearly home,' he said. He moved the beam along the tunnel wall, and then stood horrified as it picked out the skeletons of the dead children.

'Oh my word,' said Barney, simply.

Then the beam fell to the tunnel floor, and he saw Slaterbake lying there. At first, his natural instinct was to back away. But Slaterbake wasn't moving, the medicine had done its job and he felt strong; and he had Barney by his side, who was worth half a dozen ordinary men. So he not only stood his ground, he moved slowly towards his tormentor and the closer he got the more relaxed

GALWAY COUNTY LIBRARIES

he grew, because he could see that Slaterbake was asleep, unconscious.

No – Slaterbake was dead.

There was no mistaking it. His face was a mask of frozen horror, his eyes wide and staring.

Barney saw the look of recognition on Eddie's face. 'You know him?'

'He's the man responsible for all these,' said Eddie, nodding around at the skeletons. 'This must be who you bumped into. You obviously gave him a bigger fright than he gave you.'

Barney stared down at Slaterbake. 'He's dead. But if he was alive, I wouldn't like him.'

'And quite right too,' said Eddie.

Barney led Eddie back to the crematorium gates, then produced a set of keys and unlocked them. He then took his young friend past the steaming furnaces and up several sets of stairs until they reached ground level. It was still an hour before dawn. Barney gave him a running commentary as they passed through the building, explaining that when bodies were brought in for burning a service was usually held in a small room they used as a chapel, and then the coffin disappeared through a curtain. Most people thought it was burned there and then, but the reality was that the coffins were stacked up, and then burned at night, all at once, long after the mourners had gone home. It was cheaper that way. And it was Barney's job to burn them. He seemed to enjoy it almost as much as he'd enjoyed washing bodies back in the Royal Victoria Hospital.

'Even more,' said Barney, 'because I don't have to deal with creeps like Bernard Scuttles. You see much of him these days?'

'Too much,' said Eddie, without elaborating. That was the good thing about Barney. He never required much information. He had once saved him from Scuttles and from an attack by the Reservoir Pups, but he had never asked Eddie why or how he'd gotten himself into such situations. It was the same with the tunnels. He didn't ask Eddie what he'd been doing there. But he did say, 'I'm going to have to tell someone about the skeletons.'

Eddie agreed. The police would find them, they'd find Slaterbake, and they'd work out that he was to blame for their deaths. Hopefully they would also find out that the Governor was involved. He would be removed, and perhaps the Melody Hill Centre for Trouble Makers would be closed. 'Just don't mention me,' he said.

There was a small kitchen in the crematorium. Barney opened the fridge and asked Eddie what he wanted. There were sandwiches, buns, apples, chocolate bars and biscuits. 'We keep everything in here,' said Barney, 'because there's so much heat from the furnace. So help yourself.'

As he stuffed his face Barney took a look at Eddie's lacerated, weeping fingers. He thought he should go to a hospital, but Eddie just shook his head. So Barney went to a first aid box. He carefully washed the wound, applied an antiseptic cream and then began to wrap his hand in a cool, cotton bandage. As he did he said quietly, 'I saw you on TV. Your brother.'

'I didn't do it,' said Eddie.

'I know,' said Barney. Although really, he didn't *know*. That was what friendship was about, Eddie thought – trust and care. Barney took a long look at him. 'You don't look well, Eddie. You can rest here. Get some sleep. There won't be anyone here for hours.'

Eddie shook his head. There was nothing in the world he would have liked more than to stretch out in a soft bed – or even a hard one – or a bench, or under a desk. But with the medication still kicking through his veins, and with his wounds dressed and even his swollen ankle feeling better, he knew he had to press on.

His little brother was out there.

Somewhere.

And he had to find him.

Twenty-seven

An hour and a half later Eddie was limping through the cold, damp, mist-enveloped streets of early morning Belfast. Traffic had already started to build up; there were men and women going to work; schoolboys and girls off to school; postmen, milkmen, policemen.

Eddie kept his head down. This wasn't just so that he wouldn't be recognised, but because he hardly had the strength to keep it raised. He was starting to feel miserable again. His hand throbbed, and with each step he took the pain in his ankle worsened. He still had the half-pill left in his pocket, but he decided to keep this in reserve for as long as he could. He had to just plough on, grin and bear the pain – although there wasn't much grinning.

He wanted to go home. He wanted to go up to his mum and say sorry, that it really wasn't his fault; he wanted her to hug him and say she knew that. But if he went home Scuttles would surely be there, comforting her, and he would take one look at Eddie and make sure he was sent back to Melody Hill or some other ghastly place. No, what he *wanted* didn't matter. It was what he *needed* that was important, and what he needed was support and advice and help. Also known as Mo.

By the time he reached her house, he was sweating profusely. He didn't want to have to deal with her dad, so he scraped up a handful of gravel from the gutter and threw it at her bedroom window. There was no response. He threw some more. Still nothing. Eddie sighed and was limping away when a familiar voice called him back.

'Hey! Would you give a girl a chance to get some clothes on?'

He turned. She was standing in the doorway, still buttoning up her shirt, smiling widely at him – although that smile quickly faded when she saw what state he was in. She ran right up to him. He managed his own smile for her, and then more or less collapsed into her arms.

She hugged him tight, then helped him back to the house.

'Your . . . dad . . . ?' Eddie whispered.

'He's at work,' said Mo.

'Work?'

'Well, he's out stealing things – that's as close as

he gets to a job.' She guided him through the front door, then down a short hall to the living room. The TV was on, there was a half eaten bowl of cereal on a table, and a girl's dressing gown lying in a heap on the floor. She sat him down in an armchair, then took a long, critical look at him. 'Eddie – you look dreadful.'

He nodded grimly.

She sank to her knees beside him. 'I've been worried sick about you. I tried to visit, but they wouldn't let me.'

'Any word . . . about Patrick?'

'Nothing.'

'I didn't . . .'

She put a hand on his knee. 'I know, Eddie. I know.'

His head slumped forward. He quickly jerked it back up. 'We have to get moving,' he said, although his voice, even to his own ears, sounded distant and vague. 'I think if we can just . . .'

'Eddie – we're going nowhere until you have a rest.'

'We haven't time to . . .'

'Eddie – a couple of hours isn't going to make any difference. We're not doing anything until you tell me everything that's happened to you, how you got into this state . . . and you're not even going to start telling me that until you've had a sleep.'

'But—'

'But *nothing*. Sleep.'

Despite his desire to go out searching for Patrick, Eddie found that he couldn't fight the idea of sleep. He *knew* he was exhausted. He knew he needed time to rest and recover, that he wouldn't be able to think properly until . . .

It wasn't an easy sleep. The Seagulls were back, swooping down for Patrick and carrying him off. He kept trying to fly after them, but there was no strength in his wings. Yes, he had wings. He was turning into a Seagull. Eddie tossed and turned and sweated and groaned and moaned and shouted out loud, and Mo, who had guided him upstairs to bed even though he was ninety-five per cent asleep already, sat on a chair and held his hand and dabbed his forehead with a damp flannel.

When he woke, in the middle of the afternoon, he found that the bed sheets were stuck to his pale skin. He didn't feel any better, either. In fact, he felt *worse*. His hand. His foot. His head. His eyes. His throat. Everything that could hurt, *did* hurt. Eddie stumbled out of bed. His shirt and trousers were lying over a chair. He didn't remember taking them off. Had Mo taken them off for him? But he was beyond embarrassment. He needed relief from his pain. All he needed was . . .

He lifted the shirt and checked the top pocket for the half-pill. It wasn't there. He checked it again. It *must* be there. He checked his trouser pockets. Empty. He got down on his hands and knees and began to run his good hand over the bedroom carpet. It must have fallen out. It must have . . . where was it? He couldn't go on feeling this bad, he just needed the little half-pill to help him through the next few hours until his strength started to return. He moved in a wider circle. Then he checked the bed, pulling the damp sheets back one by one in case it had somehow become stuck between them.

Damn, damn, damn, damn . . .

'Is this what you're looking for?'

Eddie turned. Mo was standing in the doorway. Her hand was open, and the half-pill was sitting on her palm.

'Oh thank God,' said Eddie, relief flooding through him the way the warmth of the pill surely would in just a few moments. He hopped across to her, raising his own hand to take it. But instead of dropping it into his, she clenched her fist tightly around it.

He looked up at her, surprised, and then confused because he'd never seen her look quite so . . . hard or cross or grim. 'How could you, Eddie?' she asked, her voice calm, but cold.

Eddie laughed. 'Stop messing,' he said. He opened, closed, then opened his hand again, motioning for her to drop the half-pill on to it.

Instead she shook her head.

'Mo – please, I'm *dying* here.'

'How long have you been taking them, Eddie?'

'Mo! Will you just give it to me!'

'*No*. How long?'

'How long what? Mo, if you were in pain I wouldn't play stupid bloody games. I'm not in the mood, OK? Now give me my painkiller.'

'Painkiller, is that it?'

'*Yes*. Now will you just—'

'Painkiller. How big a fool do you think I am?'

'I don't *care*. Just give me it!' With that he grabbed suddenly for it, catching her wrist and wrenching it down. He clamped it between his arm and his chest, and with his free hand began squeezing her fist, trying to force her to open it. He had taken her by surprise . . . but it only took her a few moments to recover. She was stronger than he could ever have guessed, or was it just that he had no strength at all in his own arms? And his legs were so weak that they were nearly giving way. In seconds she'd freed herself. She spun around and then gave him one almighty shove. He almost flew across the room. Luckily the bed was there to break his fall. He lay on it for several moments, winded. He gasped for air. 'Mo . . .' he spluttered. 'I'm sorry – I just don't understand why you . . .'

'You're hooked on crush.'

Eddie blinked at her. 'What?' he said.

'Crush. You're hooked.'

Eddie laughed. He sat up. 'Don't be ridiculous. Hooked on crush? Mo, I've never even seen . . .'

And then he stopped, because if he'd never even seen crush, then how did he know he wasn't . . .

Mo could see the sudden confusion in his eyes. *Crush?*

Did Jimmy give me crush?

Oh my God.

Oh my God.

Crush!

He had seen the terrible effects of crush out on the streets, in the hospital. And now he . . .

Mo sat beside him on the bed. She put a

reassuring hand on his arm – but not the hand with the crush in it. As if she could tell what he was thinking, she slipped her other hand into her jeans pocket and deposited the half-pill there.

'Tell me what happened to you, Eddie. Tell me everything.'

GALWAY COUNTY LIBRARIES

So he did. He told her about Melody Hill and the Governor and the letter from Scuttles pretending to be his dad, and Slaterbake and what he did with kids and how he'd sliced his hand to bits and the pain had been so bad that Jimmy had given him a pill – but now that he thought about it, what kind of a painkiller was *that* good? You didn't feel like you could take on the world ten minutes after taking a couple of headache pills.

Suddenly it all made sense.

Crush. Jimmy had a supply of crush, and had given it to him to enable him to lead them in their escape bid. He hadn't meant to get him hooked on . . .

Hooked? I'm not . . .

Eddie took a deep breath. 'Mo – look, look at my hand . . .' He quickly unwrapped the bandage, only slowing down and wincing as he peeled the last few strands away. 'It's not the crush making me feel so awful – look at that, it's full of poison, I must have some kind of infection . . .'

She looked at the wounds. He looked at the wounds. They were undoubtedly raw and bloody, but whatever magical cream Barney had applied seemed to be working. The hand no longer looked quite so bad.

Mo shook her head. 'I know it's sore, Eddie. But that's not why you're feeling so rough. It's the crush. You only have to take it once and you're addicted. That's what's so awful about it. It makes you feel fantastic for a couple of hours – and then you're sick as a dog for weeks on end until you get some more. And the more you take, the shorter the good feeling lasts. So you take more and more and more, trying to get that feeling back, until eventually your body can't take any more. It kills you, Eddie.'

Eddie lay back on the bed. He rubbed at his damp brow. 'What am I supposed to do, Mo?'

'I don't know.'

'My little brother is out there and everyone thinks I've stolen him.'

'I don't.'

'I know that. But I've already been in a hell-hole like Melody Hill. If they catch me they'll probably send me back there, or somewhere even worse. The only way I can prove I didn't do something awful to my brother is to find out what really did happen to him. If he's alive out there, I have to rescue him. Every minute, every hour is vital, but I can't even begin to look for him feeling like this. And you say it'll last for weeks? I *can't* do that, Mo. Paddy's depending on me. Do you know what I'm saying?'

She gave him a long look, then nodded.

'So what are you going to do about it?'

There were suddenly tears in her eyes. She reached into her pocket and withdrew the pill. She looked at it, sitting in the palm of her hand. Eddie looked at it.

'Eddie – if I give you this now . . . you'll need another later on. And then another.'

'I know that.'

'It's like a death sentence.'

'It's a death sentence for me if I don't find Paddy. I *have* to find him, Mo. I have to.'

'I don't want to lose you, Eddie.'

Eddie took a deep breath. He felt like crying himself. 'You won't lose me, Mo.'

She wiped at her eyes. 'Eddie – you don't understand. If you get fully hooked on this, then *I will* lose you.'

He sat up. He put his arms around her and hugged her to him. 'Mo,' he said softly, 'that's a risk we're both going to have to take.'

She looked up at him, hesitated for just another moment, then closed her eyes tight shut and handed him the half-pill.

Twenty-eight

She made him wait in the shop doorway while she darted across Royal Avenue, and then down a sidestreet between the Waterstone's bookshop and Virgin Records. She was gone for perhaps ten minutes. When she reappeared she gave him the briefest nod.

Brilliant – she got them.

Mo's dad had returned very drunk from his day out stealing things. It had apparently gone well, because when he'd fallen asleep on the couch – empty bottles of beer littering the floor beside him – she'd darted downstairs and removed fifty pounds from his wallet. Even Mo seemed surprised to find so much. It was enough to buy twelve crush.

Eddie could already feel a tingle of anticipation as he watched her take out the silver foil and open it in her lap. Twelve full crush. They were sitting on a bench in the Botanic Gardens, a large public park right beside Queens University. He watched curiously as she set the foil on the bench between them, then produced a knife from her pocket and slipped down on to her knees. She moved the knife until it was hovering over the first of the pills.

'What're you doing, Mo?'

'I'm cutting them into halves. And then I'm cutting them into quarters.'

Eddie felt his stomach turn over. 'But I need—'

'It's not about what you need, Eddie – it's about what I'm prepared to give you, and that means you get the absolute bare minimum.'

Eddie suddenly felt panicky. 'But it won't be enough! What if it doesn't work, what if I still feel really crap . . . make it a half, Mo – a half works. Please.'

She shook her head. 'Eddie, you've already turned me into a drug dealer. Now, either you agree to this or you're on your own. I'm trying to look after you. Just trust me.'

Eddie took a deep breath. 'I know you are. And I do. I just . . .'

'Just trust me. Quarter-pills. And I decide when you get them. All right?'

'But . . .'

'No *buts*, Eddie.'

'But what if we fall out and you just withhold them for badness, or we get separated and I can't—'

'Eddie.'

He knew she was right. But he also knew that he wanted the crush. Needed it.

Who runs this gang anyway? Aren't I big enough to look after myself? What if I just swipe them all now? Make a run for it. I can take whole pills. Two or three of them. My God. if I feel fantastic on one, what will I feel like on two or three – Superman?

As if she could tell what he was thinking, Mo quickly wrapped the foil back into a ball and stuffed it into the black canvas bag she'd brought with her. She sat back down beside him and put the bag between her feet. 'I can cut them later,' she said.

Her eyes suddenly flicked beyond Eddie, and she tutted. He turned slowly and saw that two policemen were walking along the path towards them. They weren't paying any particular attention to them, but if they got much closer the chances were that they would probably recognise him, for as Eddie and Mo had walked through town earlier they'd seen the front page of the *Belfast Telegraph* – with a picture of Eddie. The headline said: MASS BREAK-OUT FROM MELODY HILL, and the caption beside Eddie's photo said, *Eddie Malone, suspected of murdering his own brother, is one of the escapees*. There was more, much more, but the man selling the papers had started to examine Eddie with a little too much interest, and so they'd quickly walked on to the next corner, and then run like wild.

The police were only ten metres away. If they got up and walked away now it was bound to look suspicious. But if they stayed where they were . . .

'Mo . . .' Eddie whispered, 'what'll we . . .'

She leant towards him, as if she too was going to whisper something in his ear. But instead she looped an arm around him, and kissed him full on the lips. And she was still kissing him when the policemen passed; they must have looked over because one of them gave a friendly whistle. Mo only released him when the sound of their boots on the path began to recede. She stood up and put her hands in her pockets and began to walk in the opposite direction. 'Come on,' she called back, 'we better get going.'

Eddie sat in shock for several more moments. She'd *kissed* him. Out of nowhere. This tough-looking albino kid had just *kissed* him. Right on the lips.

He hurried after her, his face bright red. 'Mo . . . ?'

'We should get a taxi instead of a bus – too many people might recognise you on a bus.'

'Mo . . .'

'You keep your hood up and let me do the talking.'

'Mo . . .'

She stopped suddenly and glared at him. Eddie was amazed to see the very vaguest hint of colour on her bone white skin. 'So I kissed you,' she snapped. 'Don't get a complex about it. I had no alternative, all right?'

Then she started walking again.

Eddie shrugged. 'All right,' he said. 'Keep your hair on.' He hurried after her. They walked the rest of the way to the taxi rank in silence. Eddie thought about the kiss some more. He felt kind of warm inside. *It's the crush*, he thought. *Definitely the crush*.

As instructed, Eddie sat quietly in the back of the taxi all the way to the Palace Barracks Army Camp. It was lucky in a way that Mo looked so weird, because the driver spent half his time staring at her in his mirror and didn't give him a second glance.

They made him stop halfway up a barely lit lane which wound up and around the back of the camp. 'You sure about this?' he asked. He was reluctant to leave a couple of kids on such a dark stretch of road.

'We're sure,' said Mo. She paid him with what was left of the money she'd stolen from her dad's wallet. As Eddie climbed out behind her, she saw beads of sweat on his brow. When the taxi drove off she said, 'Eddie – how're you doing?'

'Fine,' he said. But he wasn't. The crush had worn off, and he was trying to fight the desire to ask for more. 'So now we're here, what's the plan?' he asked.

'Well,' said Mo, 'I thought we'd go in and find the baby.'

Eddie nodded. 'Sounds like a good one,' he said.

They smiled at each other. They hadn't worked anything out, apart from the fact that there had to be some alternative way of getting in to going through the heavily guarded front gates. So they began to walk the perimeter of the camp. The front of it opened up on to the main dual carriageway into Belfast, but the rest – the houses, the community centre, the temporary buildings, the overgrown sports fields – was surrounded by the rolling green Hollywood Hills. These were beautiful during the day, but wild and windswept by night, which was a good thing, really, as there were no people and few cars to disturb them as they examined every centimetre of the high, wire fence which surrounded the camp for some means of entry.

They walked for almost a mile without finding anything. The fence wasn't only tall, but it was topped with barbed wire. If they'd been in the city, some gangster would long ago have cut a hole in it, either just for badness or to get inside to steal something; but out here, right on the edge of the countryside, it had been left well alone. When they began to encounter streetlights they realised they were approaching the entrance again, and must have completed one entire circuit of the camp.

'Now what?' said Eddie.

His ankle was aching; his throat was dry; his head throbbed.

'We look again,' said Mo. She turned, and began to retrace her steps.

'But we've—' Eddie began.

'We look again!'

Eddie bit his tongue. He was on the verge of shouting something horrible after her, even though he knew she was right. There *had* to be some way in that they'd missed. He was just feeling miserable because . . .

Crush.

As he walked, he peered through the fence at the camp below. *There's plenty of crush in there – maybe I can steal some if we get in. No need for Mo to know. Just a few pills to keep me going when she won't give me what I need. Until I get Patrick back. Then I can stop taking them. I'll throw them out. I don't really need them. Just because of my ankle. And my hand. She says it isn't infected. What does she know? She's not a doctor.*

Half an hour later they were more or less back where the taxi had dropped them, and they still hadn't found a way in.

'So what now?' Eddie asked. He was feeling even worse. His head swam. He could barely focus.

Mo shook her head. 'We need another plan.'

She crossed the road towards an iron gate leading into a field. She climbed on to it and perched herself on the top rung. Eddie began to haul himself up beside her, but lost his footing and cracked his knee on one of the metal bars.

'You all right?' Mo asked.

'Fine,' Eddie snapped.

She knows what I need, why doesn't she just give it to me?

But I'm not going to ask. I'm not going to ask.

The lights of the camp twinkled before them.

'You're sure he's in there?' Mo asked.

Eddie nodded. He *wasn't* sure, in fact – but anything else was almost too horrible to contemplate.

Mo took a deep breath. 'OK,' she said, 'let's think.'

Eddie nodded beside her.

He *couldn't* think. At least not about a plan, or about Patrick.

I won't ask her for it. I'm not that weak. I'll be all right.

But it's in her bag . . .

All I have to do is push her off the gate, pin her down, take the bag, run off into the woods.

Mo grabbed his arm suddenly, and for a moment he thought she'd caught him thinking out loud. But no – she was pointing to their left. There was a strong breeze, so all of the bushes and branches around them were moving, but there was definitely something different about it: a shaking, a definite sense of something coming towards them. Had the taxi driver tipped off the police? Or worse, the Seagulls? Were they slowly being surrounded? He felt Mo tense beside him, ready to jump. Would she fight or flee? Eddie didn't feel like jumping. He didn't have the strength to run or fight. He was feeling so miserable that he was starting not to care about anything.

'Awww.'

Eddie glanced at Mo. She was smiling. She pointed at the bushes. He tried to focus. At first he couldn't see anything, but then he detected a vague outline of something moving, then a flash of white – white fur, against a dark background – and he could just make out a creature about the size of a small dog, now beyond the bush and zigzagging through the long grass. It hesitated for a moment, its nose high in the air, then darted quickly across the road.

'I've never seen a real live badger,' Mo whispered.

Eddie tried to stifle a yawn. He'd more or less grown up in the country – playing in the woods and fields around Groomsport – and he'd seen plenty of badgers. So what. A badger. Big deal. He was dying, and Mo was getting all goggle-eyed over a bloody badger. He needed crush. Just a little. If he could just lick one of the pills, he didn't even have to swallow it . . . but then Mo was nudging him again and pointing, and he gasped in surprise as he saw the badger pop up on the other side of the fence, inside the army camp.

Mo jumped off the fence and hurried across the road. When Eddie caught up with her, she was already on her hands and knees, crawling behind a bush. There was a hole there, only a few centimetres deep, but running directly under the fence. It was a perfect fit for a badger – and with a little work, for a couple of smallish humans as well. They pulled themselves under, then crawled out into the long grass on the other side. They could see the badger already meandering away across the overgrown camp sports fields.

'Well,' Eddie whispered, 'looks like we're in.'

Mo glanced at her watch. Then she nodded towards the camp buildings. 'We should wait until the lights go out.'

'We can't afford to—'

'Eddie, if we're going to do it, we need to do it properly. If there's lights that means there's people up and around, and if there's people around, then what if they see us?'

'We'll just have to take that chance.'

'No.' She said it firmly.

Eddie fumed beside her. Who did she think she was? *Who runs this gang?*

'But . . .'

'It's just after midnight now. We'll give it another hour.'

She hauled her canvas bag around and delved inside it as Eddie shook his head. 'And then when the lights go out, we'll be in the dark as well. What's the point in . . . ?'

But Mo was now holding something out to him. 'Remember these?' she grinned.

It wasn't just that it was a dark night; his very eyeballs were aching, and he had to strain to make out what she was now reaching out to him. He took hold of them – and then smiled suddenly himself.

Night-vision goggles.

The very first time he'd teamed up with her, inside Alison Beech's cavernous warehouse, Mo had come up with night-vision goggles to help them track down the stolen babies.

'Of course,' he said, snapping them quickly over his eyes and switching them on. Immediately what had been dark, dense countryside exploded into life around him. 'Wow!' said Eddie. He snapped the eyepiece back up again. 'Are these the same . . . ?'

Mo smiled broadly. 'Updated model.' She delved back into her bag. 'I also have these . . .' She put something into Eddie's hand.

'Smoke bombs,' he said.

'And these.'

They were similar in size to the smoke bombs – small, black and hard – but were square as opposed to round.

'Flashbangs.'

'Flashbangs?'

'They flash and they bang. So it's a good name for them. They work the same way as the smoke bombs – you just light that touch-paper on the side – but they go off like hand grenades. They'll scare the pants off anyone who gets in our way.'

Eddie slipped four of them into one pocket, and three smoke bombs into another. He managed a smile for Mo. 'Just like old times,' he said.

'Just like old times,' she repeated – although it seemed to him that she said it with a hint of sadness.

They nestled down in the grass to wait. It wasn't particularly cold, but Eddie was shivering. He tried to sleep, but there were too many thoughts racing through his mind. Instead, he watched the lights of the camp winking out, one by one. Mo didn't say much. At one point the badger came wandering back towards them – then stopped, sniffed, and headed off in a different direction.

Eddie buttoned his coat tight around him and hugged himself. 'Do you think,' he asked quietly, 'that Patrick is still alive?'

'I know he is.'

'And do you think my mum will ever forgive me?'

'For what?'

'Losing him.'

'You didn't lose him, Eddie. He was stolen.'

'I left him alone.'

Mo had nothing to say to that. She glanced at her watch again, and then down at the camp. There were only one or two lights left on. She lifted her bag, reached in and withdrew the silver foil. She carefully unwrapped it and lifted a quarter crush. She held it out to Eddie. 'You've been very strong,' she said.

Eddie stared at the quarter-pill.

He knew what he should do. He should say, *No, I don't need it, I'm stronger than any damn drug.*

But the fact was – he wasn't stronger. He *needed* it.

He took it and swallowed it quickly, as if scared that she would dive after it, wrench his mouth open and claim it back.

'Thank you,' he said.

She nodded grimly. She checked her watch again. 'Another five minutes to let it work, Eddie – then we need to go.'

It was barely into his body, but he was already starting to feel better.

Crush. It wasn't so bad. There was bound to be a way to work with it, so that he could feel this good without becoming some kind of zombie drug addict like those Seagulls he'd seen slumped in doorways. *I mean, they're Seagulls, what do they know? I'll be able to handle it, I'm made of stronger stuff.*

The five minutes were up.

'You ready?'

'I'm ready.'

And he was. He felt great.

'All right then,' said Mo, lowering her glasses, 'let's go.'

As she began to move forward, Eddie put his hand out to stop her. She pushed the goggles up again and looked impatiently up at him. 'What?'

'I appreciate everything you've done, Mo,' he said.

'Uh-huh.'

'And I'm even prepared to forget about the kiss.'

'Uh-huh.'

'But one thing you've got to understand.'

'Uh-huh, what?'

'This is still my gang. I get to say "let's go".'

She giggled suddenly. 'All right then.' She bowed her head, and smiled mockingly. 'You say it.'

Eddie took a deep breath. This was it then. His little brother was down there, and if it was the last thing he did, he was going to get him back. Eddie snapped on his goggles. 'All right,' he said, 'let's go.'

Twenty-nine

Eddie and Mo raced across the grass and down a slight incline towards the dark rectangle of narrow huts which acted as the hub of the camp, confident that they wouldn't be spotted – at least at this early stage. The night-vision goggles worked perfectly; they could see everything, while being fairly confident that they couldn't be seen themselves. They reached the closest of the huts and slipped under it. They took a minute to get their breath back, then Mo whispered, 'What now?'

Eddie tried to remember the layout of the rectangle, and what each of the huts contained. There was the clinic where he'd sat with his mother, then the café, the small church ... then the larger hut which was divided into sections. Yes. That was ... on their left, about a hundred metres along. There was a workshop, a classroom, and the room which he'd supposed acted as the headquarters of the young Seagulls themselves, outside of which he'd seen the two guards in their coal-black uniforms. And then there was the crèche. His mum had said the orphan babies lived there.

Patrick has to be there.

If he isn't – we're sunk. We can't go and search hundreds of houses for him.

Eddie indicated for Mo to follow him; he crawled out from beneath the hut, jumped over the gravel path that ran alongside it, then sprinted along the edge of the grass towards the largest of the huts. He reached the edge, with Mo right behind him, then peered along the length of the hut.

Good.

The Seagulls' HQ was in complete darkness. No guards to worry about. The crèche also appeared to be dark, but with their night-vision goggles they could pick out several dots of light in its main window – curtains had been drawn, but they either weren't thick enough or were so old that they were starting to hole.

Eddie motioned Mo forward and they hurried along to the crèche window and listened. At first they heard nothing, but then a smile crept on to Eddie's face: the sound of a baby crying. Small and muffled, but definitely crying. It didn't mean it was Patrick, of course. But there was a chance.

Eddie cautiously examined the door into the crèche. It was padlocked closed. He quickly thought back to his last visit. Before he'd destroyed the statue of General Killster he'd observed the rectangle of huts from inside the well-kept quadrangle on the other side. Was there another entrance? He couldn't quite place it. But there had to be. Whoever looked after the babies needed access to them during the night for feeding and changing. They weren't about to padlock them in and let them cry all night. No, the padlock was for protection from the outside. There must be an inside door they felt safer using. He crouched down and signalled for Mo to follow him under the huts. They crawled through weeds and assorted rubbish. They parted the long grass on the other side and peered out. The rectangle of grass was as smartly kept as before. General Killster's statue was still standing – but it was missing a head and both arms, and the main body of it was surrounded by scaffolding. Half of the windows along the inside walls had temporary wooden panels nailed in place across them. He had clearly caused a lot of damage with Gary Gilmore's little bomb.

And he would do it all again.

There was a second door into the crèche just five metres along. It was closed, of course, and a curtain was pulled across its glass panel. Instead of going right up to it, and taking the risk of somebody suddenly opening it and discovering them, they moved along to the windows and checked again for holes or gaps in the curtains. At the third one along they found that the curtain had been hung short, allowing them to see into the room through a thin strip at the bottom.

Eddie pushed up his night-vision goggles and peered in. The room was lit by a single, bare light bulb. There were three rows of three cots, but he couldn't tell how many of them were occupied. At the front there was a fridge and a sofa, upon which a middle-aged woman sat. She was resting her head on her hand, and her elbow on the arm of the sofa. She was, apparently, asleep.

They knelt on the short, damp grass for a moment, trying to decide what to do. Mo thought it was a bad idea to go straight in. 'You can be sure that as soon as we open the door – if we can open it – she'll wake up and start screaming.'

'So what then?'

She thought for a moment. 'What if you cut the power, I'll go in with the night-visions and pick up the baby while the old woman's still stumbling around in the dark?'

Eddie nodded. 'All right. Except – you cut the power, and I go in.' He stopped her as she started to protest. 'Mo – I have to do it.'

'Your leg, your hand . . .'

'I'm doing it. My brother.'

She could see that it was no use arguing.

They began looking for the power source. Most buildings have their wires built into the brickwork, but because these were wooden huts, they were bound to be a lot more accessible. They moved along the near wall of the hut, then began to search directly underneath. About halfway along they found a little cube of bricks with a wooden slat for a roof. Eddie lifted the slat and was pleased to find a miniature circuit board inside. It didn't look overly complicated. He nodded at Mo. 'Count to twenty,' he whispered, 'then loosen the wires so it looks like it just happened naturally; don't cut them.'

Eddie slipped back outside and approached the door – he didn't even know whether or not it was locked. He would just have to hope for the best. He slipped his hand around the handle and waited.

Five seconds later, the light inside suddenly went out.

He gave it another five seconds, waiting for some reaction from the sleeping woman inside, then cautiously tried the handle.

It's not locked!

He eased the door open. It squeaked ever so slightly. He stepped carefully into the crèche and eased the door closed behind him. He recognised the smell immediately – you don't spend days and days with twelve stolen babies without recognising the stink of nappies and the sour aroma of spilled milk. He glanced briefly at the sleeping woman before quickly moving to his left.

Now for the babies. It was a simple matter of elimination, checking the cots one by one; but he still had to bite his lip to stop himself from calling out his brother's name. He stepped quietly along the first row – even in the weird light of the night-vision goggles he could tell that these were true Seagulls: their hair was dark, their skin an olive complexion. He turned into the second row.

Just a few seconds now, he has to be here, he has to be . . .

But he wasn't in the second row either.

Eddie turned into the third . . . just four cots to go now.

The first two were Seagulls . . . so was the third. The fourth, which was pushed up close to a cracked window, had some kind of a net over it, probably to prevent light or a draught disturbing it.

It has to be. It has to be!

Eddie carefully began to peel the netting back.

Beneath it the baby gurgled happily.

It has to be, please God!

Eddie pulled the net right back and looked in.

The baby frowned, its black eyes opening wide at the sight of this dark shape looming over it with the goggle-eyes.

Black hair. Dark skin.

No!

Eddie felt like he'd been kicked in the stomach.

He's not here! He's not here! But then where? Where?

The baby began to cry. Eddie quietly shushed it. That didn't help. The crying grew louder. Eddie glanced anxiously back at the woman as she shifted in her seat, but didn't open her eyes. The crying was threatening to move to a scream, so he stepped back out of the baby's eye-line – and banged into the cot behind. His foot hit one of its legs, which, riddled with woodworm, gave way suddenly. The corner of the cot hit the floor with a crash.

The woman at the front jumped to her feet as

babies began to scream all around him. She looked about her in a desperate panic – the room was still in complete darkness.

The woman cried out something soothing in her own language, and began fumbling her way towards the pale shadow of the door.

Eddie didn't know which way to turn. No Paddy, and now this woman about to raise the alarm. He couldn't get to the door before her, either.

OK . . . patience . . . patience . . . Once she's outside, I can slip out past her, and we can make a run for it.

They would never know for sure that there'd been a break-in, they would check the power source and see that a wire had come loose. Nothing more than that. Then Eddie and Mo would be free to try again.

He walked quickly through the rows of crying babies as the woman reached the door; but instead of going straight through it, she hesitated. She glanced behind her. Did she sense that he was there? He would surely be nothing more than the vaguest shape. She opened the door – but then instead of immediately going out she reached behind it.

She's pressing an alarm!

But no – the power is cut . . . What's that she's . . . ?

She stepped outside and raised something in her hand, and immediately Eddie knew that he was in trouble. An old-fashioned bell, the kind you would use to call a class of unruly schoolboys to dinner. One you don't need to plug in. Just one you raised and shook with all the strength you had, just exactly the way the frightened woman blocking the doorway was doing now.

Mo was lying anxiously amongst the weeds and rubbish underneath the hut as the bell peeled out. It didn't take a genius to work out that something had gone dreadfully wrong. She crawled forward, then pushed her head out through the weeds so that she could get a better idea of what was going on.

There she was – the woman with the bell, framed in the lenses of her night-vision goggles. But where was Eddie? A door opened to her right, and half a dozen young Seagulls came charging out, hurridly buttoning themselves into their dark uniforms.

There was a lot of shouting, then one of them produced a torch. More and more young gangsters were pouring out of the gang headquarters. Clearly the adults – whose houses were quite distant – would take longer to arrive. The woman with the bell was pointing back into the crèche and jabbering excitedly. She was quickly ushered away by the gangsters, and then they gathered about the door. At a signal from one of them they charged through. There came to Mo the muted sound of a brief but seemingly violent struggle, and then a few moments later she saw Eddie being carried out. Two boys on each arm, two on each leg.

As the rest of the gang saw what they'd captured there was an explosion of shouting and pointing and punching and kicking directed at Eddie. He was being carried face down, with his head slumped forward, and he didn't seem to be reacting as the blows landed again and again and again. He appeared to be unconscious.

Mo was now aware that one of the Seagulls was standing in the crèche doorway, flicking the light switch back and forth. She heard him walk across the floor above her, presumably to check the light bulb, then retrace his steps. He hurried across to another boy and took the torch from him, then knelt down and shone it along the underside of the hut.

Mo flattened herself amongst the weeds. The beam passed over her. She thanked God. But a moment later the boy eased himself under the hut and began to crawl towards the fuse box. If he knew what he was doing, it would only take him a moment to repair the lights.

She had a decision to make.

Go to Eddie's assistance.

Or escape.

Take on dozens of mad Seagulls.

Or live to fight another day.

She had no choice, really. As the boy, clutching the torch in his mouth, approached the fuse box, Mo slowly began to inch her way through the weeds along the length of the hut. When she reached the end of it she glanced back and saw that the boy was still working at the wiring. The fence was about two hundred metres away across the overgrown sports fields, which, luckily, were still in complete darkness. Mo pulled herself quietly out, got to her feet and then, without looking back, ran as fast as she could towards the fence.

I'll be back for you, Eddie, I'll be back, she said again and again under her breath. But she had no idea how or when, or whether, if she did make it back, Eddie would still be alive.

Thirty

Eddie Malone, gang leader, hero, crush addict and now – prisoner. He woke in a dank room, which felt like it was underground. The walls had a thick, ancient look about them that suggested that you could scream all you wanted, but somebody on the other side wouldn't even hear a whisper. The floor was covered in ceramic tiles, although most of them were cracked. He knew this because when he opened his eyes he found he was lying on that floor, and he actually quite liked the fact that they were tiles because they were cold and he was burning hot. Fever. His head throbbed. Every joint ached. Every muscle was yelling. He had been beaten, he was already carrying injuries to his hand and foot, and now that the crush had worn off he desperately needed some more. Wherever Mo was – captured or free – the one place she definitely *wasn't* was right where he needed her. *Here. Now.*

For a fleeting moment he thought his wish had somehow come true. The door to his room – his *cell* – suddenly opened – but it wasn't Mo, of course.

First of all two Seagulls, at least three or four years younger than Eddie, hurried across the floor and pulled him roughly to his feet. They wordlessly guided him to a table in the centre of the room and lowered him on to a red plastic chair with a cracked back. They then stood on either side of the door as another boy entered. He was taller, clearly older. Eddie had seen him before. Just once. Leading the gang of Seagulls through the centre of Belfast. His black hair was now cropped short. Eddie noticed that there were three small red stars sewn into the arm of his black shirt. Clearly he wasn't just an ordinary gangster. Behind him came the girl he'd seen at the hospital and then here in the camp at his mother's clinic. Rotavia.

They each took a seat opposite him. Eddie hardly had the strength to lift his head.

'We have met before,' said Rotavia. Eddie barely managed a shrug. She said something in her language to her comrade. Then she continued: 'My name is Rotavia Mislovich, and this is Alexander Rostocovich. He is our leader. Alexander's English is not good. So I will translate for him. Do you understand?'

Eddie nodded. Alexander gave him a long, hard look before he began to talk. Eddie could feel this boy's hatred and contempt burning into his skull.

He talked for at least three minutes, and every thirty seconds he jabbed a threatening finger at him. Eddie had expected Alexander to stop after every sentence to allow Rotavia to translate, but once he got going he didn't seem to want to stop. It was only when Rotavia gently touched his arm that the young leader seemed to realise what he'd done. He folded his hands before him, and nodded at Rotavia to begin.

'Alexander says – you are scum.'

Eddie waited for her to continue. But she didn't.

'Is that it?' Eddie asked.

'There are . . . lot of words in Ruritanian for . . . scum.'

'Well,' said Eddie, 'the feeling's mutual.'

Rotavia glared angrily at him. Her cheeks were flushed. This time she pointed the finger. 'You dare to call us . . . *scum*? You? You who break into our home to kill our babies? You who blow up statue of our revered leader?'

'I didn't blow—'

'We know what you did! Every member of every gang in this city knows what you did!'

Eddie shrugged. He actually felt quite proud of the fact that every gang member knew what a hero he was.

'Why?' Rotavia demanded. 'Why would you do this?'

'What, blow up a statue? Why do you think? Because you attacked us!'

She looked surprised, then quickly translated Eddie's words for Alexander. He listened attentively, nodding his head. Then again he spoke at length. He pointed his finger at Eddie just as much. After a while he nodded at Rotavia, and clasped his hands before him. Rotavia looked at Eddie.

'He says that you are definitely scum.'

'Is that it?'

'More or less,' said Rotavia. 'He also said that you were a liar and a dog and deserved to die. We have never attacked you or any gang in this city.'

Eddie laughed out loud. 'Yeah. Right. The Dundonald Ice Bowl burning down – I imagined that.' And then suddenly he wasn't laughing, because his head was hurting and his body aching and he wanted crush and he wasn't in the mood to sit there being called scum. So he did the pointing, first at Rotavia, then at Alexander, then at both of them. 'You haven't done anything? You're all so perfectly innocent! You never set fire to the Ice Bowl! You never stole my brother! That's right!

Well, I'll tell you this – you'd better bloody kill me because I'm not going to rest until I get him back! I'll blow up every statue you have! I'll set fire to every hut! I'll get every last one of you, because I'm going to make your lives so miserable that you'll be begging me to take him back! Do you hear me? Do you understand?'

Even Eddie was quite surprised to find that he was on his feet and screaming at them. The two guards from the door moved forward to restrain him, but Alexander raised his hand, and they stepped back. Eddie took a deep breath; he saw stars; his legs felt suddenly weak; he kind of stumbled back into his seat. He felt like he was going to be sick. Alexander stood. He exchanged some words with one of the guards, who then hurried away. When he returned, less than a minute later, Eddie was sitting with his head bowed, staring at the floor.

'Perhaps this is what you want?'

Eddie glanced up. Rotavia had her hand out, with a single crush sitting on her palm.

Eddie snorted. 'Why would I want that?'

'You don't think we know the signs?'

'Signs. Yeah. Right.'

'So you don't want it?'

Eddie stared at it. He wanted it more than anything in the world. 'No I don't.'

'OK, then I'll send it away again.'

Rotavia said something in Ruritanian, and then handed the pill to the guard. As he began to turn away Eddie quickly snapped, 'No – wait.'

The guard stopped, and looked at Rotavia for instructions. She smiled triumphantly and took the pill back. She rolled it between her fingers, but did not offer it to Eddie.

'OK,' Eddie spat suddenly, 'so I take crush. So do you. So do all of you. You lot brought it into this country – it's your fault I'm addicted to it.'

Rotavia translated Eddie's response to Alexander.

'So are you going to give it to me or not?'

He had his good hand out. He was clicking his fingers. He could almost feel the warmth coming off the pill. He wanted it now. He needed it now.

'First, we would like you to answer some questions.'

Eddie sighed. 'Just give me the bloody pill!'

'First, answers.'

'I've given you my answers! Just give me the . . .'

Rotavia closed her fist around it again. 'I think,' she said calmly, 'that we can wait for our answers.'

The guards opened the door.

Alexander and Rotavia turned to leave.

With the crush.

'No ... look ...' Eddie said, standing himself now. 'I can answer your questions.'

'We will return later.'

'No, please ... I'll answer them now ... I'm sorry for shouting – I just want my brother back ... please ...'

But they were already going through the door. And then it was closed and Eddie was hammering against it, shouting and yelling and demanding that they come back and give him his crush.

There was no response. Eddie rested against the door, then allowed himself to slip down it. His head fell forward and he began to sob – great, miserable, defeated sobs; sobs because he was a prisoner of the Seagulls, sobs for his mum who hated him and sobs for his dad who'd run away, sobs for his stolen brother, but mostly sobs for the crush he couldn't have.

Crush was, truly, a terrible thing. He knew that now.

But he would do anything just to feel that lovely warmth once more.

·

Thirty-one

Eddie was a prisoner of the Seagulls, and in order to get him out alive Mo knew she was going to need help. If she could have done it by herself, or even, say, with the help of another Gary Gilmore bomb, then she would certainly have done so. But this was beyond what one or two could manage. The Council of War had started it all by sending Eddie into the enemy camp. Now they would have to save him.

The first thing she did was call Billy Cobb. She quickly explained what had happened and he agreed to recall the Council. He told her to go to the Pups' headquarters at midnight. It was only nine in the morning, and she protested that that was far too late – they needed to act *right now*. But Cobb was firm; it would take a while to get all of the leaders together. Mo reluctantly agreed, and then spent a very, very long day pacing her room, watching the clock and fighting with her dad – who'd discovered that quite a lot of his money was missing from his wallet. She eventually convinced him that he'd been so drunk he must have spent it and forgotten.

Then it was dinnertime, then she sat in front of the TV, all the time wondering why the hands of the clock were going round so slowly; and how Eddie was – if he was being tortured or beaten or secretly buried in an unmarked grave.

She was hurrying through the Rivers by eleven-fifteen. There were Pups on guard duty on every single corner, obviously nervous about a possible attack by the Seagulls, but they had clearly been told that Mo was coming, as she wasn't challenged for a password once. She was admitted into their headquarters at 11.30 pm, and then shown directly to the boardroom. It was still empty when she entered. She walked anxiously around the table, willing the Council to appear so that they could get some sort of plan together. Eddie had been captured at around two o'clock in the morning. It was now almost midnight. He had been a prisoner of the Seagulls for nearly twenty-two hours.

Eventually, eventually, the boardroom door opened and Billy Cobb came in. He held the door open for Captain Black in his motorised wheelchair. Four Pups came in behind them, closing the doors and then taking up their posts in front of them.

Mo was confused. 'The rest of the Council, are they . . . ?'

'The others aren't coming,' said Billy Cobb.

As he took his seat at the head of the table, Captain Black's wheelchair hummed into place beside him.

'I don't understand,' said Mo. 'Doesn't the whole Council have to agree to . . .'

But Billy Cobb was holding his hand up to stop her. 'Mo,' he said, 'I thought it might save any . . . embarrassment if just the three of us met for now.'

'Embarrassment? What are you talking about? Eddie's been taken prisoner, God knows what they're doing to him, we have to get the gangs together, we have to attack, Billy, we have to—'

'Perhaps you should sit down, Mo.' It was Captain Black. His voice was cool and calm and it seemed like the kind suggestion of a concerned leader. But she knew him too well. Captain Black had never done anything kind in his life. Nevertheless, she took her seat. She didn't trust him in the slightest, but she had no choice, she needed his help as much as she needed Cobb's. 'What's going on?' she asked.

Cobb looked genuinely concerned. He liked Mo.

He liked Eddie Malone. But the evidence against them was mounting. 'Mo,' he said, 'we appreciate the . . . ahm, urgency of the situation. We do. Honestly. However – it has been brought to our attention – to *my* attention as the Chairman of the War Council – that you . . . you and Eddie Malone, haven't been exactly straight with us.'

'Straight?'

'Honest.'

She turned her gaze on Captain Black. 'What sort of crap have you been giving him?' she snapped.

Black responded with a thin smile. 'The truth, merely. The blindingly obvious, indeed. The facts that only a moron could ignore. The fact that Eddie Malone is a murderer, that he has killed his brother and disposed of the body.'

'That's a lie!' Mo exploded. 'The Seagulls took him!'

'Did they really? You have evidence of that?'

'No of course I don't have evidence. We were getting evidence when Eddie was captured. We were going to bring his brother home.'

'You saw him, then? You saw the baby?'

'No – we . . .'

'You didn't see him? So how do you know he's there?'

330

'Because . . . they *must* have taken him.'

'Oh right – I see, the sum total of your evidence is that they *must* have taken him. I'm sure that would stand up in a court of law.'

'And what would you know about a court of law?' Mo exploded. 'This has happened because you, the War Council, told us to attack the Seagulls. This is their revenge. Just because we haven't been able to find the baby doesn't mean—'

Captain Black slammed his fist down on the table. 'Yes, we ordered an attack! We ordered a full-scale gang attack! And what did your mighty gang do? It sent *one* person. Why was that?'

'Because we thought it—'

'I'll tell you why! Because there is no gang! The only members of this Gang With No Name are members with no names, because there aren't any! There's only you and Eddie Malone!'

'That's rubbish! We have dozens of—'

'Where are they, then? Where are they now? What are their names?'

'That's none of your business!'

Captain Black turned slightly in his chair. 'I've told you, Billy, there is no gang, not now, not ever. They've been lying to us all along!'

Billy Cobb folded his hands before him. 'Well, Mo? Is there a gang?'

Mo laughed. 'You think just Eddie and I could outwit the Babysnatchers? Do you think Eddie and I could rescue the head of Oliver Plunkett? Just the two of us?'

'Just answer the question.'

She stared at Billy Cobb. Captain Black stared at her. Billy Cobb glared at her. There was a lot of staring and glaring going on, and all the time Eddie was probably being tortured. She had to make a decision. Either preserve the reputation of their mythical gang, or tell the truth. Neither answer guaranteed their support, she knew that much.

Eventually she gave a little shrug. 'We have a fluid membership.'

'What exactly does that mean?' Cobb asked.

'It means people come, people go, as we need them.'

'Listen to her!' Black cried. 'There are no other members!'

This time Mo struck the table, bringing her fist down hard. 'We've enough to sort you out!'

Captain Black laughed sarcastically, but before either of them could shout anything else, Billy Cobb raised his hands for quiet. 'OK – OK. Let's keep this civilised. Mo, Eddie *misled* us, do you agree with that?'

Mo nodded reluctantly.

'And you agree that he was twice able to gain access to the Seagulls' heavily guarded camp? Once when the statue was blown up, and once when he was captured?'

'Yes.'

'And you don't think that was strange, that you were able to get in twice, undetected?'

Mo shook her head. 'We're good at what we do.'

Captain Black snorted. 'Billy – let's stop this charade now.'

'Well I think it's better if I—' Billy began to respond, but was immediately cut off.

'If you won't say it, I will.' Cobb fell silent. It was clear that although he was the Chairman of the Council of War and a powerful gang leader in his own right, Captain Black was absolutely in control. He turned his attention back to Mo, and as he spoke his upper lip seemed to curl up in distaste. 'Listen here, little Mo. We know exactly what's going on.'

'What are you talking about?'

'We know that we've been betrayed.'

'*Betrayed?*'

'Do you really think we're that gullible? Eddie

Malone has planned all this; he's gone over to the other side.'

'What?'

'He's addicted to crush; they've promised to supply him in return for information about us. He's sold us out!'

'That's rubbish! Eddie would never . . .'

'You're denying he's a crush addict?'

'Eddie's . . .'

'Are you denying it?'

How could he know? How could he possibly know?

Mo shook her head. 'He would never betray—'

'An addict will betray anyone in order to safeguard his supply.' It was Billy Cobb, his face grave, his voice depressed.

'Eddie wouldn't . . . Billy, I swear to God!'

'Mo – you've been on the streets long enough, you know what crush does to people.'

Mo nodded reluctantly. 'Yes, but . . .'

'Then you must agree that addicts are not to be trusted.'

Again, she had no alternative but to agree.

'And that the only thing worse than an addict, who really can't help himself once he's hooked, is the dealer who supplies the drugs. That they're the scum of the earth and that no gang which deals in drugs can have anything to do with our Alliance. You agree with that?'

'Yes, of course.'

Billy nodded slowly. Captain Black leant back in his chair with a self-satisfied smile.

'Then, Mo,' Billy began, 'I'm going to ask you to turn out your pockets.'

'*What?*'

'Empty your pockets, Mo.'

'I don't understand.'

'It's quite simple, Mo,' said Billy. 'Captain Black alleges that both you and Eddie Malone are addicted to crush. He alleges that you are Eddie's dealer. And that you get your crush directly from the Seagulls. He is accusing both you and Eddie of trading our secrets for crush.'

Mo was stunned.

And shocked.

Because the crush she had bought for Eddie was still burning a hole in her pocket.

Captain Black smiled triumphantly at her. 'You see, Mo, we have a mole inside the Seagulls' camp. We know you're a dealer. We know you've sold us out, you and Malone.'

'Is this true, Mo?' Billy Cobb demanded.

'No – don't be ridiculous. It's absolute . . .'

'Then turn out your pockets.'

Mo shook her head at them defiantly. 'I won't do it,' she said. She pointed at Black. 'You've set me up.'

'You're a liar, and a dealer!'

'Billy – Eddie attacked the Seagulls! He risked his life to blow up that statue, and he risked it again to try and find his brother! He needs your help now! Don't believe *him*. You know what he's like! He twists everything!'

Billy Cobb looked sadly at her. 'Mo – I'd like to believe you.'

'Then do it!'

'I will. As soon as you turn out your pockets and prove Captain Black wrong.'

Mo shook her head. Captain Black suddenly clicked his fingers, and the guards from the door rushed forward and grabbed her. She kicked out at one, hitting him hard, right in the willy, but even as he fell another grabbed her foot, and then they had her arms and were forcing her to the floor. They pinned her there. One guard looked up at Captain Black, who nodded. The guard then roughly searched her pockets. He produced a number of coins, a penknife, a packet of Polo mints, a battery, a lighter, string, an elastic band, a pencil, three needles, a key, an MP3 player, a conker, a straw, a tissue, a bus ticket, a razor blade, a single earring, a magnet, a directional compass, a computer disk, a small cross, a head and shoulders photograph of Eddie, a shoelace, a lipstick, four cotton buds and finally, a folded square of tinfoil, which they unfolded and then laid on the table before Captain Black and Billy Cobb.

They looked down at the crush tablets.

Billy Cobb tutted.

'You don't understand . . .' Mo started to say, but Captain Black cut her off by barking for her to be released.

The guards stepped back and she climbed warily to her feet.

Captain Black scowled at her across the table. 'You're finished, Mo,' he said. 'Your boyfriend is finished, and your gang is finished. Billy – with your permission?' Billy Cobb nodded. 'I'm doing you a favour, Mo. The easiest thing would be to just make you disappear the way Eddie Malone did to that baby. He probably sold it to get money for crush. But we're not like that. We're going to give you five minutes to get out of here, Mo. Then we're going to declare you an enemy of the Alliance. You step foot in Alliance territory ever again and we'll destroy you. Now get out of here while you still can. Go back to your drugs and your Seagulls.'

Black nodded at the guards, and they came forward again. Mo glared at Black, and then turned her attention to Cobb. 'You're making a mistake,' she said.

But Billy Cobb merely shook his head. 'Get her out of here,' he said.

They tried to grab her again, but she quickly raised her fists. 'Keep your bloody hands off me,' she hissed, with enough venom to make them hesitate. Then she strode forward, opened the boardroom door, and hurried away down the hall, and from there out of the building, still looking defiant, but feeling utterly lost and totally alone.

Thirty-two

'Are you ready to answer my questions *now*, Eddie Malone?'

It had been a long, cold, lonely night. It had also been a long, hot and crowded night. Because when he wasn't shivering, he was sweating. And when he wasn't feeling totally alone and abandoned, he had vivid nightmares filled with screaming Seagulls. At some point someone had opened the door and thrown some blankets in for him and he had flopped down on them like an exhausted, rabid dog. There were no windows in the little room, and they'd taken his watch from him, so he could only guess at what time it was. In fact, he didn't guess, because he didn't care. He only cared about one thing, and that was crush, and now Rotavia was standing over him, offering it to him once again.

Eddie looked up at her, and the crush in her hand. His throat was sore, his voice dry and raspy. 'I'll tell you anything you want, I just want to know what you've done with my brother.'

'We have done nothing with your brother.'

'He's OK then?'

'We have done nothing with your brother, because we have no idea who your brother is or where he is or why we should even care who he is or where he is. We only care about what you tried to do to us, about the babies you tried to kill. We want to know why you did this, we want to know what your gangs are planning next, we want to know why you don't leave us alone. We want answers, and we want them now.'

What was she saying to him? She didn't know who his brother was? *Of course she knows. She's playing tricks. She's trying to confuse me. Mind games. Brain washing.* He couldn't think straight, couldn't focus. He needed to clear his head. Only the crush could do that. Only the crush. Just one pill. Feel better. Think. She held the pill out to him. He reached for it – and she closed her fingers around it again.

'Do we have a deal?' she asked.

Eddie nodded quickly. She opened her hand. He reached for it again, and he almost, almost picked it up. The tips of his fingers were touching it. One quick lift and it would be into his mouth. Heaven was seconds away . . .

And yet he managed to stop himself.

He stared at it, at his own hand, shaking above it. Sweat dripped off his brow. His clothes were already stuck to him. The answer to *everything* was there in Rotavia's hand; in five minutes he could be feeling fantastic. He could make up any old nonsense to keep them happy. He could invent great battle plans and imaginary gangs, he could feel superb and still scare the pants off them with predictions of the terrible things that were going to happen to them once the Alliance attacked. And they might decide to kill him because of it, to make an example of him, but he didn't care, because he would have the crush, the crush!

And yet, still, he hesitated.

'I want my brother back.'

Rotavia rolled her eyes in frustration. 'We don't have your brother!'

'You kidnapped him! If he's dead, then just tell me, that's all I want to know!'

'For the last time – we do not have him or know of him.'

'I need to know what—'

'This isn't about what you need to know!' Rotavia exploded. 'You are our prisoner and you will answer our questions or you will suffer the consequences!'

'I don't care about the consequences!' Eddie roared back. 'I want my . . .'

She thrust the pill towards him again. 'Take it!'

His eyes flitted up to her. 'Do you . . . are you . . . still taking it?'

Rotavia glared at him for a moment, then quickly shook her head.

'How did you . . . stop?'

'Alexander locked me in a room and didn't let me out for three days.'

'How terrible was it?'

'It was like death! But worse! You do not want to try it! Now take the pill, answer my questions, then you will feel better. Take it!'

But instead of taking it, Eddie sat back on his blankets.

Rotavia stood in disbelief. 'What . . . what are you doing? You cannot! I have questions that need . . .'

Eddie shook his head. 'Close the door on your way out. And don't open it for three days.'

Rotavia stared at him, then abruptly turned for the door. She opened it, then paused for a moment. 'You will not do it. This crush . . .' and she held the pill up again, 'is different to what I took. It is even stronger. It will take more than three days. And look at you. You are weak. You can hardly stand. You will not beat it. You *cannot* beat it.'

Eddie rested his pounding head back against the cool wall. He closed his eyes. 'Watch me,' he said.

Of course, it was quite easy to say, 'Watch me', like he was a cool hero-type who could overcome the odds in a way that ordinary mortals could never hope to. But the truth is he regretted saying it almost immediately. Rotavia left the room and locked the door and suddenly he was all alone again, facing the prospect of continued and escalating misery, with the only bright light at the end of the tunnel being the faint possibility of the onset of death. That would cure his pain once and for all, although with his luck he'd probably find himself burning in hell.

Eddie lay on his blankets. He examined his injured hand – it was healing quite well now. His twisted ankle no longer ached. This fever, the pains, the sickness – it was all due to crush, or the lack of it. He had to beat it. *Beat the addiction. Get my strength back. Sort out my head.*

If I can just hold out.

If I can just hold out!

Rotavia kept a close eye on the prisoner during the next three days. She hated this Eddie Malone for what he had tried to do to her people – blowing up the statue, trying to steal their babies – but part of her admired him as well.

He was clearly sick and weak – that was the crush doing its work, and she had seen many of her fellow gang members in a similar state. Only a few of them, including herself, had ever been able to recover from their crush addiction. And she knew of none who had come off this new, stronger version of the drug. What's more – she'd actually offered Eddie Malone crush and he'd turned it down. If she'd been offered crush when she was in the middle of coming off it, she would have grabbed it with both hands. But he'd fought the temptation, and now he was paying the price – a living hell in that cold, dank cell.

Alexander was furious with her, though. He wanted answers. The whole camp was in a state of turmoil, afraid that at any time they were going to be attacked by the Alliance gangs. Guards relentlessly patrolled the perimeter; many had been on duty for so long that they were dead on their feet. All in all they had about one hundred and fifty gangsters. This made it very big for a single gang – but tiny compared to the numbers the Alliance could pull together. And of those one hundred and fifty members, at least forty of them were addicted to crush, and therefore liable to betray their comrades at the first offer of a fix.

Rotavia had been lucky – she'd escaped its deadly grip. But many hadn't, many had died; and others would, and soon.

There was a small peephole in the cell door, through which she could watch Eddie Malone as he tossed and turned and shouted and moaned. It was like watching an animal in a laboratory being given poison just to see how long it took to kill it. On the rare occasions when he did sleep, Rotavia quietly entered the room and left water and food for him. When he woke he always drank all of the water at once, but ignored the food. Or hurled it around the room.

'Will he survive?'

It was Alexander, standing behind her as she peered into the cell.

'I do not know.'

'We must know their plans, Rotavia.'

'I know. And we will. I promise.' She decided to change the subject. 'Any word from home?'

Alexander shook his head sadly. A ship

containing refugees was due to leave their devastated homeland any day now – a thousand more earthquake survivors would soon be crammed into this very camp. The adults already there were dreading their arrival because it was already so overcrowded, but the Seagulls themselves couldn't wait – an influx of new recruits would surely even up the sides in the coming war with the Alliance gangs. 'They keep postponing the departure,' said Alexander. 'If they don't leave soon, it's going to be too late for us.'

Rotavia nodded grimly and returned her attention to the cell. 'What if he dies?' she asked.

'Then we bury him.'

'But isn't he some kind of hero to them? Won't that make the Alliance even angrier?'

'What are you suggesting, Rotavia – that we release him? That we try to buy them off by freeing the dog they sent to kill our children?'

'He says he was looking for his brother.'

'Of course he does! He's trying to save his miserable skin!' Alexander shook his head angrily. 'I don't care whether he lives or dies in there – but I do care about the information he must have. Get me that information, Rotavia. We're running out of time.'

'If I get it – then what will we do with him?'

'We do what we always do to dogs that bite. We put them down. He is weak now – go to him, find out what you can.'

Rotavia nodded. He was right. Eddie Malone was a dog. A sick dog. But sometimes if you were nice to a sick dog, it wagged its tail – and that was exactly what she planned to do with Eddie Malone.

Thirty-three

Eddie became aware of the coolness only gradually. He had been in the grip of another relentless, pounding, horrific dream, set somewhere in the fires of hell, and then there had been some slight slither of hope which manifested itself in the shape of a freezing river into which he could dive and then be carried away on the fast currents. But when his eyes fluttered open there was no hell, and no river, just the bare cell and Rotavia kneeling beside him, pressing a damp sponge to his brow and looking very concerned.

'Thank you,' Eddie whispered through his cracked lips.

She had a basin full of water beside her. She dipped the sponge in again, then set it softly back on his brow. She gave it the slightest squeeze. Refreshing drops of water chased down the dry riverbeds of sweat on his cheeks and into his mouth. Eddie had never been one for drinking water – give him Coke any day – but this was something else entirely. He couldn't remember anything ever tasting so good. He raised his hand slowly, and pressed it down on the sponge. Again the water cascaded down his cheeks and into his mouth.

After a while, she helped him to sit up. She had brought soup as well, and at first he resisted, but eventually she managed to get several spoonfuls into him.

'Do you think . . .' he whispered, 'that I'm doing . . . OK?'

'You're doing . . . OK,' she said. She seemed warmer, friendlier than he remembered – perhaps because she had been an addict as well. She knew what he was going through.

'How . . . much . . . longer do you think?' he asked.

'Not long . . .' she said, although, thinking about it, he wasn't sure if she meant not long until he died or before he recovered. She gave him another spoonful of the soup, then asked quietly, 'Why do you want to make war with us?'

Eddie swallowed noisily. 'We . . . don't . . . you started it.'

She hesitated as she went to feed him the next spoonful. 'We did not start . . . anything.' She gave him the soup. 'We come to your country – not out of choice, but because our country is destroyed by earthquake. But as soon as we arrive . . . you people hate us.'

Eddie rested his head back against the wall. When she tried to give him more soup he raised his hand. 'No. No more. I think I'm going to be sick again.' He took a deep breath. He willed himself not to be. After a few moments the feeling of nausea passed.

'Why do you hate us?' Rotavia asked.

'We . . . don't . . . we . . . *they* . . . hate what you . . . *bring* . . .'

'Bring?'

'Crush.'

She looked at him incredulously. 'We . . . did not bring crush here. We never had crush before we came here. There is no crush in Ruritania.'

Eddie managed to shake his head without it falling off. 'That's . . . *rubbish*. That's what the whole war is about, you trying to . . . take over our gangs . . . by getting us hooked on . . . crush.'

Her mouth had dropped half open. 'Why would we want to take over your gangs?' she snapped, not trying to hide her anger now. 'Do you think we want to stay here? We want to go home to Ruritania. We want nothing to do with your country! We come here with no money, no jobs, we have nothing to do . . . then your gangs sell us crush and we get addicted and we die!'

Eddie gave a dry, grating laugh. 'That's . . . just . . . crap . . .' His head was starting to pound again. He closed his eyes. He allowed himself to slip down the wall and back on to his blankets. Surely this couldn't go on for much longer? This *agony*. He could still feel her beside him. Why didn't she just go and let him die in peace instead of trying to poison his mind further with her murky lies? Well he wasn't going to let her get away with it. He forced his eyes open again.

'You . . . started this war – you attacked *us* . . .'

'Oh no. *You* attacked us . . . you blew up General Killster's statue.'

'Only because . . . you attacked our meeting. The Ice Bowl. You . . . set fire to it . . .'

'That wasn't us . . .'

Eddie's anger was now masking the worst of his symptoms. 'You were bloody spotted! And I saw you later at the clinic – you had burns on your arm!'

He nodded down at her arm, and yes, there was definitely a scar there. She didn't try to hide it. She shook her head. 'I got burned trying to put the fire *out*.'

'Yeah. *Right*.'

'I swear.'

'Uh-huh. You were seen.'

Rotavia jumped angrily to her feet. She snarled down at him. Any pretence of concern was now gone. 'I do not deny being there, Eddie Malone,' she said sternly. 'We knew there was a big meeting of all the gangs, so we sneaked in to try and find out what you were planning. We are entitled to do that if it concerns us.'

'You were spying, you didn't like what you heard, so you set fire to the building!'

'No! We sneaked around to the back to try and find a way in . . . and there was this boy there . . . and he was setting fire to all these boxes at the back – he caused the fire. I knew there were lots of people inside and I didn't want them hurt so I tried to put the fire out, but I didn't have anything to use but my bare hands, and that's how I got burned.'

'So you were actually trying to save us? Yeah. *Right*.'

'I swear. If I saw the boy today, I could point him out to you.'

'Uh-huh.'

'Ginger hair. He had ginger hair. And glasses.

He was laughing like a madman. Ginger. That's what he was. There are no ginger Seagulls! *He* set fire to your precious meeting – not me, not us! But you're never going to believe us, are you? Because we're Seagulls and we lie and we cheat and we sell you drugs, isn't that right!'

She stormed from the room, slamming the door behind her.

Eddie stared after her.

Ginger.

Ginger and glasses.

And a liking for setting fire to things. *My God! Gary Gilmore!*

Thirty-four

Rotavia did not return until the next morning, and when she did it was only because Eddie hammered on the cell door for an hour and a half, exhausting himself completely, demanding with every breath he could manage that she be summoned. When she arrived, ready for another fight, she found Eddie completely transformed. Yes – he still looked dreadful, his hair plastered across his head, his clothes dirty and stinking, but there was a brightness in his eyes, a new determination written across his face. It was clear that he was over the worst of his fight to come off crush. He was winning. She had expected that he would lose the battle, that Alexander would order his body buried in some quiet corner of the camp under cover of darkness – but here he was, looking considerably stronger and seemingly desperate to talk to her. But she wasn't about to give him an easy time. He had destroyed General Killster's statue, he had been caught red-handed trying to do something to the little orphan babies. However, she was thrown by his first words.

'I'm sorry,' Eddie said.

'*What?*'

'I'm sorry. For blowing up the statue. For breaking into the crèche. I'm sorry.'

Rotavia looked suspiciously at him. 'Why are you sorry now? If you think we're going to let you go just because you're—'

'It's not that. There's been a massive misunderstanding. I know you didn't set fire to the Ice Bowl. I know who did it. As soon as you described him I knew.'

Rotavia gave a little shrug. 'So what difference does that make?'

'Well,' said Eddie, 'it means I shouldn't have blown the statue up.'

'And I say again, what difference does that make? The fact is – you did blow it up and must be punished for it.'

Eddie came towards her, and she tensed suddenly, ready for a fight. There were two guards standing just outside the door. All she had to do was call.

'I know that, I know . . . but don't you see, war was declared between you and us because of the fire – but if you didn't start the fire, there's no reason for the war. If you let me go I could explain it to them and . . .' He stopped. She was shaking her head. 'What?'

'Do you think they would really stop the war because you said it was a mistake?'

'Well, of course . . .'

'I am not a fool, Eddie Malone! They mean to have war! The meeting you had at your Dundonald Ice Bowl was to plan a war!'

'No it wasn't! It was just to . . . well it was just to – you know – talk about . . .'

She laughed dryly. 'What do you have – a debating society? A nice little talk over your nice cups of tea?'

He had to admit she had a point. War had been in the air long before the fire broke out.

But why?

Because we don't like the Seagulls and their drugs.

Yet Rotavia says the drugs don't come from their side.

If she told the truth about the fire, what if she's also telling it about the drugs?

Eddie's thoughts were interrupted by Rotavia pulling out one of the chairs at the table and sitting down. She indicated for him to sit opposite. 'Now you must tell us how many gangs will be involved in the attack, and where they will strike. You must answer these questions now. Alexander has run out of patience with you. He has allowed you time to recover only on my word that you will provide this information. Now . . . ?'

'I can't.'

'You must. Otherwise you will be . . . disposed of.'

'And I'm telling you I can't. I don't know anything about their battle plans.'

'You must know. You are one of their leaders. They talk of you as a great hero.'

Had he been his normal self, he might have blushed at this. But things were too serious for that now. He just said, 'I'm not a hero . . . I'm just trying to find my brother.'

Rotavia sighed. 'You *must* tell us. If I go back without . . .'

'And I'm telling you I can't. I don't know.'

'Don't know . . . or won't tell? It seems to me, Eddie Malone, that you have gone through a terrible time coming off crush – only to waste your life now in this way. And how will you ever find your brother if you are dead?'

'And I'm telling you – I don't know.'

'That is your final word?'

Eddie looked at her for a long time. In a strange way, this angry young woman reminded him of Mo. He thought she would probably be just as good to have on an adventure. But he would never find out. His final word? Eddie had been so close to death so many times in the last few days and weeks that final words had lost any real meaning. Every time he came up with final words or thoughts or images, he had to rethink them all again at a later date, because he always came through, he always survived, he always worked out how to escape or confuse or defeat his enemy. Rotavia wasn't his enemy, exactly, but Alexander – he didn't doubt for one moment that Alexander would have him killed.

'Well?'

Still he didn't respond. So Rotavia stood and walked to the door.

Eddie knew he had to say something now, or he might not have another chance. Even he knew that he must be close to using up his lucky escapes and fortunate rescues. Sooner or later he was going to end up dead. It might be right *now* if he didn't say the right thing.

She opened the door. She glanced back at him, raised a final questioning eyebrow, then turned to leave.

Finally, just as the door was almost closed, he said, 'Rotavia.'

She stopped, then slowly turned back.

'I cannot tell you the battle plans, because I don't know them.' She went to snap something back at him about wasting her time, but he quickly followed it with, 'But I do know how to stop this war.'

Her brow furrowed. She took half a step back into the room. 'How?'

Eddie explained that it was all to do with crush. The Alliance disliked and feared the Seagulls mainly because they had introduced crush to the city and wanted to control its distribution. The Seagulls, on the other hand, disliked and feared the Alliance mainly because the Alliance had been selling them crush and turning their members into brainless zombies.

'Don't you see?' he asked Rotavia. 'Each side thinks the other is to blame.'

She considered this for a long moment, then shrugged. 'So?'

'Well *somebody* introduced crush. *Somebody* is manufacturing it. *Somebody* is making vast amounts of money from it. And *somebody* is causing kids on both sides to die or get sick or turn into great steaming brainless vegetables. If we find out who that is, then maybe we can stop crush being made at all – and then there'll be no reason to fight. Or at least one less reason.'

Her eyes narrowed. Eddie could almost see her brain cells jabbering excitedly with each other, trying to work out if this was indeed a sensible suggestion or a wasted-looking Irish kid's lame attempt to squirm out of his richly deserved punishment.

'So you're suggesting what?'

'I find who that somebody is.'

'You?' Rotavia didn't do a very good job of hiding her disbelief. 'You? So, we just let you go. Then you go straight back to the Alliance and lead them into war against us.'

'I won't. I swear. I don't want a war. I just want to find out where my brother is, and who's behind these drugs.'

Rotavia shook her head. 'You really think we should trust *you* to do this?'

Eddie sighed. 'Rotavia – if you're going to live in this country, sooner or later you have to start trusting someone, don't you?'

Eddie spent the next hour sitting at the table, worrying about the ten thousand things that had gone wrong in the last few days and weeks. Starting with Paddy's disappearance – no, even before that, with him snubbing Mo at the train station – no, even before that, with his discovery of the letters from his dad. No – even before that, with Scuttles moving into the apartment. No – his dad having an affair with Spaghetti Legs and running away to Liverpool. Yes – that's where it all started. He tried to think of anything that was messed up in his life before his dad left, and he couldn't. Everything was perfect. At least, perfect for him. Obviously something had gone dreadfully wrong between his mum and dad.

But that wasn't my fault.

Or was it?

He was just beginning to think about that depressing subject, when the door opened again and Rotavia was standing there. 'You are to come with me,' she said crisply, then turned on her heel and led him out of the cell and down a short corridor. They climbed a set of stairs, went along another corridor, then up a second set of steps before emerging into what Eddie recognised as the inside of one of the wooden huts. Clearly he had been held prisoner in some kind of secret underground complex. Alexander was standing against a window on the far side, looking out. There were three doors in all – the one Eddie was standing in, one on the far side leading out to the rectangle of grass, and the third, opening on to the main camp itself. Two guards stood by this door. Eddie stood where he was for a moment, then Rotavia put a hand on his shoulder and indicated for him to approach Alexander.

Eddie crossed the room and stopped a couple of metres behind him. He was wearing his black Seagulls uniform. Rotavia stood behind Eddie.

'Do you see . . . *this* . . . Eddie Malone?' Alexander spoke without turning. He also spoke in more or less perfect English. Unless he'd undertaken a crash course in languages in the past few days, it seemed clear that he'd been able to speak it all along. Eddie realised that his double act with Rotavia during his interrogation must have been an attempt to unnerve him. Alexander was nodding out of the window. Eddie moved a little closer. Outside he could see the rectangle of grass where he'd blown up General Killster's statue. Except the statue was no longer in bits – it had been completely repaired and now stood towering over the ranks of Seagulls standing in dark rows before it. Eddie could only guess at how many of them there were – a hundred at least, quite possibly more. 'These are our warriors. When the battle comes, they will fight to the death.'

'It's, uhm, very impressive,' said Eddie.

'Impressive – yes. They are brave, but there are not enough of us. Not yet. Very soon, however, our comrades from across the sea will land, and then we *will* have enough.' Alexander turned from the window. 'Rotavia has told me what you have said about the crush. And while I do not truly believe all that you say, I would like to know more. You also spoke to her of trust – and now I am going to show you that I understand the concept; that despite the fact that you destroyed our most revered statue and were caught in the act of trying to harm our orphaned children, I am going to release you – on your word that you will find out the source of this crush and report it back to me. Do I have your word?'

Eddie nodded 'You have it.'

'Very well.'

Alexander turned back to the window. At the far end of the room the two guards opened the door leading into the outer camp. Eddie hesitated for a moment, then began to move towards the doorway.

Freedom.

I can hardly believe it.

But he had barely started before Alexander spoke again, stopping him in his tracks.

'Just one thing,' he said.

I knew it. Too good to be true.

'Yes?'

'Rotavia must go with you.'

'*What?*' It was Rotavia.

Alexander turned and smiled benevolently at her. 'One from our side, one from his, Rotavia.'

'But I cannot go with this . . .' She glared at Eddie as she struggled for the right word. In the end she said something in her own language. It didn't sound very complimentary.

Alexander shook his head. 'You must go, Rotavia. It is in our interests.'

'But the war, the battle – I must lead the—'

'Rotavia, if what he says is right, then perhaps we can avert the war.' Alexander turned his gaze on Eddie. 'Yes, Eddie Malone, there is a place for trust. But many trusting people have ended up stabbed in the back. Rotavia will go with you. If you find this – *source* – of crush . . . then each of our sides will be informed and perhaps the war might be averted. I do not hold out much hope – but it is right that we try.' With that he turned and walked quickly toward the door leading into the inner rectangle. As he appeared in the entrance, his troops, his soldiers, his Seagulls, quickly sprang to attention.

Eddie glanced across at Rotavia, standing quietly fuming, staring after Alexander.

'Well?' he asked.

'Well *what*?' Rotavia snarled back.

Eddie shrugged. Rotavia *did* remind him of Mo. And he suspected she would turn out to be just as big a pain in the neck.

Thirty-five

The first thing he wanted to do, he told Rotavia on the bus back into the city centre, was to contact one of his senior officers. Mo. She knew the city much better than he did – she knew every street and alley, every gang, every scam, every everything he could think of. Eddie made it sound like she was just one member of his huge gang. Rotavia didn't need to know that she was just about the only other one there was. There was Gary Gilmore of course – but as he had almost started the war single-handedly by setting fire to the Ice Bowl, he thought it was a better idea to keep him out of the picture entirely.

Rotavia nodded wisely as he sang Mo's praises, and then said, 'No.'

'No? What do you mean no?'

'No one else. Just us.'

'Us? You? We can't do this ourselves. We need Mo. And not just Mo. We need back-up. Support. Surveillance. Somewhere we can conduct interviews and plan raids and—'

'Just us.'

'Just us?'

'Just us.'

'You make it sound like you're in charge.'

'I am in charge.'

'Are not.'

'Yes I am.'

'No you're not.'

'I am.'

'You're not.'

'Yes I am.'

'No you're not.'

Eddie sighed.

Rotavia sighed.

Eddie said, 'We should be an example to others. A shining example of how two young people from either side of a divided community can work together to solve their shared problems.'

Rotavia thought about this for a moment. 'I agree.'

'Good, so let's call for Mo and then we can—'

'No.'

'No what?'

'No, we cannot call for anyone.'

'Excuse me, but you're making it sound like you're in charge again.'

'I am in charge. Do I have to remind you that I secured your release, that but for me you'd still be in that cell, or quite possibly lying in an unmarked grave? I persuaded Alexander to let you go. I accepted the responsibility. And I agreed to go on this crazy mission with you. It is clear that I am in charge. And I say we don't need any help.'

Eddie cleared his throat. 'I appreciate what you've done. I know I could still be in the cell. I'm aware that I could also be in a shallow grave somewhere. However, Alexander did not specify who was in charge. I was there. I heard it all.'

Rotavia cleared her throat. 'You are a prisoner. I am in charge.'

'With respect,' said Eddie, 'I am no longer a prisoner. And you are no longer in charge.'

They sat quietly for another ten minutes. As they approached the city centre Eddie began to spot small groups of boys and girls he recognised as members of different gangs moving through the streets – all in the same direction.

They're gathering for war.

Rotavia had a small, black canvas bag sitting on her lap. She opened it up and withdrew a mobile phone. She keyed in a number. A moment later she said, 'Alexander?' And then she spoke for about three minutes in her mother tongue. She seemed quite angry, but for all that Eddie understood she might have been discussing the weather. Then she snapped the phone shut and said, 'Alexander says you are in charge. It is your city. I observe and report.'

Eddie nodded wisely. He tried his best not to smile. 'Well,' he said, 'we'll work something out.'

He asked to borrow her phone, and called Mo. Her dad answered and demanded to know who this was.

'Uhm, Eddie,' he said.

'Eddie? That little creep friend of hers?'

'Uhm, yes,' said Eddie.

'Well she's gone and bloody disappeared with my bloody money! You see her you tell her I'm gonna beat her to death, you hear? You hear me?'

Then he slammed the phone down.

Eddie nodded at the mobile for a few seconds longer, then turned to Rotavia and said, 'She's out on a mission and can't be contacted.'

But Rotavia wasn't paying attention. The bus had pulled into the station now, and all she could see were dozens and dozens of kids milling about. They weren't exactly wearing uniforms like her own gang did, but they were undeniably gangsters.

GALWAY COUNTY LIBRARIES

You could tell by the way they moved in groups. The way some of them wore a particular style of trouser, or a type of haircut, or baseball cap. Eddie recognised a couple of Cobb's Commandos, the skull and crossbones of the Ormeau Pirates . . . the Churchill Regulars . . . three Ramsey Street Wheelers he'd once been attacked by. The thing was, although they were all standing in their own groups, there was no apparent animosity between them. Usually, if you got even two different gangs in the same area, there'd be tension, threats, perhaps some violence. They might be members of the Alliance together, but it didn't mean they were friends. But here, in the bus station, they were all standing in the same general area without a cross word between them. Waiting. To be taken to some assembly point. To go to war.

Eddie looked at his watch. It was a little after one-thirty in the afternoon. If there was to be an attack, or a battle, it wouldn't be until night-time, he was fairly certain of that. That was when the gangs really did their work – when everyone else was sleeping, when there was less chance of them being disturbed. But darkness wouldn't be long in coming. They needed to get to work. And fast.

* * *

They kept their heads down as they exited the bus station via an under-used back entrance. Luckily Rotavia had changed out of her Seagulls uniform into a pair of blue jeans and a zip-up jersey with a baseball cap pulled down low over her distinctive black hair and olive complexion. Eddie also wore a baseball cap, again pulled low, so that the assembled gangsters wouldn't recognise their hero – or child killer, depending on their point of view.

From the station they made their way to what Rotavia called 'Drug Alley'. Eddie recognised it as the place Mo had gone to buy him the crush. According to Rotavia it was also where the majority of the drug-addicted Seagulls bought their supplies. It was one of those city-centre streets which didn't quite fall under the control of any particular gang, so it was a natural haunt for those who weren't gangsters, or who'd been thrown out for being too violent, or mad, or both. It was only about a hundred metres long, but situated as it was between two huge buildings which blocked out the sun, and with its streetlights permanently smashed, it existed in a kind of permanent twilight. There had once been shops and offices on either side, but these had long ago been closed down, locked and boarded up. Some were still like that, others had been broken into. Crush victims lay in doorways, out of their heads or sick as dogs. Drug dealers sat in the darkness of the empty shops, hissing out at Eddie and Rotavia as soon as they entered the alley.

'Get crush, get crush . . .' 'Best crush . . .' 'Cheap crush . . .'

Usually, when Eddie got into trouble and was attacked or chased, there was a fairly good reason for it. Here, in this alley, it felt like you could be attacked for no reason at all. Just because you were there. Eddie glanced at Rotavia. She didn't look any happier to be there than he did. 'Well,' he said, 'let's get started.'

When the next voice slithered out, whispering, 'Crush . . . great crush . . . get your crush,' they moved towards it, but stopped short of the darkened shop doorway. 'Here – in here . . .' came the voice again. But they stood their ground, and a moment later a hunched figure, his skin almost translucent, scurried halfway towards them, then waved them back. 'Here . . . here . . .'

'*Here*,' Eddie said firmly.

The boy – and he was definitely a boy, even though he looked like a hundred-year-old corpse – hesitated. He didn't like to make his deals in full view of the alley's other denizens, but when he saw movement coming from the other doorways he suddenly realised that he could lose this deal to his neighbours, so he came right out to them, his hand out already, showing them two pills of crush. Eddie stared down at it. He felt the very slightest tingle in his fingers. A vague hint of a warm glow in his stomach. The crush had been so wonderful for a while, an amazing feeling of . . .

'Eddie . . .'

He looked up sharply. Rotavia was glaring at him. *What's wrong with her? I'm only looking at—* What was he thinking of? Crush had nearly killed him. It destroyed everything it touched. Eddie quickly shook his head at the ancient-looking boy. 'Not enough,' he said.

The boy's dull eyes seemed to brighten with possibility. 'How much you want?'

Rotavia pulled off her baseball cap. 'How much do you have?'

The boy quickly noted her hair and complexion. 'Ah,' he said, 'you come from the camp. Good Seagulls, good Seagulls. I have twenty. You buy twenty?'

'Not enough,' said Eddie.

A kind of gurgling sound came from the boy's

throat. It was probably a laugh, but it sounded like he was choking. 'Not enough? Twenty-plenty!' He began to gurgle again, but it was cut off in midstream by Rotavia grabbing him by his grubby T-shirt and pushing him back hard against the boarded-up shop-front.

'There's a war coming,' she barked, 'the camp might be cut off for weeks. We need to buy crush now, lots of it.'

'How . . . how much . . . ?' the boy stammered.

'Two hundred.'

'*Two hundred?*' The boy stared at Rotavia in disbelief, then at Eddie, to see if they were joking. 'I . . . don't have two hundred . . .'

'Then find us someone who has.'

The boy seemed to gulp for air for a moment, then darted away along the street. About twenty metres up he ducked into another shop doorway and disappeared. Eddie said, 'This place gives me the creeps.'

Rotavia shrugged. 'I used to come here all the time.'

'So the dealers must know you.'

'Every time I came back, there were new dealers. The old ones died.'

There was movement up ahead. The boy was

ushering someone else out on to the footpath – an older boy, sixteen, seventeen, in a smart green suit, hurried towards them. But as he drew closer they saw that the suit was not so smart, that the knees were stained and one arm was ripped. The boy himself had red, watery eyes and a dark stubble on his chin.

'I hear you want two hundred.' Eddie nodded. 'How'd I know you're not cops?'

'We're *thirteen*,' said Eddie.

'Don't prove nothing,' said the boy. He reached into his suit pocket and withdrew a single crush. He held it out to Eddie. 'Here – swallow this. Cops won't take crush, that's for sure, you swallow, you prove you're no cop.'

Eddie knew he couldn't afford to hesitate. Too much depended on getting to the source of the crush. He took the little white pill and popped it into his mouth. He was aware of Rotavia staring at him. But he had no choice. He swallowed, then opened his mouth to prove it.

'OK,' said the green-suited boy. 'You have money?'

'We have it,' said Rotavia. Her voice sounded dry and harsh and angry. She opened her bag and gave the boy a quick flash of a wallet full of twenty-pound notes which Alexander had provided for them.

The boy nodded appreciatively. 'OK. We know there's a war coming, so price goes up. But let me call the boss, then we can do business.'

He turned and hurried back up to his doorway, followed by the other boy, who kept glancing back at them and gurgling as he went. As they both disappeared back into the darkness, Rotavia spun angrily towards him.

'How could you?' she hissed. 'You nearly die on crush – but as soon as he offers you take! Now you are right back to start – only worse! Why did you do it? You could have refused! We could have found someone else! Why did you . . . ?'

And then she stopped, because Eddie was sticking his tongue out at her.

More importantly, sitting on the tongue, completely complete, was the crush.

A smile instantly raced across her face. 'You didn't . . . ?'

Eddie said, 'Awwwwwahburrrawaaaahawah hhey . . .' Or at least that's what it sounded like, because it is practically impossible to speak without moving your tongue. So he held his hand up, and then for the benefit of whoever might still be watching them, he pretended to cough. He then surreptitiously indicated for Rotavia to look at the footpath. And there it sat, the crush. An instant later Eddie brought his foot down on it, and ground it into a million pieces.

Further up the alley, the boy in the green suit reappeared in his doorway. He waved them up. 'Boss wants to see you,' he shouted.

As they moved towards him Rotavia whispered, 'Thank you for doing that – it must have been very hard.'

'No problem,' said Eddie.

In fact, it was one of the hardest things he had ever done. And every cell in his body wanted to go back there and lick the footpath.

Thirty-six

The boy in the dirty green suit led them up a set of dank, evil-smelling stairs to the first floor of the abandoned shop and into a large, empty room. At the far end a hole had been knocked in the wall, and beyond it they could see an identical room, presumably belonging to the shop next door. Identical, save for the desk, and the boy sitting behind it. He was also wearing a suit, but this one was clean, and looked expensive. He had a gold chain around his neck, a big gold watch on his wrist and a diamond stud in each earlobe. He clearly wasn't short of a few pounds. He also looked like he was about nine years old.

He stood up, came round from his desk and strode towards them with his hand out. 'Hi – I'm Tommy, have a seat. Do you want a cigar?' His hair was slicked back, his eyes were bright and his teeth were white and shining.

Eddie glanced at Rotavia. Under normal circumstances they might have burst into laughter at the sight of this little boy pretending to be a big, flashy businessman. But they didn't, because they guessed that he actually *was* a flashy, big businessman. Big in the business sense. Small in the physical sense.

So instead of laughing they shook hands and Eddie said, 'We want to buy – we want to buy a lot.'

'I hear two hundred.'

'Four.'

'Four? I heard two.'

'You look like a man who can get us four.'

Tommy nodded appreciatively. He walked back behind his desk, sat down and proceeded to punch numbers into a pocket calculator. 'Four would cost you . . .' He didn't tell them the figure. He just smiled to himself. Eddie had no idea what percentage Tommy was on, but clearly his cut of four hundred crush would buy him an awful lot of new jewellery. Tommy looked up at them. 'I can do four. When do you want them?'

'Now,' Eddie said firmly.

Rotavia nodded beside him. 'We don't want them from the losers around here, we don't want crush that's been sitting in someone's pants for the past six months. We want fresh, and we want the new stuff. The stronger stuff.'

Tommy rocked back in his leather swivel chair. Eddie heard a noise from the stairs behind. He turned to find that three boys in denim jackets had arrived and were standing with baseball bats in their hands. They weren't waiting for a game to start.

'What is this?' Rotavia demanded.

Tommy smiled. 'Well, a leading Seagull and Eddie Malone, hero on the run – I have to protect myself, no?'

So, he was recognised.

'We don't want any trouble,' said Eddie.

Tommy shrugged. 'There's also the fact that you appear to have enough money with you to buy four hundred crush. That would keep me in cigars for quite a while.'

Eddie quickly scanned the room – there was a set of stairs behind Tommy's desk, but there was no way of knowing where they led. Then there were the stairs they'd come up on, but the hole in the wall leading to them was guarded by the boys with the bats. Eddie had recovered well from his struggle with crush, but he was still far from his full strength. He had never seen Rotavia in a scrap, but he suspected she was pretty good. If it came to it, they would put up a good fight.

We didn't come for this. We cannot be sidetracked.

Eddie shook his head. 'Sure – you can take our money. And sure, you'll live nicely for a couple of weeks. That's if you live at all.' He nodded at Rotavia. 'She's second in command at the camp. They know we're here. Anything happens to us, you'll have every Seagull in Belfast after you.'

Tommy didn't seem particularly worried by this. 'From what I hear,' he said, 'maybe by tomorrow there won't be any Seagulls left.' He opened a side drawer on his desk and removed a cigar. He lit it. He coughed a little, then puffed out smoke towards them. It stank. The cigar was so big, and his mouth was so small, that he looked like he was smoking a tree-trunk. 'Or perhaps they'll just be an endangered species.'

Rotavia didn't like this one bit. 'We're going to be here long after you're dead and buried,' she growled.

Tommy paused in his smoking. 'Well then,' he said, 'whatever I do – it's a bit of a gamble.'

Rotavia was about to snap something else, but Eddie cut in. 'Well, Tommy, yes it is. And sure you could take our money. But we're not just talking about four hundred crush today, we're talking about four hundred crush every week. Think about how much you'd make off that.'

'If they're still here.'

'If they're still here.'

'Every week?'

Eddie nodded.

Tommy's fingers shot back to the calculator, jabbed excitedly at the buttons; and then he stared at whatever figure appeared on the little screen. When he looked up, he was smiling widely. 'Ladies and gentlemen,' he said, 'let's talk business.'

He stood and put his hand out. Eddie shook it immediately. Rotavia hesitated, but Eddie gave her a hard look and she reluctantly offered her hand. He could tell she thought Tommy was a slime-ball, but they needed to play along with him for now.

So they spent another fifteen minutes haggling over the money. Eventually they agreed on a figure, then endured another round of handshaking.

'OK,' Tommy said at last, 'now I need the money. Then I go and collect the stuff.' Rotavia glanced at Eddie, who nodded. She opened her bag and withdrew the notes Alexander had given her. She handed them to Tommy. He counted through them quickly. 'All right,' he said, 'you give me, say, one hour. Then meet me back here. All right?'

'All right.'

Eddie turned for the hole in the wall. Rotavia hurried after him.

'Hey – Eddie?'

Eddie stopped. He was right at the hole. The boys with the baseball bats had moved to one side to let them through. 'What?'

'Word on the street is you betrayed the Alliance – joined the Seagulls. I guess it's true.' Eddie didn't say anything. Tommy shrugged. 'Doesn't worry me – why do you think I'm here? You're just like me, Eddie, you'll betray anyone if the price is right, isn't that so?'

Eddie still didn't say anything. He gave Tommy a hard look, then ducked through the hole.

Thirty-seven

It was a simple plan, but its success depended almost entirely on something they had no control over: good luck. Their thinking was that by insisting on such a huge amount of crush Tommy wouldn't be able to put his hands on it right there in his office. He would have to leave the building and go to whoever supplied him. That would either be an even bigger dealer, or whoever was manufacturing the stuff. Either way, Eddie and Rotavia had to follow him, and make sure they weren't spotted. That was where the good luck was required.

They took up a position just inside a Waterstone's bookshop, about twenty metres down from the entrance to Drug Alley. The shop's front window gave them a good view of the alley; luckily the far end had been blocked off years ago, so there was no escaping that way. They supposed the empty shops had rear exits as well, but as there was no way they could keep watch on all of them, they just had to hope that a boy like Tommy, who seemed to take such pride in being seen in the flashiest clothes and jewellery, would prefer to parade down the main street like the little peacock he was, rather than sneak along dangerous back alleys.

'But what if he sends someone else, someone we don't recognise?' Rotavia whispered over a cookbook she was pretending to read.

'He won't – he wouldn't trust anyone else to collect the four hundred crush. He'll get it himself.'

Eddie sounded more confident than he was. War was about to break out and he was standing reading a Spiderman comic in a Belfast bookshop. How long should they give him? Tommy had told them to come back in an hour. Ten minutes had already passed and there was still no sign of him. That left fifty minutes – say it took twenty minutes to get wherever the drugs were, ten minutes to get them, twenty minutes to get back. But what if he didn't leave for another ten minutes, or ... the possibilities were endless. His head would explode if he tried to work them all out. But he couldn't stop himself. What he needed was something to calm him down, something to help him relax. A good lick at that pavement. Or if Tommy came back with four hundred crush perhaps he could sneak a few of them into his pocket when no one was looking.

No.

No.

No.

And suddenly there he was, striding purposefully past the bookshop window. If he had bothered to look to his left he would have spotted them, but he walked straight on. Rotavia immediately moved to follow – but Eddie held her back. She looked surprised, and was trying to twist away when she saw the three boys with baseball bats pass their window.

'Bodyguards,' whispered Eddie.

'Sorry.'

They gave it another ten seconds, then slipped out of the bookshop and began to follow Tommy and his entourage. They were careful to keep crowds of shoppers between them, at least for the first five minutes. But then as they began to move away from Royal Avenue, both the shops and the shoppers began to thin out and they had to drop back even further.

Luckily, Tommy was very much lost in his own dreams about all the money he was about to make while his bodyguards were too busy laughing and joking amongst themselves to pay much attention to what was going on around them. Just to be extra safe, Rotavia took off her zip-up jersey and slipped it into her bag and turned her baseball cap back to front; then she crossed the road and followed from the other side. Eddie took his jumper off and tied it around his waist; he tossed his baseball cap away. Hopefully, if any of the baseball squad looked around they wouldn't give either of them a second glance.

They walked for another ten minutes, following the curve of the Lagan River towards the docks. They entered a huge industrial area full of warehouses used for the storage of goods either brought in from abroad by ship, or waiting to be shipped out to other countries. Eddie and Rotavia dropped back even further, because there was less cover here; the warehouses weren't packed up close together like rows of shops, but separated by wide open spaces, and car parks, and many of them were fenced off. There were security gates and security guards and at some of the fences Alsatian dogs barked and yelped as they passed. Luckily, the road running between the warehouses was wide and rumbled loudly with the steady flow of articulated lorries, so that when the dogs barked the sound was quickly drowned out. Eddie tried to remember the map on his wall that showed which parts of the city were controlled by which gangs. He knew there had once been a gang called the Docking Squad, but he seemed to recall that they'd been swallowed by a larger outfit. He thought perhaps that there were so many rich pickings here that the area was constantly being fought over; that the warehouses were probably controlled by different gangs at different times. Not that it seemed to matter right now – there were no gangsters to be seen anywhere.

They're all off to war.

Up ahead, Tommy and the baseball boys had now stopped. They were gathered around a hole in a fence surrounding what appeared to be an empty warehouse. Eddie and Rotavia, about a hundred metres away, pressed themselves against another fence and watched as the boys waited for a gap in the traffic before jumping through the hole. They hurried across a car park, stood for a moment in the shadow of the warehouse, then darted around a corner and out of sight.

Rotavia pulled her bag around and reached inside for her mobile phone. As she opened it and began to dial Eddie said, 'What are you doing?'

'I am letting Alexander know that we have found source of crush.'

Eddie reached across to cut the line. 'We haven't found anything yet. All we've found is a hole in a fence.'

'But they must—'

'They might have just gone in for a pee.'

'I think not. This has to be where they get it.'

She pulled the phone away from him and began to dial again.

'Rotavia – *no*. We have to find out.'

'And how do we do that?'

'How do you think? We go in and see.'

She looked surprised. 'In there?'

'Yes!'

'But . . . I am here only to observe and report.'

'I know that – so we go in, we observe, we report. Rotavia – what are you going to tell him? Alexander, put the war on hold, we've found a big building? I don't think so. Now come on.'

Eddie started walking towards the hole in the fence. Rotavia hesitated. She looked at her phone again. Following people was one thing. Acting tough was easy enough. But she'd never done anything like this before, even though she had no idea what 'this' was. However, she knew she couldn't let Alexander down. She couldn't let the rest of the Seagulls down, or all of the people of Ruritania. So she took a deep breath and hurried after Eddie.

The warehouse *appeared* from the outside to be disused – there were huge padlocks on the gates, and the car park surrounding it was covered in broken glass and littered with rubbish – but Eddie knew from past experience how appearances could be deceptive. They squeezed through a broken door and on to the floor of the warehouse. There was rubble everywhere, and the air was thick with dust. Abandoned crates and cardboard boxes lay all around. Pigeons flew about. There were huge, green-tinged puddles where the rain had come in through holes in the roof but had been unable to drain away. And there was also . . . well, a *smell*. Not a rotting smell, or a polluted smell, or a damp one, but . . .

Rotavia was sniffing too. 'Crush,' she whispered.

She was right.

The light was poor inside, and he wished he had the night-vision goggles with him. They crept along the inside wall of the warehouse, feeling their way, listening for the slightest noise, following their noses more than anything. It was clearly a huge building, and although this storage end of it was deserted, they could see in the distance a three-storey bank of dark offices, which must once have been used as the administration area.

There was more than enough discarded packing material to provide cover for them as they hurried forward. As they drew closer to the offices they knelt down behind a large wooden box which was lying on its side, with squares of polystyrene hanging out of it, and peered up at a set of stairs which led to what appeared to be the reception area.

'You keep watch on the stairs,' Eddie whispered, 'I'll go and see if there's another way in around the back.'

'No, I go where you go.'

Eddie was about to argue with her, but then a door suddenly opened above them. They ducked down as two boys – each of them wearing white coats and what appeared to be gas masks and carrying a heavy bucket between them – carefully began to negotiate the steps. It was gloomy enough for Eddie and Rotavia to watch without there being much danger of them being discovered. The boys reached the floor of the warehouse, then crossed to a metal grating. They began to cautiously pour the steaming contents of their bucket into it. Clearly it was some kind of chemical waste. As it gurgled away a misty cloud wafted towards Eddie and Rotavia – and they were soon enveloped by *that* smell. Eddie couldn't help himself. Although he tried to mask it from his companion, he nevertheless breathed deeply in. Immediately a tantalising hint of crush spread through him.

My God, he thought, *no wonder they're wearing gas masks!*

As the boys disappeared back up the stairs Rotavia excitedly whispered, 'They're making it here!'

Less than a minute later the doors opened again and the boys reappeared with another bucket.

If they were making crush here, it seemed that they were making *a lot* of it. Part of him wanted to just stay where they were and breath in that delicious cloud again. It would be so easy just to lapse back into it. But he forced himself to focus on his mission. He had to. He had to think of Patrick. If he fell under the sway of crush again, then all hope of finding his little brother would surely be lost.

Rotavia tugged lightly on his arm.

'Now we know crush is made here, now we call.'

But again, Eddie shook his head. 'So far we've only seen two boys in gas masks. We need to know who's in charge.'

Rotavia nodded reluctantly.

'What else have you got in your bag?'

'My bag? Nothing. My phone. My – well,' and even in the dark she looked a bit sheepish, 'my . . . make-up . . .'

'Let me see.'

She was confused, but she handed Eddie the bag. He quickly found what he was looking for – a nail file.

'It's not much of a weapon, but it'll have to do.'

'A weapon?'

He nodded. He had a vague kind of a plan, and he quickly outlined it. She quickly outlined the fact that she thought he was mad. He said that it could work. She said he was mental. He asked her if she had a better plan and she said no, but it was still mad and mental. But she reluctantly agreed.

They spent five minutes sneaking around in the darkness, scouring the discarded packing cases for lengths of sticky tape and string. Then they waited for the boys in gas masks to reappear again.

Five minutes passed and Eddie was just starting

to worry that perhaps they'd finished with their task when the door opened and they appeared, lugging another of the buckets between them. They laboured down the stairs and then approached the drain. As they tipped the bucket up and the crush-flavoured cloud briefly enveloped them, Eddie whispered, 'Now!' and they rushed forward.

Eddie grabbed the nearest boy from behind, put one hand over his eyes and with the other pressed the point of the nail file into the narrow gap between the bottom of his gas mask and his collar. 'Don't move a muscle!' he hissed.

At the same time Rotavia knocked the other boy – who was kneeling down so that he could properly guide the edge of the bucket towards the drain – forward with her knee. As he sprawled on the ground she pounced on top of him. She pushed the front of her mobile phone into the small of his back and whispered, 'This is a gun, one little noise and you're dead.'

Neither boy moved nor made a noise.

Eddie and Rotavia produced their tape and string. They ripped off the boys' white coats and wrenched off their gas masks. Then they stretched sticky tape across their mouths. They tied their hands. Then their feet. Then they tied their hands to their feet so that they couldn't move at all. Then they dragged them, one at a time, huffing and puffing, into a discarded packing case.

Eddie looked down at the two helpless boys. 'So far so good,' he said to himself; then slipped on one of the white coats and lifted one of the gas masks and pulled it down over his head. Rotavia put the other coat on, and then the gas mask. She lifted the empty bucket. They both turned and faced the stairs.

'Ready?' Eddie asked.

'No,' said Rotavia. 'But I'm still going.' Then they set off into the unknown.

Thirty-eight

Eddie had no idea exactly how crush was made. He didn't particularly care. All he knew was that what was spread out before him, covering an area of perhaps two of his classrooms at Brown's Academy, was a laboratory. Flasks bubbled. Liquid ran along tubes and dropped into moulds. There were little cookers, microwaves and fridges. They all played their part in the manufacture of vast quantities of crush. As did the dozen or so boys in gas masks who were supervising and masterminding the operation before them.

Eddie and Rotavia hesitated for just a moment in the doorway, drinking it all in, but thankfully – at least as far as Rotavia was concerned – not sniffing it all in. If you worked in here without a gas mask, you would almost certainly be permanently off your head on crush, or, in fact, dead. Eddie thought it looked like a very slick operation. It clearly wasn't just a case of a crowd of druggies turning up now and again and mixing themselves up some crush. These were scientists –

evil, corrupt scientists to be sure – but scientists nevertheless, undertaking a chemical process professionally, efficiently, clinically. They were going to a lot of trouble to make a lot of people's lives a complete misery, and some other people a great deal of money.

'Hey! We haven't got all day! Hurry up!'

One of the scientists was waving them over to the far side of the lab. They hurried across with their bucket.

'What took you so long?'

'Pee,' said Eddie.

Luckily, with the gas masks, their voices all sounded the same.

The boy indicated a bucket on the floor beside the dripping end of a lengthy, curving plastic tube. It was close to overflowing with the same bubbling liquid that had been poured down the drain outside.

'Get that outside,' the young scientist snapped, 'before we have a bloody flood.'

Eddie took hold of the bucket and manoeuvred it gently to one side, while Rotavia slipped the empty bucket into its place. Then they lifted the full bucket together and headed back towards the door. As they walked Eddie spotted a set of stairs at the far end of the lab leading up to what appeared to be a suite of offices. The baseball boys were sitting on the top steps, watching the scientists at work. They had pulled their jumpers up over the lower half of their faces to stop them breathing in the crush, but even from the floor of the laboratory Eddie could see that their eyes were red and watering.

As soon as they reached the drain outside, Eddie darted across to check that their two prisoners were still securely tied, then hurried back to help Rotavia pour out the chemical waste. When it was empty, Rotavia set down the bucket for a moment and snapped out her mobile phone again. For a moment Eddie thought she was once again going to phone Alexander and he was about to tell her it was still too early, but instead she clicked on the menu, and then he was looking at a small but clear photograph of the lab. He hadn't seen her take it. He gave the thumbs-up.

Behind and above them, the lab door opened again, and this time it was Tommy who emerged, quickly followed by the baseball boys. He had a small leather holdall slung over one shoulder. Four hundred crush, no doubt. He passed by without looking at them, although the boys shouted a couple of smart comments at Eddie and Rotavia as they bent over the drain.

Eddie gave them the thumbs-up as well.

They waited until Tommy and the boys had exited the warehouse before turning back towards the lab.

'OK,' said Eddie, 'here we go with part two.'

They mounted the steps again with the empty bucket. Once inside the lab they approached the drainage tube. Rotavia set down the empty bucket, and Eddie took hold of the one they'd replaced only a few minutes before. It was already three-quarters full. He looked at Rotavia. She gave the slightest nod. Then Eddie tipped the bucket over. The steaming chemical hissed across the floor.

'Watch out!' Eddie yelled as both he and Rotavia jumped back, away from it.

Immediately the boy-scientists turned towards them, and then scuttled away themselves, panic-stricken at the sight of the boiling liquid.

The boy who'd shouted at them for taking their time charged forward, yelling, 'You bloody idiots! Keep away from it! Keep back! Keep it away from the equipment! You bloody fools!'

The whole place was in uproar. The lab floor was covered in white tiles, which made it easy for the chemical to spread. Those scientists who hadn't made it to the back of the lab sat on their chairs with their feet raised, like old women afraid of mice. Suddenly the high, trill sound of a smoke alarm began to ring.

The boy in charge twirled and pointed. 'Switch that off!' he shouted. 'It's not the end of the bloody world!'

But before it could be switched off, the door at the top of the stairs opened, and two boys hurried out to see what the problem was.

Eddie was stunned. It was Bacon and Bap. Two of the leading Reservoir Pups. And then from behind them came an angry shout. 'Well? What is it?'

A voice that was burned into his soul.

Bacon and Bap turned to answer, but before they could say a word the source of the shout emerged, his wheelchair purring across the soft office carpet.

Captain Black.

Captain Black.

His nemesis. His greatest enemy. Leader of the Pups. The most powerful force in the Alliance. It was suddenly all so crystal clear. Black manufactured crush. He sold it mainly to the Seagulls. If the Seagulls were defeated in battle, if they were weak and leaderless, then there would be nothing to stop Black taking over, enslaving them all to the dreaded crush.

'What's going on?' Black demanded, glaring down from the top of the stairs.

'Nothing, sir . . . slight spill . . . slight spill, that's all . . .'

'Well get it cleared up!'

'Yes, sir!'

'And turn that racket off!'

'Yes, sir!'

Black turned his chair, and began to whirr back into his office. Bacon and Bap looked haughtily down at the still-panicked scientists for a moment, then followed him.

Eddie glanced across at Rotavia. He could just see the silver glint of her mobile phone in her left hand. Had she managed to take a picture of Captain Black? She knew exactly what he was thinking. She nodded.

'You!' The boy in charge was shouting at Eddie. 'There's a chemical protection pack back there! Get it!'

Eddie gave him the thumbs-up, then turned away. Beneath his mask he was smiling widely. While every bone in his body wanted to rush up and grab Black's wheelchair and then hurl him down the stairs into his own deadly chemical stew, he knew that wasn't the way. They had the evidence they needed. Now they just had to take their time, clean up the mess, fill the next bucket, then sneak out of the warehouse and get the photos back to Billy Cobb and Alexander. Black would be finished. Alexander would call off his troops; Cobb would cancel the attack.

Just a few more minutes.

Bacon and Bap closed the office door.

The alarm was switched off.

But then in the almost perfect silence that always seems to follow a very loud noise, there came one sound that Eddie had never expected to hear in a million years, a sound which froze him to the spot even as the boy in charge yelled at him to get moving.

Somewhere, far away . . . a baby was crying.

Thirty-nine

It was Patrick, of course.

It *had* to be Patrick.

Eddie's mind was reeling. Black had stolen Paddy. *Black!*

But why? *Why?*

Revenge.

Because he was evil.

Because he *could*.

'Move!'

The scientist was shouting again. Eddie stepped forward, stumbled slightly; he looked about him, quite lost.

'Down there, you imbecile!'

The boy was pointing to a door at the back of the lab. Eddie nodded, then walked towards it. He felt like he was moving through a thick soup. His senses were dulled, but his mind was racing.

Patrick, Patrick, Paddy, Paddy, Paddy . . .

Why? Why? Why? Why?

All this time Black's had him.

He's put me through hell!

No – wait, wait, make sure.

I've been wrong once before, in the Seagulls' crèche. Make sure it's him, make sure!

Eddie pulled the door open. There was a short corridor with several other doors leading off it, and at the end a second set of stairs.

What will I do? What will I do!

Concentrate, concentrate, concentrate . . .

But Paddy . . .

Concentrate now!

He forced himself. He had to. He only had a few seconds to make the right decision. He knew that the sensible thing would be to stick to the plan. Get the photos out. Have Cobb and the rest of the Alliance confront Black, then force him to hand Patrick over.

But what did sensible mean when his own flesh and blood was probably upstairs now, possibly up *those* stairs, right in front of him? He couldn't leave him *now*, he couldn't leave him for one minute longer. He had to see him. Had to make sure at the very least that (a) it really was Paddy and (b) that he was all right. Then he could . . . get Rotavia to cause another distraction, knock something else over. Or just bundle him up and sneak out a back way without even telling her. She could fend for herself. She would understand being abandoned. If Black was to find out that Paddy was gone, and then discovered Rotavia, it would surely be the end of her . . . but who was more important? Some Seagull who'd held him prisoner, or his own flesh and blood?

The fact was, he didn't know what to do.

And then, in a way, the decision was made for him. The door he'd come through opened again and Eddie spun around, ready for a fight. But it was Rotavia.

'He sent me to help you,' she said.

Eddie pointed up the stairs. 'My brother's up there,' he said.

She took it very calmly. 'Then go and find him. I will take the cleaning materials.'

'But . . .'

'If there is a way to get him out safely, then take it.'

'But what about you?'

'I will follow, when I can.'

'But . . .'

'Just go.'

She gave him a gentle push. He hesitated for a moment, just long enough to say, 'Thanks,' then he charged forward and took the stairs three at a time.

He came to a short landing. He paused there, listening, and heard the baby cry somewhere above him. The next floor. Again he leapt up the steps. He came to a door, listened for a moment, then gently opened it. Another hallway, with doors on either side. He listened at each door in turn. The third, on the left – a baby was crying.

It's him. It has to be him.

Eddie opened the door and peered in. A large room, in almost complete darkness. The only light came from a small, slowly revolving lamp which was clipped on to the side of a large wooden cot. The lamp shade was covered in animal shapes, and their shadows were being thrown on to the ceiling. The baby cried again. Perhaps it was scared by the parade of ghostly animals above it. Scarcely able to breathe, Eddie tiptoed across the room. He stopped a metre away from the cot, crossed all of his fingers, and said a silent prayer that this was indeed his long-lost brother.

Then he stepped up to the cot and looked in.

A tiny pink baby blinked up at him. Its eyes were red from crying. Its cheeks flushed. And it was beginning to look like a miniature Bernard J. Scuttles. But it was also, absolutely and definitely, his little baby brother.

'Patrick.'

Eddie reached into the cot. He extended his index finger and the little one clenched it tightly and gave the gentlest of gurgles.

'Patrick.'

And then, as suddenly as an explosion, the main light went on. Eddie froze. His body froze. His heart froze.

'You know, you don't have to wear your gas mask in here, Eddie, his farts aren't that bad.'

Bacon. He'd been waiting behind the door.

'What took you so long, Curly? We've been expecting you for ages.'

Bap, on the other side of the room.

Then the purr of something electric, and Eddie turned slowly to find Captain Black in his wheelchair, in the doorway, smirking up at him. 'Oh – family reunions, they're so emotional, don't you think?'

A trap. And he'd walked right into it.

Why hadn't he suspected something?

It was all suddenly clear to him. Tommy had arrived, looking for four hundred crush. Black must have wanted to know who this rich new customer was. And once he found out, he would have known it was a ruse and that Eddie couldn't be far behind.

Paddy's little fist was still clamped tightly to his finger. He gently removed it, then pushed up his gas mask. He glared at Captain Black. 'You evil—'

But before he could say anything else Bacon and Bap rushed forward and attacked him. Their fists rained down on him, pummelling his head and stomach and arms and chest. They were too quick, too strong. In just a few moments he was lying stunned on the ground; the punching continued, now joined by vicious kicking, but in a strange way he was hardly aware of it – he was much more focussed on the sound of his little brother crying as Captain Black lifted him from his cot.

Forty

Water splashed on to his face, and he sat up suddenly, shouting 'Paddy!' and reaching out, but what he touched wasn't Paddy, it was Rotavia, kneeling beside him, with a bottle of water in her hand. She was looking concerned and terrified, but she still managed to say, 'It's OK, it's OK,' even though he knew instantly that it was anything but OK. They were, after all, prisoners of Captain Black and the Reservoir Pups. Eddie blinked against the harsh light of the room – the same room – and even though he ached from his beating he leapt to his feet and charged across to the cot.

It was empty.

So close, and yet so far away.

'What did they do with him?' Eddie asked, his voice full of despair.

Rotavia came up beside him. 'I don't know. He was gone by the time they threw me in here.'

He saw now that she had been attacked as well. Her top lip was bloody, and there was an ugly swelling under her left eye.

'How long was I unconscious for?' Eddie asked.

'Not long. An hour maybe.'

'And what did Black have to say for himself?'

'Nothing. This boy – he is an . . . enemy of yours?'

Eddie nodded. 'I did not like him. He is . . . evil.'

'That's for sure.'

'But he has gone now. He leaves to go to war. I think perhaps the battle has already started. Or will soon.'

Eddie sighted. 'We're too late then. And Paddy's gone and . . .'

Rotavia put her hand on his shoulder. 'We did everything we could.'

Eddie nodded slowly, still standing, staring down at the empty cot, at the vague impression on the blankets where his little brother had lain. They *had* done everything they could. But it hadn't been enough.

Black had won, and they were doomed to . . . what? Eddie shuddered. What would Black do with them? He couldn't afford to have Eddie tell the Alliance about his drugs manufacturing business. So there were only two ways he could stop him – keep Paddy a prisoner, with the threat that he would be harmed if Eddie breathed a word about the crush. Or simply kill Eddie and Rotavia to keep them quiet.

The answer was not long in coming.

Twenty minutes in fact.

Bacon unlocked the door and came in, followed by Bap and four Pups. 'All right, Curly, time to go. You too, Seagull.'

The four boys came across and stood over them. Eddie and Rotavia, sitting together against the wall, reluctantly got to their feet and were then pushed and prodded across the room and out into the hall.

'Where are you taking us?' Rotavia asked.

'Just for a nice little walk,' said Bap.

They were escorted down the first flight of stairs, then the second, until they were once again on the ground floor. They were then marched through the crush lab which was efficiently working away. Nobody stopped to look at them. Eddie, now minus his gas mask, couldn't help himself – he breathed the fumes in deeply. Then he saw that Bacon was smirking at him – he knew what Eddie was doing. Eddie suddenly felt even smaller and more worthless than he already felt.

They reached the lab door and were then hurried down into the vast warehouse. They passed the broken packing crate where they'd hidden the two tied-up boys, and saw that they were gone. Bacon led the way across the damp, rubbled, puddled floor until they came to an area where the concrete beneath them was so cracked and broken that large expanses of earth were exposed. Evidently Black had ordered that repairs be made to the floor, because there was a large cement mixer chugging away over to the left, its mixer bin revolving smoothly. Two boys were working it, another was standing over a small mountain of fresh cement, ready to apply it to one of the cracks. Bacon stopped at the edge of the largest of these cracks, and indicated for Eddie and Rotavia to be brought up beside him.

'Don't you think this looks like somewhere good to hide a body?' Bacon asked.

Bap, standing behind them, added, 'Of course, you'd need to throw some fresh cement in there afterwards, paper over the cracks, as it were. Luckily, we have some.'

'In fact,' said Bacon, 'if we throw you in there alive, then cover you in cement, it'll look just like an accident. No need to shoot you first, then, or bash your head in with a spade. Just give you a gentle little push.'

He suddenly gave Rotavia one of his gentle little pushes – in fact it was a hard shove and she let out a shout of surprise and fear as she toppled over the edge and fell the metre and a half on to the soft soil below. It happened so quickly that Eddie couldn't even begin to reach out to try and save her.

'Look at that,' Bap laughed, 'she just fell straight in – and I thought Seagulls could fly.' Bacon cackled in response. Eddie just glared at them. 'Aw, come on, Curly,' Bap continued, 'you knew it had to end sooner or later . . . you've had a good run, you even outwitted us a couple of times, but you knew we'd get you in the end.'

'You've not got me yet,' Eddie hissed.

'Try saying that when you're chewing a mouthful of cement.'

He laughed again, and then turned to signal to the boys in charge of the mixer to begin bringing the cement forward.

Except – they weren't there any longer.

They were . . . lying on the ground. They appeared to be . . . well, asleep. Unconscious. And standing in their place was a girl with brilliant white hair and the palest skin in the history of the world. She held a long thin stick, like the shaft of a broom, in her two hands, and was turning it slowly.

'Mo?'

It was Eddie, looking incredulously at his best

friend. The last person in the world he expected to see.

Bap shook his head in disbelief. Bacon laughed.

'Well look who it is,' said Bap, 'little Mo.'

'Come to rescue your boyfriend, is it?' said Bacon.

Mo gave the slightest nod.

'Well why don't you just join him instead?' Bap asked. 'Plenty cement for all of you.'

Still she didn't speak.

'What's wrong?' Bacon asked. 'Cat got your tongue? Or do you think we're just going to run away at the very sight of you? You might have surprised those eejits,' and he nodded down at the boys lying on the ground, 'but you don't scare us. Unless, of course, you have the rest of the Andytown Albinos with you. Oh sorry – I forgot, that's your old nonexistent gang. I meant the Gang With No Name. Oh – sorry, there's no one else in that gang either, is there?'

He took a step towards her now. Two of the Pups moved with him.

She was brave, there was no doubting that, but Eddie knew it was useless. There was no point in sacrificing herself. If she moved quickly enough she could still escape from the warehouse and alert someone to what was happening. 'Mo!' Eddie shouted suddenly. 'Get out of here!'

But instead of moving, she merely twirled the stick in her hand slightly faster. Bap moved closer to Eddie and took a firm hold of his arm. 'Rescued by a girl,' he laughed sarcastically, 'that'll be the day.'

Bacon stayed right in front of her – but the other boys moved to either side.

'You're wrong,' Mo said.

'About what?' said Bacon.

'About there not being any other members.'

Her eyes flitted for a moment to her left, just as Gary Gilmore emerged from behind one of the packing cases.

'Hi,' he said.

'Oh,' said Bacon, 'now I'm really scared. An Albino and a ginger nut.'

'Don't forget me.' It was another, vaguely familiar voice, from off to the right, and at first Eddie couldn't make out who it was emerging from the shadows.

'Or me,' and he was joined by someone else.

As they drew closer Eddie caught his breath. Sean. And Pat. The two Drogheda orphans who'd helped him retrieve the head of Oliver Plunkett.

'Or us.'

Three others appeared behind them. Two boys and a girl, in baseball caps. Eddie was getting completely confused now. There was certainly something familiar about them. But . . .

And then the boy at the front removed his cap.

Even in such poor light, it was his eyes which gave him away.

It wasn't his left eye. That was fine.

It wasn't his right. That was just perfect.

It was his third eye, right in the middle, that told Eddie that this was Diet Coke, one of the Forgotten, the products of Alison Beech's evil experiments under the Mourne Mountains. And with Diet Coke were Beans and Snickers, and then quickly following them out of the darkness there came a dozen more of the Forgotten, all of them different in some way – one had webbed hands, one had three arms, one had no nose, one had a fist shaped like a hammer.

Eddie was in shock.

But he wasn't half as shocked as Bacon or Bap, standing there, suddenly outnumbered by these bizarre-looking kids.

And it wasn't over yet.

From a gap in the warehouse wall on the far

side of the crack another face appeared – Jimmy McCabe, his friend from Melody Hill. Jimmy stepped into the warehouse, then turned and waved behind him. There came a sudden flurry of footsteps as Jimmy led in what appeared at first glance to be every single boy who'd escaped from the home with him. They formed up in two lines right along the edge of the crack.

Eddie felt Bap's grip on his arm loosen. He took a step back from him. Bacon and his boys began to back away from Mo.

Eddie was almost overcome by this sudden, spectacular reversal. He could feel the sheer excited thrill of it coursing through his veins, a thousand times greater than any crush.

He turned, his eyes wide with disbelief, towards Mo. 'Mo – I don't under—'

But before he could finish there was yet more noise, this time from the other side of the warehouse, and Eddie had a sudden, and, given the way his life had been in recent months, totally understandable feeling that this brief moment of hope was about to be snatched away again – but instead a huge smile enveloped his face as the familiar purple uniform of Brown's Academy emerged on the first of dozens and dozens and dozens of his school friends, marching in in perfect formation, as if they were going to a school assembly.

As they came to a halt, Mo shouted across, 'What took you so long?'

'Sorry,' said the closest boy, a big bruiser called Unsworth, that Eddie had seen crack manys a head on the rugby field, 'transport problems. Had to steal the school bus in the end.'

Mo nodded, twirled her stick once, then suddenly flicked it out sideways. It whacked into the side of Bap's head, and he was unconscious before he hit the ground.

The other four boys tried to run away, but were quickly captured. Bacon dropped suddenly to his knees. He looked desperately from one advancing group to the other. 'Please . . .' he said, raising his hands almost in prayer, 'we weren't really going to . . . and if we did . . . we were just following orders—'

But he wasn't able to finish. Mo whacked him as well.

Eddie stood in the middle of it all, quite unable to move.

There were at least a hundred boys standing around him now.

'Mo?'

'Eddie.'

'I don't understand – what are you . . . how did you . . . I don't understand . . .'

She smiled. She came forward. She went up on her toes, and kissed him on the cheek. 'Eddie . . . I told your friends you were in trouble. They wanted to help.'

His friends?

Eddie was so used to thinking that he didn't have any friends in the entire world, that the very thought that any of these boys or girls might really care enough to come to his rescue just astonished him. He didn't know what to say or how to respond. He just looked around all of them, shaking his head.

'We were just planning how to rescue you from the camp when one of my spies reported you'd left with the girl, he followed you here and . . . well, I called in the troops. I'm just sorry it took so long to get here.'

Eddie laughed. 'Don't worry about it. The timing was perfect.'

Mo turned and knelt by the crack in the ground; she reached down, and Rotavia grasped her hand and hauled herself up. As she scrambled over the edge her mouth dropped open in surprise as she saw the huge numbers of kids standing around her.

'Hi, I'm Mo.'

'I am Rotavia.'

The two girls looked at each other for several long moments.

'Thank you,' Rotavia said, finally breaking what was threatening to become an awkward silence.

'My pleasure,' said Mo. She turned to Eddie, then nodded around the huge crowd of boys and girls now standing watching them expectantly. 'Well,' said Mo, 'I guess the Gang With No Name just got a little bigger. Now what do you want us to do?'

Eddie shook himself. Every pair of eyes – and even several sets of three – was upon him.

His gang.

His gang.

His eyes flitted up to the office complex at the other end of the warehouse. The lights were on, the production of crush continued at full speed. He now had enough manpower to seize Black's business. *He* could control the distribution of crush all over the city. Make huge amounts of money. And have access to as much of the wonderful drug as his brain could cope with.

Could.

A few days ago, in the grip of his addiction, he certainly would have.

But not now.

Not today, with this mighty gang around him.

He raised his hand and pointed at the laboratory and the offices. 'Burn it!' he shouted. 'Burn it down!'

Forty-one

Just three miles away, the gangs of the Alliance were gathered in complete darkness in a field overlooking the Palace Barracks camp. Billy Cobb wore night-vision goggles to survey his troops; it was indeed an awesome sight. Off to the left were the Ramsey Street Wheelers, the Churchill Regulars, the Malone Marauders and seven or eight others; the centre of the field was taken up by the Reservoir Pups, who hugely outnumbered the other gangs. To the right he noted the Ormeau Pirates, the Ballysillan Spidermen and many of the smaller gangs with less than a dozen members each. All stood in utter silence, waiting for the word to move forward. Every one of them was heavily armed – hard, knotted sticks, baseball bats, knives, catapults, crossbows, rocks, hammers, hatchets, metal spikes. Blood would be shed.

Cobb's throat was dry. There had never before been a battle on this scale. He looked at his watch. The attack would start at midnight. A tent had been pitched just below the brow of the hill; Captain

Black and the other members of the War Council were in there, going over the battle plan for the final time.

It was relatively simple.

The Seagulls would not expect the Alliance just to charge up to the front gate of the camp and attack. But they would think to themselves, that's just what the Alliance wants us to think, and decide that the front gate was *exactly* where the attack would come. They would mass their forces there as a result. To reinforce this bluff, Cobb would send a hundred gangsters to attack the front gate. Meanwhile, Alliance engineers, under the cover of darkness, had already removed the poles securing the fence at the rear of the camp. At a given signal, the fence would be pushed over and the gangsters would sweep down the hill and hopefully take the defenders by surprise.

The Alliance had: around one thousand fighters.

In the camp below, they were also getting ready for battle. Alexander was already aware of enemy activity close to the front gate. There was no way of telling if this would be where the main attack took place. Perhaps it was a bluff. Perhaps it was a double bluff. It didn't really matter – he didn't have a big enough army to properly defend the camp. He knew that.

The Seagulls had: two hundred and thirty fighters.

Of those, around forty were crush addicts, and you couldn't rely on them to follow orders.

It was going through his mind that it might be better just to surrender. To agree to whatever the Alliance demanded. What was the worst they could ask for? That his Seagulls never leave the camp again? That they give up their weapons and what little money they had? That they agree to pay every time they crossed Alliance territory? That the Seagulls work as slaves for the Alliance gangs? Or that they all become enslaved to the crush?

The bulk of his fighters were formed up in four rows before him in the centre of the interior rectangle. Their uniforms were clean and they stood to attention like the trained soldiers they were, their faces grim with determination. They would be overrun, injured, humiliated. But they would fight.

Alexander raised his hand and pointed at the repaired statue behind him. 'General Killster was our leader,' he shouted, 'and is now our inspiration! He led our country to victory against overwhelming odds, and now we face the same situation! We are strangers in this strange land, and until the day we can return to our own country, we must make it our home! And if that means fighting for our right to be here, that is what we must do!'

A cheer went up from his fighters.

'I will not lie to you! We are outnumbered! They may have better weapons! But they do not have our spirit, they do not have our bravery . . . they are not Seagulls!'

Another roar went up.

'We will fight to the last man!'

A third roar.

'Now go to your positions! And fight for Killster!'

'Killster!' roared his troops.

The Seagulls filed away, their faces set hard for the coming battle.

Alexander looked at his watch. It was just five minutes until midnight.

On the hill overlooking the camp, Billy Cobb heard a familiar grinding, metallic sound, and turned to find Captain Black coming towards him in his wheelchair, which had been adapted for use on rough terrain. It boasted the kind of caterpillar tracks that were found on bulldozers – or tanks.

'What's the delay?' Black snapped.

'Just a few more minutes.'

'We need to go now! We need to crush them!'

Cobb had always disliked Black, but he had to work with him, because his gang was by far the largest in the city. But Cobb was in charge, and he was determined to show Black that *he* would order the attack when he saw fit. He was sending a lot of gangsters into battle and he wanted to be sure he wasn't sending them into any kind of a trap. He knew they outnumbered the Seagulls. But then Goliath had been much bigger than David.

'Sir?'

It was one of Cobb's lieutenants, pointing down the hill towards the camp gates. Cobb had his hundred gangsters hidden in the long grass on the opposite side of the dual carriageway, waiting to make the first attack, and for a moment he was worried that they'd sprung into action too early – but instead he saw that the gates were opening . . . and that a bus was approaching. No – not one bus, two . . . then three, four, five, six . . . dozens and dozens of buses were coming through the gates.

Cobb watched in consternation. *What is this? What's going on?*

Then he began to hear a whisper, at first only

half carried on the breeze, and then growing louder and louder, and it was coming from his own men, lined up on the hill, ready to attack. It also came from the Pups and from the other gangs to the left and right.

The Seagulls have landed!

The Seagulls have landed!

Cobb pushed up his night-vision goggles and snatched up the binoculars offered by his lieutenant. He focussed on the first of the buses, which was now pulling to a halt on the car park in front of the rectangular community centre complex. Tired and bedraggled-looking adults began to climb out of the vehicle. They moved around to the side to collect their luggage. But in amongst them, decked out in the familiar black uniform of the Seagulls, were a number of kids. Seven . . . ten . . . fifteen off the first bus alone. And there were . . . how many buses? His glasses swept along the road leading back to the gate. He quickly counted thirty buses. If there were fifteen Seagulls in each bus – that would mean more than five hundred new fighters.

Suddenly the odds didn't favour the Alliance quite so much.

'Order the attack now!'

It was Black, furiously pointing towards the camp.

Cobb hesitated. With so many women and little children coming off the buses, many would be hurt when the first wave of stone-throwing landed. And if they attacked now, wouldn't the men from the buses also join in the defence?

'You must attack now!' Black yelled again. 'Before they have a chance to organise!'

The other War Council leaders were now streaming out of the planning tent as word of the Seagulls' arrival finally reached them. They anxiously gathered about Cobb and Black.

Cobb had the toughest decision of his life to make. And it came to him surprisingly easily, because he was at heart a cautious boy.

'Too many innocent people will be hurt,' he said. 'We must delay!'

'Innocent Seagulls?' Black bellowed. 'No such thing! We must strike now while their attention is diverted! Give the command!'

But Cobb stood firm. 'No, Captain.'

Black looked stunned. He wasn't used to being disobeyed. He turned to the War Council. 'I demand that we attack *now*.'

The council members looked warily at each

other. They'd put Cobb in charge of the battle. They thought he was a good leader. But they were also terrified of Captain Black and what he would do if they defied him. And in the end this is what decided them. One by one they said, 'We must attack.'

Cobb shook his head unhappily. He had no alternative now. If he tried to stand up to the entire War Council, he would be removed from his command. 'Very well,' he said without enthusiasm. He turned to his second in command. 'Signal the company by the gate. Begin the attack!'

Forty-two

There are certain safety precautions which the driver of a school bus must adhere to. No standing in the aisles. No overcrowding. He must not speed or drive in a manner that might constitute a risk to either his passengers or members of the general public. It is fairly safe to say that Barry Unsworth, driver of the Brown's Academy school bus, did not adhere to any of these precautions. He drove with the pedal to the metal, hurling them all from side to side, then forwards, then backwards. Every single gangster was squeezed on to the bus – they were crushed under seats, squashed into overhead lockers, they stood four abreast in the aisles and three on top of each other in the seats. Unsworth drove with his hand on the horn and every light flashing. Other terrified drivers threw their vehicles out of his way; when he found himself caught up in traffic, he turned the bus on to the footpath and then it was the turn of the pedestrians, small dogs and wandering cats to jump for their lives.

Eddie hung on to a pole near the front, and

watched admiringly as Unsworth negotiated each new obstacle. He had never exchanged a single word with the boy. Until tonight he'd thought of him just as a snotty, stuck-up, blond-haired, rugby-playing prefect too in love with himself to talk to someone like him. Well, he supposed he shouldn't judge a book by its cover. Just as he had once misjudged Rotavia. She stood right beside him. She was brave and strong and had risked her life for him. She had battled the crush and beaten it. And then there was Mo, on his other side, whom he'd almost forgotten about. When she'd escaped from the camp he'd been too caught up in his own fight for survival to worry about her. But he should have guessed that she wouldn't just leave him to his fate. She had gone to extraordinary lengths to recruit this gang, which now bristled with excitement around him as they thundered through Belfast towards the Seagulls' camp.

Mo caught him looking at her. She smiled up and said, 'You beat it, didn't you?'

She didn't have to spell it out. She was talking about his addiction to crush. 'So far,' he said. He turned his attention to Rotavia. 'Is it safe?'

She patted her pocket. 'It is safe.'

That's where her mobile was. They'd rescued it

from Black's offices and endured a nerve-wracking few moments while Rotavia checked to see if the photographs of the Reservoir Pups leader and his drug production facility were still intact. And they were fine. Perfect evidence. As soon as they'd found it, they'd sent the pictures to Alexander and to Billy Cobb. But neither had responded. They knew why. Who had time to check their messages when there was a huge battle about to take place? No, all they could do now was physically take the pictures to the battlefield, and hope to confront and expose Black before the war really started. If only they were in time.

The first wave of stones came out of the darkness and smashed into the last half-dozen buses with venomous force. The windows shattered, spraying both those inside and those outside with glass. The women screamed, then screamed harder as they saw that their children were cut and bleeding. A second wave rained down, cracking heads and smashing bones. They struck the old men clambering off the buses, men already weary and destitute, men who had been plucked out of the ruins of the earthquake back in Ruritania, men who were too weak to fight. The strong men, the fathers, the brothers, who would have fought off this attack, were still back in the old country, desperately trying to rebuild their homes.

Alexander, standing outside the community centre, watched this initial attack through his binoculars. He counted roughly a hundred Alliance stone throwers approaching the gates. They were wearing crash helmets to protect them. Behind them there were other boys, hurrying up with bags full of stones, resupplying them. Alexander ordered thirty boys forward to meet them. One of his officers demanded more, but he refused. It wasn't clear yet if this was the main attack – he couldn't commit everyone to the defence of the gates and leave other parts of the camp vulnerable.

His people were now streaming off their buses in sheer panic. They had been warned by those who had gone ahead of them that Belfast was a hostile place, but they hadn't expected this kind of violence. Now they hurried up the slight incline towards the shelter of the community centre, which was already bursting at the seams.

Down at the gate, the first bus was now burning. *My God*, thought Alexander, *what if the community centre catches fire when the main attack comes?* Hundreds might be burned alive. And yet he couldn't leave them out in the open, because whatever attack there was would surely start with a wave of similar stone throwing – but this time from potentially thousands of attackers rather than just the hundred at the gate.

Alexander turned and gave a signal. Immediately, the security lights surrounding the camp erupted into life, illuminating every inch of the overgrown grounds.

There!

The security lights were throwing enough light on to the back fields to show up where the Alliance army was even now moving forward to attack. Alexander watched as its forward patrols seized hold of the security fence. For a moment he thought they were going to climb it, but instead they barely seemed to touch it and it gave way, one section, then another, and another. There was now a huge gap, through which the Alliance troops began to pour. All around him stones were now beginning to land. The community centre's roof was under a sudden and terrifying bombardment.

Alexander gave another signal. Two hundred Seagulls surged forward to meet the attack. Hopefully they would hold up the Alliance for long enough to arm the newly arrived Seagulls with as many stones and sticks and bats and knives as they could muster, before sending them to join the battle.

Thousands of stones had now rained down both on the Seagulls and on the Alliance. So many in fact, that instead of either side running out, they each ended up resupplying each other. Dozens of gangsters from each side lay injured on the grass; many cried for help; others were completely unconscious. With each volley of stones, the two sides drew closer, closer and then even closer until there was only twenty or thirty metres separating them.

Gradually, the throwing stopped. The time for stones was over.

It was time for weapons. For the sticks, with nails in the end; for the baseball bats, sharpened to a point. For biscuit-tin armour and crash helmets. For punching and kicking and gouging and biting and strangling and head-butting. It wasn't going to be pleasant. It was going to be bloody.

Alexander looked at his army. It had now been joined by the new arrivals. He looked at the Alliance troops.

The two sides appeared to be equally matched.

Now it would be about strength, determination and spirit.

For the Seagulls, it was a fight for survival.

For the Alliance, a fight to save their land from invasion.

They inched closer and closer, and as they did a fearful roaring came from both sides. It was rich with bravery and fear, and seemed to envelop everything. This was it then, this was it – the two armies awaited only the signal to attack. Alexander raised his hand. On top of the hill Billy Cobb raised his.

In the very instant before the order was given to launch the full attack, there came the roar of an engine from the country lane running up the side of the hill and a yellow school bus burst through the gap in the fence and careered across the overgrown sports fields. It raced down the right flank of the Alliance army, then turned into the expanse of damp grass between the two armies and skidded to a halt.

Each battle leader assumed that his opposite number had introduced some deadly new weapon to the field and was about to give the order for it to be stoned – but then the door opened and Eddie

Malone jumped out. He was followed by Mo, Rotavia and a steady stream of boys who were clearly neither Seagulls nor members of any of the Alliance gangs. They blinked in the harsh glare of the security lights as they emerged, looking slightly stunned to find themselves between two such huge armies, but it didn't stop them forming a protective circle around their bus.

Then Eddie Malone spoke to the driver, who was standing now on the top step. Barry Unsworth clasped his hands together and gave him a hoist up until he was able to clamber up on to the roof of the bus. A moment later Rotavia joined him. Mo tried to join them, but Eddie knelt quickly down at the edge and said no, this was something he and Rotavia had to do alone. Mo nodded reluctantly and stepped down. She understood. Kind of.

They then stood and looked out at their respective sides: Rotavia towards the solid black mass of Seagulls; Eddie at the Alliance soldiers – the smaller gangs grouped to the left and right, the centre held by the Pups, the Council of War standing in a line on the brow of the hill.

'Billy Cobb!' Eddie bellowed.

'Alexander!' yelled Rotavia.

'We must talk to you and the leaders of the

Assembly!' Eddie shouted. 'Please! Before this starts!'

'Alexander!' Rotavia yelled again. 'You must talk to us!'

Up on the hill Captain Black hissed, 'Start the attack! Start it now!'

Billy Cobb hesitated. He looked to the War Council. They'd already backed Black once, but now they seemed less sure. In the end they said nothing.

Down below Alexander raised his binoculars and studied Rotavia – was she being held captive? Was she being forced to invite him forward into a trap? He saw her face close up, full of terror and concern. She was waving frantically in his general direction, but with the lights and the mass of bodies around him, he was sure she couldn't see him.

'Please!' Eddie yelled. 'We have evidence which will stop this war!'

Up on the hill, Billy Cobb said, 'We should hear what he has to say!'

'Are you mad?' Captain Black yelled. 'That's Eddie Malone! He killed his brother! He's a crush addict! We attack the bus, we attack the Seagulls, we finish them all for good!'

Beside him, several of the gang leaders nodded.

The gangs spread out in attack formation on the hill below were beginning to get restless. They were primed for attack. All they needed was their leader to let them off the leash.

Still Cobb hesitated.

Black's eyes blazed furiously. 'You're a coward, that's what you are! You're scared of fighting! Any excuse not to attack!'

This time Cobb lost his temper as well. 'I will order the attack as soon as I'm happy that we're attacking for the right reasons!'

'Coward!' Black turned his wheelchair to face the other gang leaders. 'Must we do this again? Vote for an attack! Vote for it now!'

But before they could respond, Cobb leapt to his own defence. 'I'm not against an attack, but if Eddie Malone has information that will stop a lot of our guys getting hurt, then we should hear it.'

'Attack!' screamed Black.

'You can scream all you want, Captain!' Cobb pointed at each leader in a slow rotation. 'Listen to me, you made me leader of the Alliance and Chairman of the War Council, and the reason you made me leader was to stop *him* having his own way all the time. If you let him decide this now then there's no point in having me in charge, and if I'm not in charge, which of you is going to stand up to him? He will be in control, and then how long will it be before he gets rid of you and takes over your gangs? We are an Alliance, we all have an equal say; I say we agree to talk to Eddie Malone. Five minutes, then if he's talking crap, yes, I'll give the order.'

The leaders exchanged worried looks.

'Don't listen to him!' screamed Black. 'He's chicken! He's a friend of Eddie Malone! Look at him down there – he's in with the Seagulls! So if he's in with the Seagulls, how do we know *you* aren't as well?' Black pointed at Cobb. 'How do we know you're not going down there to betray our plans? To sell us out?'

Cobb shook his head. He had never seen Black so angry. But it seemed to him that it was an anger that was masking something else. 'What are you so scared of?' he asked.

Black ignored him. He waved his finger at the other leaders. 'You must decide now, or the advantage will be lost!'

The leaders quickly huddled together, and spoke in hushed tones. Then they turned back to Cobb. The leader of the Ramsey Street Wheelers said, 'We delay by five minutes – and three of us go with you.'

'No!' Black exploded.

'That's our decision,' the lead Wheeler said, somewhat apologetically.

'You will not go down there! If you take one step towards that bus, I will withdraw the Pups!'

Again the leaders exchanged glances. This time Cobb answered for them. 'That's your choice, Captain. Though it would kind of make it look like it was you who was the chicken.'

With that he stepped forward and began to make his way through the troops, quickly followed by three of his fellow gang leaders.

Alexander and two of his officers hurried forward from their battle lines and approached the bus. The gang surrounding it parted to allow them through, and they were then helped one by one up on to the roof of the bus. Rotavia immediately ran up to Alexander and gave him a hug. Her eyes were red, she was clearly exhausted, but she was also shaking with excitement.

'Alexander!' she exclaimed, and was about to launch into their story, but he silenced her with a finger to her lips.

'Shhhh,' he said. 'Wait.' He nodded forward, to where the Alliance leader, Billy Cobb, was just being pulled up on to the roof. When the other Alliance leaders joined him, the two sides advanced towards each other. Eddie and Rotavia stood between them.

Cobb eyed Alexander warily.

Alexander eyed Cobb warily.

Everybody eyed everybody warily.

'Well?' Cobb asked eventually.

Eddie put his hand out, and Rotavia passed him the mobile phone. He opened it up, and quickly found the most incriminating of the photos she'd taken. Before he showed it to them he said: 'This war is being fought for the wrong reasons. The Ruritanians—'

'We are Seagulls,' Alexander said crisply.

'The Seagulls . . . just want to be left in peace, they don't want to take over anything. And the Alliance . . . they're scared you *will* take over because they think you're going to get everyone addicted to crush—'

'We do not—!' Alexander began to explode.

'I know, I know,' Eddie quickly cut in. 'You are not responsible for crush.' The Alliance leaders exchanged looks.

'How do you know this?' Cobb asked.

'Because we found the lab where it is produced.' Eddie turned, and pointed away across the city. From their elevated position they had a perfect view. 'There . . .' he said. 'The fire.'

In the far distance, they could see the glow of a massive fire, and a cloud so black it made the night sky seem almost light.

'We burned it down.'

They watched it, as if hypnotised, for several long moments before Cobb said, 'Who was running it?'

Eddie passed the phone to the Alliance leader. Cobb took a deep breath. He then handed it to the other gang leaders. They looked genuinely shocked. Eddie took the phone back, then held it out for Alexander. He too then saw the picture of the lab, and in the background, at the top of the stairs, Captain Black and two of his men.

'He's been behind it all,' said Eddie. 'He wants to get everyone addicted, to take over the whole city.' Eddie's voice began to crack. 'And he stole my little brother.'

Rotavia put a hand on his arm. She gave it the gentlest squeeze.

Cobb nodded, then turned and wordlessly stared

up the hill towards Captain Black. And even though he was several hundred metres away, Black knew.

He knew that they knew.

He knew that what they knew would soon be known by the soldiers waiting to fight. By his own Reservoir Pups. He was their leader – but for how long, once they found out about the crush? He had run its production as a secret division within the gang, and only his most trusted officers, like Bacon and Bap, had known about it. Many of the Pups were already addicted to crush; some were in hospital, several had died. Everyone knew the devastation it was causing and had hated the Seagulls because of it. But now they would know that it wasn't the Seagulls at all, that they'd been lied to by the one man they trusted above all others.

Black spun in his wheelchair. 'Get me out of here,' he hissed to one of his officers, one who knew about the crush and whose loyalty would never be in doubt. The rest of the Pups were still watching the discussions on the top of the bus. So Black was able to guide his chair across the coarse, tramped-down grass towards the adapted people carrier he used as a mobile headquarters, without being noticed.

* * *

Down below, Cobb snapped up his binoculars. He picked out Black, positioning his wheelchair on the small electric lift which allowed him direct access to the people carrier without him having to get out of his chair.

'He's making a run for it!' Cobb exclaimed, pointing.

The soldiers on the hill turned and saw what was happening. They didn't know anything about the crush factory. But they could see that Black was leaving, and suddenly the ranks were alive with whispers. *Where's he going, what's he doing, why's he leaving, what does he know, what has he done, how can we fight without our leader . . . ?*

And then Cobb began to shout from the top of the bus. 'Captain Black has betrayed you! Captain Black makes crush!'

The Reservoir Pups looked at each other in confusion. What was Cobb shouting? *Their leader makes crush? How could that be? The great Captain!* But there was no doubt that he was leaving. The people carrier was reversing up the hill, back towards the lane. *Why is he leaving? If he's done nothing wrong, why would he go?*

Cobb was yelling again. 'Stop him! He must be stopped!'

And now it was clear to everyone that Cobb must be right. That Captain Black was guilty, guilty of *something*, guilty of something so bad that he wasn't even brave enough to stay and plead his case to his own gang.

The people carrier turned on to the lane, but suddenly there were gangsters running after it.

'Faster! Faster!' Black yelled.

There were gangsters – even some of his own men – hammering on the side of the vehicle, there were others on the road in front of them.

'Captain!' the driver shouted. 'They're blocking—'

'Run them down!' Black screamed.

So the driver increased his speed and aimed directly at the gangsters now spilling on to the road in increasing numbers. Most saved themselves by diving out of the way. Three were struck, and spun off into a ditch.

He's even knocking down his own men!

The stones they'd saved to pound the Seagulls with were hurled towards the vehicle. They smashed through the side and rear windows, but still the driver kept his foot down, and before very long he was clear of his pursuers and the stones began to fall short.

Then the people carrier rounded a bend in the road, and Captain Black was gone.

Forty-three

Dawn was beginning to break over Belfast as Eddie finally arrived at the one place he most wanted to be in all the world – home. But it was also the one place in all the world that he dreaded approaching, because of Patrick. Captain Black's flight, and the somewhat hesitant peace which had been agreed between the warring factions, had lifted his spirits for only a few minutes. Yes, his greatest enemy had fled; yes, he had triumphed over adversity once again, but Black's escape had only emphasised the fact that Eddie had no clue as to where Patrick was, or even if he *was* at all. Black's little empire had crumbled and Eddie was very much to blame for it. So what hope was there for Patrick?

None at all.

Eddie was on the stolen school bus. He had insisted that Barry Unsworth drop the other gangsters off first; not because he was a kind and caring leader – which he was, actually – but because he was putting off the inevitable moment when he would have to knock on his front door. His mum would scream at him. Scuttles would have him arrested again or sent straight back to Melody Hill.

Why go home at all?

Jimmy McCabe and his boys had set up a headquarters in a disused factory just outside the city. 'Come live with us – there's fifty-nine of us, Eddie, one more won't make any difference!'

But he'd said no.

He'd said no to Rotavia as well. 'You stopped a war, Eddie, you're a hero – if you can't go home, come and stay at the camp.'

But he'd said no to that as well. 'You stopped the war as well, Rotavia – and I have to go home.'

She understood. She went back to the camp with Alexander and the rest of the Seagulls. They said goodbye somewhat awkwardly. They had shared a glorious adventure, but they still hardly knew each other. In the end she kissed him on both cheeks. It was some weird foreign custom, he guessed. As the bus pulled away, she waved after it.

Alexander saluted.

Eddie felt a bit silly saluting back.

But he did it all the same.

Mo said she understood as well. She stood beside

him at the front of the bus, with one arm looped protectively across his shoulders. She was so proud of what he had done. But part of her was jealous that he had managed to do it with Rotavia, and not with her.

'Next time we do something exciting – I'm going too,' she whispered in his ear. She meant it as light-hearted, funny; but he just nodded wearily. He wanted everything to be as it was before. Patrick crying in bed. His mum shouting at him to do something simple like tidy his room. He would even put up with Scuttles, despite the fact that he'd been instrumental in sending him to Melody Hill. When you believe that someone kidnaps or kills your only son, you don't want to have to face him at breakfast every morning.

Eventually, even Mo went home. She was the last off the bus, but for Barry the driver. She hugged Eddie again and kissed one cheek, then the other, just the way Rotavia had. Then she said, 'Oh crap,' and kissed him full on the lips. She hurried away then before he could say anything. In truth, he was hardly aware of it.

'Where now, boss?' Barry asked.

Eddie took a deep breath. 'Take me home,' he said.

* * *

He took the lift to the apartment. He stood outside his door. One minute, two, three.

It had to be done.

He knocked.

After a moment the door opened and his mum was standing there. Her mouth dropped open in surprise. He could see that her eyes were red rimmed and there were huge, grey, sleepless bags under her eyes.

'Mum . . .'

'Eddie!'

She was suddenly beaming. She jumped forward and grabbed him and hugged him so tightly that she almost squeezed the life out of him.

'Eddie!' she shouted again. 'Oh Eddie, Eddie, Eddie . . .'

'Mum . . .'

She was *delighted* to see him.

'Eddie! You're home!'

'Mum, I'm so sorr—'

But then his eyes flitted down the hall behind her. And Scuttles was standing there, with Patrick in his arms.

'Paddy . . . ?' Eddie felt tears spring into his eyes. His mum loosened her bear-like grip. 'Paddy's home . . . ?'

She clapped her hands together. 'Isn't it fantastic! Oh Eddie, I'm so happy, I'm so proud of you! Thank you . . . thank you . . . thank you . . .' With each expression of gratitude she kissed him – on the forehead, on the cheek, on the neck. Even Scuttles gave him a thumbs-up sign.

Eddie almost staggered down the hall towards his little brother. 'I don't understand . . .' he began.

Scuttles held Paddy out to him. Eddie took him into his arms. He hugged him close. 'Paddy . . . Paddy . . . Paddy . . .'

His mum came up behind him and smiled down at her two sons. 'The doorbell just went about an hour ago, and there he was sitting on the step, happy as can be.'

Scuttles reached into his dressing-gown pocket and produced a folded sheet of paper. 'This was pinned to his blanket.' He shook it out straight, cleared his throat and read:

'*Dear Mrs Malone*

Here's your son back. He has been well looked after. The only reason I took him was to get back at Eddie. Eddie did everything he could to get him back. He's brave and resourceful and he's finally defeated me. You should be proud of him.

Yours sincerely,'

But there was no name.

Although it was perfectly clear who it was from.

'And then there was this as well.' His mum was holding out an envelope. 'Bernie wanted to open it – but it's addressed to you, it's your business.'

Eddie kissed Paddy once more, then placed him in his mother's arms. He could scarcely believe what was happening. Not only had Captain Black been defeated and fled, he had even delivered Patrick back to his parents and praised Eddie into the bargain!

Everything, finally, was perfect in Eddie's life.

Black gone. Baby back. What more could he ask for?

Eddie examined the envelope. His name was on the front, written in the same handwriting as the note. He quickly tore it open. Another single sheet of paper with writing on one side.

Dear Eddie, it read, *I hope you don't believe any of the crap I wrote about you in the other note. You've been lucky, very lucky. You might think you've won, but what you've actually done is just make me angry. So I'll be back to get you. Watch your back, because one day I'll be behind you, and then I'll have my revenge.*

Yours sincerely, Captain Black.

PS I'm giving this puking, stinking little creature

back only because I don't want you sent to some prison where I can't get you.

On any other day, this letter would have sent the chills through him. But not today. Not now that he was back with his family, not now that the war was over. Black didn't scare him now. He was gone. He could threaten all he wanted, but his power was broken, he was finished. For the first time in months Eddie felt truly safe.

He sat with his mum and Paddy and Scuttles for another hour. He told them a little of what had happened, but most he held back. He told them about the crush and the factory and how they'd destroyed it, but he didn't mention that he'd become addicted. His mum interrupted him at one point, went to the cupboard, and brought out a fresh box of Jaffa Cakes and insisted that he ate them all as he talked. So he did, and she was soon peppered in spat-out crumbs as he tried to explain what had happened with his mouth crammed full of biscuits. But she didn't mind. She couldn't stop hugging him and saying how sorry she was, and even Scuttle said he might have been wrong about him.

Just *might*, of course.

* * *

He slept without dreaming. No Seagulls. No babies.

For the first time in days he woke without a sudden craving for crush. It was still there, somewhere deep down, but he would not let it out. Not now that everything was OK in the world.

They let him sleep late. Then his mum came in with Paddy in her arms and said, 'Eddie, there's someone at the door for you.'

And he jumped up, feeling totally refreshed – even after only a few hours' sleep. He supposed it was Mo, and he felt excited and happy to see her again, even though they'd only been apart for a short while.

His mum had pushed the door half open, and just before he reached it Eddie stopped suddenly and thought – *What if it's Captain Black, with a huge knife or gun or . . . ?*

He took a deep breath. No. Black was gone. If he ever did return, it wouldn't be for a long time.

It had to be Mo.

Eddie opened the door.

It wasn't Mo.

It wasn't Black either.

It was Billy Cobb.

'Hi, Eddie,' he said.

'Oh. Hi.'

'That was fun last night, wasn't it?'

Eddie cleared his throat. 'Something like that,' he said.

Cobb was looking quite embarrassed. He shifted uneasily from one foot to another. 'Well,' he said, 'no point in beating around the bush. I've resigned as leader of the Alliance.'

'What?' Eddie asked, surprised. 'But why?'

'Because – well, I let Black have too much influence, and I should have realised what he was up to. The crush and all. So I've resigned. Before I was sacked, really.'

'But . . . but we *won* . . . didn't we? Black's gone. You made the right decision.'

Cobb shrugged. 'Well. That's just the way it is.'

'Well,' said Eddie. 'I'm sorry.'

Cobb nodded.

Eddie nodded.

Cobb nodded some more.

Eddie nodded some more.

Eventually, as Eddie began to feel a little dizzy, he stopped the nodding and said, 'I appreciate you coming round to tell me. Was there, uh, anything else?'

Cobb started to shake his head. Then suddenly

remembered. 'Oh yes – I forgot. You've been elected the new leader of the Alliance. You start on Monday.'

'What?'

'Yep, you're in charge, Eddie.'

'What?'

'Oh yes, it was unanimous. Everyone agreed. We need a hero for a leader, that's what we need. And you're a hero. So you're in charge.'

Cobb gave him a broad, theatrical kind of a wink, then spun on his heel and hurried away.

Leader . . . of the Alliance?

Leader . . . of the Alliance!!!!

Am I imagining this?

'Eddie!'

It was his mum, shouting from the kitchen.

Eddie couldn't talk. His mouth was dry and his tongue felt like a lead weight.

'Eddie!'

He couldn't move. Leader of the Alliance! One of the most powerful boys in the city. It was everything he'd ever dreamed of, and more – but did he want it after all the horrors of the last few days, and if he did want it, was he up to it? And what about Mo, what would she think? And what about his own gang? And what about the leaderless

Reservoir Pups, would they remain in the Alliance? And what about the Seagulls, what would—

'Eddie! Your Rice Krispies are getting soggy!'

Eddie took the deepest breath he could manage. The city was his, and his Rice Krispies were getting soggy. He let the air out slowly. As he did he looked out over Belfast. It looked so calm. Most people had no idea what went on out on those streets, day and night. The schemes and scams, the fights and brawls, the wars, the fear and the sheer bloody excitement of it all. And the fact was, that despite everything, despite all of the horrors he had experienced – deep down, he loved every minute of it.

GALWAY COUNTY LIBRARIES